DEATH
IN CAPTIVITY

DEATH
IN CAPTIVITY

MICHAEL GILBERT

with an introduction by
MARTIN EDWARDS

This edition published 2019 by
The British Library
96 Euston Road
London
NW1 2DB

Originally published in 1952 by Hodder & Stoughton, London

Cataloguing in Publication Data
A catalogue record for this book is
available from the British Library

ISBN 978 0 7123 5213 0
eISBN 978 0 7123 6478 2

Typeset by Tetragon, London
Printed and bound by CPI Group (UK) Ltd, Croydon CR0 4YY

CONTENTS

INTRODUCTION

The aftermath of the Second World War saw the publication of many novels set in prisoner of war camps, ranging from *The Colditz Story* and *The Wooden Horse* to *The Great Escape*. Michael Gilbert's *Death in Captivity* is unique, however, in offering an "impossible crime" murder mystery set in an Italian P.O.W. camp.

There is a good deal in the story to delight the fan of classic Golden Age detective fiction. Take, for instance, the central puzzle, which is neatly summarized in Robert Adey's survey *Locked Room Murders*: it concerns the "death by suffocation of the only man in an escape tunnel that could only be entered with the help of at least three men." As if that isn't tantalizing enough, the prison camp setting ensures a "closed circle" of suspects in the finest Agatha Christie tradition. And there is even an amateur detective— "Cuckoo" Goyles, alias Henry Goyles, a bespectacled schoolmaster who was the son of a solicitor. Given that Michael Gilbert was a bespectacled schoolmaster who became a solicitor after the war, there is perhaps an element of self-portrait, or at least witty self-caricature, in the way Goyles is presented.

The murder victim is an unpopular Greek prisoner, a suspected informer called Cyriakos Coutoules. His body is found beneath a fall of sand in Campo 127's most promising escape tunnel. The challenge for Goyles is to conduct a murder investigation with no help from the official police in a community where the camp's inmates "really did know everything about everybody else". Ultimately, he comes up with a solution to the crime neat enough to satisfy lovers of "fair play" detective fiction.

All this would be enough to guarantee an enjoyable read. But there is more. As he did in other novels, Michael Gilbert combines a teasing mystery with a pacy action thriller. The battle of wits between the prisoners desperate to get away from Campo 127 and their Italian captors is conveyed amusingly yet with an underlying seriousness. Gilbert does not flinch from the brutalities of war, including torture and other vicious punishments, but he does not dwell on them, or describe them in graphic and extensive detail.

Perhaps this habitual restraint—discretion, rather than caution—is the reason why his work has occasionally been damned with faint praise by critics (including his illustrious friends and contemporaries Julian Symons and Harry Keating, both of whom admired his work) who suggested that his gifts as a novelist were such that he should have been more ambitious in exploiting them. Yet as Gilbert said, in a characteristically mild but no doubt deeply felt rejoinder in *Twentieth Century Crime and Mystery Writers*: "I find the whole thing puzzling. What is a writer to do if he is not allowed to entertain?" Taken as a whole, the quality of his fiction does not, in my opinion, suffer in comparison with that of the similarly excellent work of Symons and Keating.

Entertaining the reader always remained Gilbert's priority as a storyteller, and his tales were told with such elegance and economy that they have stood the test of time far better than the work of most of his contemporaries. A facet of his writing that has, however, often been under-estimated is its authenticity. *Death in Captivity* is an outstanding example of his flair for making use of his own knowledge in the service of an enjoyable crime story. For

Gilbert had himself endured the wretched experience of being a prisoner in an Italian P.O.W. camp.

At the start of the Second World War, he joined the Royal Horse Artillery, and was mentioned in dispatches in 1943, before being captured in Africa, and transferred to Italy. A bold initial escape attempt—by jumping from a moving train—failed, but accompanied by two friends, he escaped from the Fontanellato camp at the time of the Italian surrender, eventually fictionalizing his adventures in *The Long Journey Home* (1943); his companions, the travel writer Eric Newby and Tony Davies, also wrote about their joint exploits, in *Love and War in the Apennines* and *When the Moon Rises* respectively.

Together with Davies and another escapee, Toby Graham, Gilbert was later joined by a South African called Hans Becker; they made it to the front line before Becker was shot dead and Davies was wounded. *Death in Captivity* is dedicated to Davies and Graham. Many years later, Gilbert learned that four members of a family which had given them shelter during the journey had been shot dead in reprisal by German troops. Local farmers often helped them, and after the war, as a mark of his gratitude for their courage, Gilbert subscribed to a charity, the Monte San Martino Trust, which gives study bursaries to young Italians. Among the many other charities to which he subscribed was the Red Cross, without whose food parcels, he said, he and the other prisoners would have starved.

The novel's excellence was quickly recognized on both sides of the Atlantic. In the US, it was called *The Danger Within*, and a film version released in 1959 was given the title *Danger Within* in Britain and *Breakout* in the US. The director was Don Chaffey (whose other movies included *Jason and the Argonauts*) and the script was co-written by Bryan Forbes. Richard Todd led an excellent cast, which included such stalwarts of British film and television as Richard Attenborough, Bernard Lee, Michael Wilding, Dennis Price, Donald Houston, William Franklyn, and Terence Alexander. Peter Arne, who was himself murdered in 1983, played Benucci. An uncredited part as a love-lorn prisoner of war was played by the young Michael Caine. To this day, the film remains well worth watching.

But the novel is even better. It ranks as one of the finest achievements of a crime writer of distinction.

MARTIN EDWARDS
www.martinedwardsbooks.com

To
LIEUTENANT A. P. DAVIES R.H.A.
and
CAPTAIN D. S. GRAHAM M.C., R.A.

CHAPTER ONE

THE CAMP—EVENING AND NIGHT

I

"IS IT TRUE, CAPTAIN," ASKED COLONEL LAVERY, "THAT Pantellaria has been invaded?"

"Quite true," said Captain Benucci. He added, without a great deal of conviction, "After heroic resistance our gallant troops, greatly outnumbered, were forced to yield. Many laid down their lives but their deeds live on. Our Duce will not forget them."

"Quite so," said Colonel Lavery. "I believe you had something you wished to discuss with me."

"It arises from the invasion of Pantellaria. That affords me, so to speak, my context for what I wished to say. From now on there may be other assaults—small assaults, you understand—on outlying islands in the Mediterranean. Your troops may even land in Sicily."

"So," said Colonel Lavery.

"Frankly, if they make such an attempt, I do not think that many will survive it. Our German allies are there in great strength. However, there may be temporary successes. All this may serve to inflame the prisoners. They may try to organize something." He paused for a moment and added, "Something stupid."

"We have some very high-spirited officers here," agreed the Colonel.

Captain Benucci seemed suddenly completely serious. He turned his head so that his black eyes looked directly into the Colonel's washed-out blue ones, and he said, "If any such thing were encouraged, you yourself would incur a terrible responsibility."

"Yes," said the Colonel.

He looked out of the little window, across the bare, stamped earth of the exercise ground, at the red-brick boundary wall. Without troubling to move his head he could see three platforms, on each of which stood two men. One man controlled a search-light, the other a machine gun mounted on a tripod. He visualized, for a moment, an unarmed crowd attempting to scale the walls. When he turned back he found that Captain Benucci was still looking at him.

"I demand your full co-operation," went on the Italian. "Otherwise I shall not answer for the consequences. If any unto-ward incident were to take place, no one would regret it more than myself."

"On the whole," said the Colonel, "I'm inclined to agree with you."

Silence fell again in the wooden, cabin-like room.

Shrill in the distance sounded the yelps of the Italian soldiers as they herded the last of their obstinate flock into the five big huts. From the Italian quarters a bugle was blowing for evening mess.

It was the Colonel who broke the silence.

"Is that just a general warning," he said, "or have you any concrete suggestions?"

"Two suggestions," said Benucci. "First, I was told—I do not know if it is true—I am naturally not in the confidence of the people concerned—that there might be some attempt to rush the wall. The people who made such an attempt might rely on the fact that the sentries would hesitate to shoot down unarmed men. Such a suggestion is fallacious. They would shoot them."

"I can assure you that I know of no such plan at the moment."

"Even if the ordinary soldiers might hesitate to do their duty, I am giving orders that, during the hours of darkness, one of the pair on each sentry platform shall be a member of my own regiment, the Carabinieri. That order will come into effect to-night."

"Very well," said the Colonel.

"Secondly, I must insist that the rule is observed, *without exception*, that no one shall move from hut to hut after evening roll-call when the huts have been closed. After all, it is not a difficult rule to keep. Each hut is self-contained. Each hut has dormitories, latrines and kitchen. The camp was designed with forethought."

"It was indeed," said the Colonel. During the short period of his captivity, he had been confined, in varying degrees of discomfort, in a museum, a station hotel, a castle and a monastery. Campo 127 was easily the best camp he had ever seen.

"There is no reason at all to leave the hut from the time it is locked after evening roll-call, until after breakfast, when morning roll-call has been completed. If a prisoner should be sick, you have your own medical man in each hut. Even if he should die"— Benucci showed his white teeth for a moment under his clipped moustache—"he will keep till morning."

"Oh, quite," said the Colonel.

"Yet, in spite of this, during the last two months there have been three cases of prisoners being found outside their huts after dark—for trivial reasons, in each case."

The Colonel nodded. He knew that a certain amount of "visiting" went on.

"In each case the guards have shot high, as a warning. Those were their orders. The orders have now been changed. They will shoot to kill."

"Yes, I understand," said the Colonel. As always, with Benucci, he wondered how much of it was truth and how much propaganda. He remembered the last case of "visiting" only a few days previously, and a quite impenitent Roger Byfold saying, "As a matter of fact, I'd just gone over to make up a fourth at bridge in Hut A. One of them spotted me on the way back and the silly bastards spent five minutes shooting all round me."

"I quite understand," he repeated. "I'll give something out. Is that all?"

"That is all." Captain Benucci clicked his heels and walked stiffly out of the room. The Colonel went to the window and watched him, as he strutted away towards the main gate of the camp, a solitary, dapper little figure.

It was nine o'clock of a perfect summer evening. The sun had disappeared, at last and reluctantly, behind the buttress of the Apennine mountains which ran up to the west of the camp. It left behind it the deep blue, almost green, light which the sky drew from the hidden Adriatic.

It was the moment in the day which the Colonel liked best.

The last of the five big huts was locked, and the last of his obstreperous four hundred children was locked away in them. He, a few senior officers, his Adjutant and half a dozen camp officials, had rooms in the end of the sixth hut, which held the camp offices, the stores, the library, the barber's shop—dignified names for tiny, partitioned cubicles.

As a privilege the outer door of this sixth hut was not locked at night. It was, incidentally, a privilege that the Colonel was determined to maintain.

He shuffled the papers on his table into some sort of order, for his bedroom was also his office, and went to look for his Adjutant.

II

Room 10 in Hut C—which was the end room on the south side, next to the kitchen—had a neat label on its door headed "Smokey Joe's". Underneath, in the same meticulous handwriting, were six names, in two sets of three:

> Major Grimsdale
> Capt. Baierlein
> Capt. Overstrand
> —
> Capt. Goyles
> Capt. Byfold
> Lieut. Long

It was the only room in the building which had as few as six names on its door and this exclusiveness was due entirely to the forethought of the Italians. Reckoning that if he had six dangerous criminals to watch it was easier, on the whole, to have them together, Captain Benucci had ordered the six to occupy a single room at the end of C Block. It was almost the only order of Captain Benucci which they had obeyed with enthusiasm.

All of them were notorious escapers. All of them had spent long hours undermining Italian property, destroying Italian buildings, cutting up Italian furniture and threatening Italian self-respect and peace of mind. All of them had been, at least once, at large in the

Italian countryside, pursuing the will o' wisp freedom in a variety of unlikely disguises.

"Cuckoo" Goyles, Roger Byfold and Tony Long—they worked as a trio, finding the concord which often comes from three discrepant natures—had jumped from a train, and spent fifteen days of unspeakable discomfort in the Apennines before convincing themselves that there was no future in night marching in mountainous country. Alec Overstrand had been out three times, on the last occasion in the company of Martin Grimsdale, when, dressed as Roumanian commercial travellers they had got as far as Bologna before arousing the suspicions of the ever-alert Railway Police. Hugo Baierlein, who was later to prove one of the outstanding escapers of the war, had already made a remarkable four-day journey by goods train from Caserta Hospital to Chiasso on the Swiss frontier. He had actually crossed the frontier and had been shunted back again into Italy, to fall into the hands of the Customs guard.

Although Room 10 had six beds in it, only three of them were occupied. Grimsdale, Baierlein and Long were all, at that moment, concluding a seven-day spell in the Punishment Block for organized insolence to Captain Benucci.

"It may be different in the big world outside these walls," Roger Byfold was saying, "but in a prisoner-of-war camp, there's no doubt about it. Crime does pay."

Alec Overstrand, who was copying a map on to a small roll of waterproof silk, nodded his agreement. "Cuckoo" Goyles, lying on his bunk absorbed in a phrase book of modern Greek, said nothing. Only the electric light glinted on his steel-rimmed spectacles as he moved his head.

"In the Union of Soviet Socialist Republics," went on Byfold, "which a prison camp in many ways resembles, a man's status and consequence are measured by the amount of living room he is permitted to occupy. Here we are, six of us, none of us of great seniority, yet comfortably lodged in a room designed to hold eight, whilst all around us similar sized rooms are full to overflowing with eight, ten or even twelve less fortunate prisoners. We enjoy the additional chance—almost, I might say, the certainty—that from time to time our numbers will be even further depleted by the vigilance of Captain Benucci, or the offended dignity of Il Colonello Aletti—"

"Do you suppose he's anything to do with the Hôtel Aletti in Algiers?"

Byfold considered the matter. "It's possible," he said at last. "He has, now you come to mention it, a certain resemblance to a hôtelier. Not a very high-class hôtelier. The proprietor, possibly, of one of the less well-known eating houses in Soho."

"It's all very well shooting a line about your criminal reputation." Goyles looked up from his book. "It hasn't got you a room all to yourself yet."

"Like Coutoules?"

"The little rat." Overstrand's rather heavy, red face took on a look of distaste. "Why don't we string him up and have done with it?"

"Stringing up's too good," said Byfold. "I should recommend slow immersion in canteen vermouth—head first, of course."

"He's not such a bad little beast really," said Goyles. "I had quite a long talk with him the other day."

"You're out of this world, Cuckoo. He's an informer and a stool pigeon."

"How do you know?"

"Didn't the caribs go straight to Desmond's tunnel last week—and hadn't Tony seen Coutoules snooping round the trap-door only the night before?"

"Coincidence," said Goyles. "Desmond's such an ass. He's been leaving sand all over his bedroom floor for weeks."

"Coutoules can't do much more harm, anyway," said Byfold. "Not now that he's tucked away, all by himself, in a little room in the Senior Officers' Block. And no one ever talks to him now—except 'Cuckoo' here."

"Schoolboy stuff," said Goyles calmly. "What's the use of sending him to Coventry, even if he is a stool-pigeon. If you talk to him you may get something useful out of him."

He returned to his studies and silence fell.

Ten minutes later he looked up and said, "Can anyone think of any situation in which it might be useful to know the modern Greek for 'Please inform me, sir or madam, whether the cabinet of easement is nearer to the cathedral or the railway terminus?'"

No one could.

III

Other parties were also discussing Cyriakos Coutoules.

Colonel Lavery said to his Adjutant, "I'm worried about Coutoules, Pat."

"It's he who should be worrying, sir," said the Adjutant.

"Yes, I know. He's not exactly popular. That's one of the things I was thinking about."

"Are you expecting trouble?"

"Well—not at the moment. Byfold and that young ass, Overstrand, have both threatened to lynch him. But it's nothing more than a threat—as yet."

"You mean—?"

"What do you think would happen if two or three of our hot heads—and we're not short of hot heads—"

"Who'll get hotter as the war comes closer."

"Exactly. Well, supposing some of them try to rush the walls. And the guards, instead of being distracted by whatever distraction is offered, are wide awake, and turn a searchlight on them and shoot them down. And suppose someone starts a little story that 'they had no chance because Coutoules tipped off the Italians.'"

"It might be sticky," agreed the Adjutant. "Tell me, sir, do you really think he's an informer."

"I don't know," said the Colonel. "It's so easy to imagine these things. We know nothing about him. He just says he was landed in Sicily to do sabotage. He's got Greek Army papers, only no one here knows enough about the Greek Army to say whether they're genuine or not. We can't check up on his home background—regiment and school and so on—as we could if he was a British officer. That makes him automatically subject to suspicion."

"One couldn't condemn him on that sort of thing alone," said the Adjutant. "But Desmond Foster's tunnel—that was a bit too coincidental to be nice."

"I wasn't too happy about that," agreed the Colonel. "But tunnels get found in hundreds of ways. The Italians may have known about it for weeks and just chosen that moment to pounce. If that had been all there was against him I shouldn't have worried."

"Has something else happened, sir?"

"Yes. Something I haven't quite worked out yet. Coutoules came to me this afternoon and practically begged me to put him back in one of the main huts."

"He *what?*"

"Yes, I know. It didn't seem quite natural to me. After all, he's got a room to himself in our hut here. Almost anyone in the camp would give a year's pay for a private room."

"Besides," said the Adjutant, "he must know he's not popular. So why does he want to go and put himself back into the lion's den?"

"Exactly. There's no doubt he did want to, though. No doubt at all. I've never seen anyone more anxious in my life. Practically went down on his knees."

"Did he say why?"

"Not really—just a lot of talk. He didn't like being alone."

"Do you think he was play-acting?"

"I didn't get that impression," said the Colonel. "If you want my real opinion, I think he was scared stiff."

IV

The Punishment Block lay in the north-west corner of the camp, alongside the Carabinieri Office. With the Camp Guard Quarters and other Italian administrative huts, it lay outside the inner line of defences that guarded the camp proper. This was one of its advantages, and it was not entirely by chance that three such hardened escapers as Tony Long, Hugo Baierlein and "Hefty" Grimsdale should have been guilty of the simultaneous offences which had landed them into the cooler together.

As nine o'clock struck Tony Long was standing on his bed looking out of the single barred window of his cell. He was reflecting, in a detached way, on the problem of escape from a prison camp. Camp 127 was not an easy place to escape from. It had been designed, as Captain Benucci had pointed out to Colonel Lavery, with a good deal of forethought. Miracles apart, there only were three ways of getting out of any camp. You could tunnel under the walls, you could climb over the walls, or you could walk out of the gate.

All these methods had their own drawbacks. The real disadvantage of tunnelling was the length of time it involved. What with the constant watchfulness of the Italians, their security checks and their sudden searches, any tunnel was almost certain to be spotted in the end. To suppose that you could keep it entirely hidden for the six or eight months necessary to reach the open was like gambling on the same number coming up six or eight times running at the roulette table. It could happen, but it didn't very often.

To get over the walls was a proposition of much greater risk but carrying with it that fundamental chance of success which must attend any bold and unexpected manœuvre. Three months before, a particularly well-organized effort of this sort had been completely successful. The camp lights had been fused and, in the few seconds that the darkness had lasted, four officers armed with hooked ladders had crossed the wall midway between sentry and sentry and had disappeared. (It is true that all of them had eventually been recaptured and were now in the fortress prison of Gavi for their pains.)

Lastly there was the gate. To crash the gate was a project which needed expert disguise, nerve and plenty of luck. At 127 you needed a double portion of luck, for there were, in fact, two gates, an inner gate and an outer gate, and a very elaborate security system of passes and checks existed between the two, which no one had yet entirely succeeded in defeating.

Standing at his window, that evening, Tony watched the system at work. A small open laundry van came across the prisoners compound and approached the inner gate. Despite the fact that it was driven by one carabinier and had another seated on the back the sentry abated nothing of his caution. He checked both passes and then went round and thrust his long needle bayonet through one or two of the larger bundles. The carib in the back said something and the driver laughed. The sentry walked across to the telephone, and spoke to the Guard House. Not till he had had a reply would he even open the inner gate. At the outer gate, although it was in full view of the inner one, and not more than thirty yards away, the whole performance was repeated.

Tony sighed, shifted his weight on to his other foot, and wondered how long it would be before it was dark. He had blond hair and a Nordic, rather serious face, which looked deceptively youthful. Only his mouth and chin had the hard lines of a generation which had been brought up to war.

By half-past ten most of the light was out of the sky, but it was eleven o'clock before he moved.

The first thing he did was to take out a short piece of wire which appeared to form part of his bed and thrust it through the ventilation between his cell and the next. He jerked it once or twice and then pulled it out, and put his ear to the ventilator.

He could hear Baierlein's voice quite distinctly.

"Not yet. The outer gate guard is the other side, looking this way. I'll knock when he changes over."

Ten minutes later a quiet knock sounded.

Tony put his hand up and appeared to be fumbling with one of the bricks which formed the sill of the window. Then he put his other hand up, and twisted one of the bars. Then bar and brick came clean out of the window. The whole operation took less than thirty seconds.

The gap left by the removal of the bar was not much more than twelve inches, but it was enough.

Tony climbed from the bed on to the sill, put a long arm through, caught the gutter above the window, and pulled.

A minute later he was on the roof of the Punishment Block, hidden in the deep shadow behind a buttress.

Baierlein, in Cell 2, turned to Grimsdale with a smile and said: "He's up."

"Should be all right now," said Grimsdale. "They won't see him so long as he keeps still."

"They certainly won't hear him," said Baierlein. "Not with that filthy row going on."

In the Carabinieri Office next door a loud-speaker, full on, was relaying a dance band from Radio Romā.

The two men lay in silence in the dark cell. Each was deep in his own thoughts. There was an occasional rustle as Baierlein turned on his bed to look at the illuminated face of his watch.

Outside the saxophones laughed and sobbed and the high trumpets screamed.

v

"Three hearts gives us game, you know."

"Pass," said Billy Moxhay.

"Four hearts."

"Three hearts," said Tag Burchnall.

"Oh, so it does. Sorry, I'm sure," said Rollo Betts-Hanger. "Pass then."

"Pass," said Gerry Parsons. "Good fun this afternoon, wasn't it?"

"First class," said Rollo. "I thought we were a bit weak in the scrum."

"Definitely weak."

"We want a bit more weight."

"A lot more weight. Aubrey and Peter don't push their weight at all."

"We really need a first-class man behind them. Someone who can lock the back row."

"What about—oh, sorry. I didn't know you were waiting for me. I thought you were pondering. I'm playing the queen. I was going to say, what about Grimsdale? He's a Hirburnian, isn't he?"

"I tried him—of course. He won't do it."

"Won't play rugger?"

"That's what he told me. He said he'd always been made to play at school and in the army. In a prisoner-of-war camp he was going to please himself."

"Must have been pulling your leg. Why, he played for Middlesex, didn't he?"

"The truth of the matter is," said Rollo, "that he spends so much time over this escaping stuff that he hasn't got time for anything else."

"Of course, in theory, I'm all for escaping," said Gerry Parsons. "It's one's duty, and so forth. But the fact of the matter is—oh, it's me again is it?—the fact of the matter is that no one ever really gets anywhere. It isn't as if there was any chance even of getting out of this camp—to say nothing of getting out of the country—and when anyone does try, what happens—?"

"They cut off the showers," said Tag Burchnall. "You can't trump that, Billy. Hearts *are* trumps."

"That's what I mean. They just make everyone uncomfortable."

"Still," said Tag, "one doesn't exactly want to stand in their way. One wouldn't want to do a Coutoules," he added.

"I can't think why someone hasn't taken the little beast right apart," said Billy Moxhay. "I should have thought the S.B.O. ought to take it up. All that's happened to the little blot is that he's got a room of his own. I'm trumping that."

"You can't trump with that card," said Tag. "I know it looks like the knave of hearts but it isn't really. It's been crossed out. It's the three of clubs."

"I thought the other knave of hearts was the three of clubs."

"No, that is the knave of hearts. It's turned down in one corner. That makes ten tricks. Game with one overtrick. Eight hundred on the rubber."

Scores were carefully checked and eight small figs were pushed across the table.

The president of the Old Hirburnian Rugby Football Club cut, and the cards were dealt again.

VI

At two o'clock Hugo Baierlein turned over on his bunk and sat up. He had many of the talents of the true escaper. One was the ability to sleep anywhere and wake on demand.

He got out of bed, picked up a chair, put it on the table which was under the high, barred window and climbed on to it. He manoeuvred the bars in much the same way that Tony Long had done in his cell and after a few minutes he also had the middle one loose. He then put his arm and shoulder out, reached up and scratched very gently on the iron gutter.

He waited, and scratched again, until he heard the muffled sounds which indicated that Tony Long was on his way down. He gave him a few minutes and then crossed to the ventilator.

He heard Tony's voice, still puffed from his descent.

"Went very well. The chap on the corner turned his search-light at me twice. He couldn't see me, of course; I was behind the parapet. Don't think he was suspicious. Just jumpy. I think I've spotted how the gate sentry works, too. He spends most of his time in the box with his back to us, but he comes out every half-hour, just before the Sergeant arrives on his rounds. I've written down the time."

"Good," said Baierlein. "I'll make a note of that myself."

"You'll have to be damned quiet getting up," said Tony. "You haven't got a ruddy great dance band to cover you like I had. I'll give you the word when to start."

Five minutes later Baierlein was on the roof.

It was cold enough to make him feel glad of his double layer of underclothes.

He was lying alongside the low parapet which divided the flat roof. His wrist-watch was strapped with its luminous face on the inside of his left wrist. In his right hand he had a tiny black notebook and pencil. His job was to note down every movement of the sentry on the main gate and of the pair on the north-west guard platform.

He faced the prospect of approximately two and a half hours of immobility.

Under the full Italian moon, which paled even the arc-lamps round the perimeter, the camp lay black and sharp. Every few minutes a searchlight from one of the guard platforms blinked its frosty carbon-blue eye and swept across the enclosure.

Baierlein lay safely in the long black shadow of the parapet. His eyes were on the gate sentry. He saw exactly what Tony had meant. The chap was too slack to stand his post properly. He preferred to lounge in the comparative comfort of the box. Only,

every half-hour, just before the Sergeant of the Guard announced
to the world the start of his rounds by throwing open the guard-
room door, the sentry left the box, crossed the gateway, and stood
facing the Punishment Block.

In that position alone was he a danger.

Baierlein glanced at the watch face, and made a meticulous
note in his book. It was for moments like this that he lived—and
was nearly to die, once or twice, before he finally hobbled across
the Swiss frontier at Gottmadingen eighteen months later.

VII

On the guard platform at the north-east corner Ordinary Soldier
Biancelli stamped his feet and prayed for his relief. He hated guard
duty at the best of times but he hated it still more now that, in
place of his friend, Moderno, he had this unspeakable, unsociable,
Marzotto beside him. His dislike was not personal. It was the dislike
of a member of an ordinary corps for the member of a privileged
corps. He, Biancelli, was a soldier. A soldier of the king. Marzotto,
although he styled himself "of the Regiment of Carabinieri Reali"
was a policeman. He took his orders from Captain Benucci,
who took them from some Colonel of Carabinieri at District
Headquarters, who took them, in the long run, from Il Duce.

Biancelli was distressed both by his discomforts and his
responsibilities.

In the old days it had been simple. If you saw an English prisoner
escaping you shot at him. Now things were more complicated.

He looked sideways at Marzotto, who avoided his gaze.

As an ordinary soldier he was not told much about how the war
was going, or what was happening in the camp he was guarding.

But he could not help being aware of certain undercurrents of feeling, certain possibilities.

He stamped his feet again and watched the sky lightening imperceptibly towards morning.

CHAPTER TWO

THE CAMP—MORNING

I

THE CAMP CAME TO LIFE SLOWLY.

In Hut C the first sound was usually the clatter of the orderly cook as he hurried along the passage to light the kitchen stove and heat the coffee which, with a slice of Red Cross biscuit, made up the normal prisoner-of-war breakfast.

At eight-thirty the Italians were due to open the huts and conduct their morning roll-call. It was an operation which might take anything from fifteen minutes to an hour according to the temper and efficiency of the Italian officer conducting it and the degree of co-operation which he succeeded in obtaining from his charges. During roll-call no one was allowed to leave his room.

Opinion varied from hut to hut as to whether it was better to heat the breakfast coffee before or after roll-call. There were advantages either way. In Hut C, at that time, for reasons which will appear, the cooking was done as early as possible.

Immediately roll-call had been concluded and the last Italian had left the hut quite a lot of things happened. None of them, in themselves, was significant or suspicious; but the total would have added up to the same answer in the mind of any experienced prisoner.

Certain officers, lying on their beds beside windows, hung out towels to dry. One prisoner fixed his shaving mirror to a nail beside the window and seemed to be experiencing some difficulty in tilting it to the exact angle he required, for the mirror could be seen, for some minutes, winking like a semaphore in the morning sun. In a room in Hut C a tall Major, wearing the green flashes of the 'I' Corps, sat at a table filling in what appeared to be a chart of the inter-related Royal dynasties of England and Hanover, and a stream of visitors came and went with items of information which he found helpful in his strange, self-imposed task.

All over the camp, from each of the five big living huts, from the Senior Officers' quarters, from the Orderlies' Billet, from the barber's shop, from the canteen, and the shower baths, the quiet, invisible, network floated out, like a thousand spiders' webs of gossamer over an early morning field. A subaltern in the Royal Corps of Signals—in peace time a professor of history at Oxford—who was sitting in a deck-chair against the wall of the camp theatre, found himself reminded of Oman's description of Craufurd and the Light Brigade at their watch on the Portuguese frontier. "The whole web of communication quivered at the slightest touch." He himself had a tiny part to play: the outer main gate was under his observation. If it opened he would drop his book. If anyone dangerous came through he would stand up.

The gate remaining shut he was able to continue his reading in peace.

The object of all this organization, the heart of the labyrinth around which this watchful maze of attention had been constructed, lay in the kitchen of Hut C.

In the middle of the kitchen, set in a six-foot square slab of concrete let into the tiled floor, stood the stove. It was a huge cauldron, shaped like a laundry copper, and it still hissed and bubbled from its morning coffee-making. Apart from a few shelves, almost the only other fitting in the room was a pair of hanging clothes-driers of a sort not uncommon in old-fashioned kitchens, made of slats of wood, and suspended, on two pulleys each, from the ceiling. They were covered, as usual, with prisoners' private laundry, underclothes, stockings and sports kit. The only odd thing about them—and no doubt the matter was so obvious that it never occurred to the Italians as being odd at all—was that the racks appeared to be a trifle too well made for their function. However great the weight of damp laundry to be hung on them it seemed an unnecessary precaution to have bolted the pulleys right through, at both ends, to the solid beams of the roof. Nor did it seem really necessary that the racks, instead of being raised by a single pulley, should be operated at each end by a small double block and tackle. The obvious is rarely apparent.

At five minutes past nine four officers entered the kitchen. Two of them went to the clothes racks and lowered them to their fullest extent so that they hung just above the stove. They then took out, each of them, a short length of wire rope with a hook at both ends. One hook went over the pulley, the other round one of the four legs of the stove. No word was spoken; nor was any word necessary since they had been performing this particular operation twice every day for several months.

Each man took up the slack on his pulley. There was a moment's pause. Then, in tug-of-war parlance, they "took the strain".

For a moment nothing happened.

"Ease her a little on the left," said the leader. "You're jamming her."

Suddenly, with no perceptible jerk, smoothly as a hydraulic press, the whole of the concrete slab came up out of the floor, with the stove fixed to it. When it was about three feet up the leader gave the sign, ropes were fastened, and, as silently as they had come, the men departed.

The stove, despite its ascension, continued to bubble and hiss merrily.

Such was the entrance to the oldest of the existing undiscovered tunnels in a camp whose Commandant had boasted that no tunnel was possible.

One had only to see it in operation to realize why it had escaped all searches. Like the African elephant in its native jungle, it defied detection by its immensity. The Italian Security Police, as they probed and searched with ant-like zeal each night, running steel spikes between bricks and tapping on floors with leather hammers, were looking for something altogether different—something smaller and slighter. A trap-door which consisted of a single slab of concrete, six feet by six feet and over two feet deep; a trap-door which weighed nearly half a ton and needed four men, assisted by double-pulleys, to lift it was something outside their ambit. It evaded search by being too big to see.

(It might as well be admitted that only a fluke had rendered its construction possible. The Italians had made the mistake of letting the prisoners into Camp 127 a fortnight before it was really ready—a fortnight during which construction work was still proceeding on the shower baths and the drainage. Despite all their precautions it had proved possible to get hold of cement and certain tools and the escape committee had immediately ordered the construction of this monster trap. The original base of the stove, a lighter piece of work, was taken out, broken into pieces, and dropped into the water-storage tank. The new base was cast in one piece and the lifting apparatus installed. Before the camp had even been completed, therefore, the foundation stone for a way out had been well and truly laid.)

Overstrand and Byfold were already dressed for work.

It was their job, every morning, to open up the tunnel, connect up the electric lighting system, see that the hand pump and airline were in order and that the trolley, which ran from the trap-door to the digging face, was working without hitch. With the tunnel now more than a hundred feet long these details were becoming of increasing importance. When they gave the word that all was ready the first shift of diggers would go down and the trap would be lowered on them. They would dig for four hours and would then be replaced by an afternoon shift.

Although they had dressed for tunnelling often enough not to feel self-conscious about it, both Overstrand and Byfold might have presented, to the unaccustomed eye, somewhat remarkable figures. From the waist downwards, they were clothed in that useful army garment known to the Quartermaster as "pants, woollen, long", the ends tucked into the tops of their socks, of which they wore two pairs. Their top halves were covered by skin-tight association football jerseys. (Of no known club, they were part of an issue of sports kit by the Protecting Power, and were believed to be the colours of the Zermatt Wanderers.) Both wore balaclava helmets and were shoeless.

"Where's Cuckoo?" said Overstrand.

"He's along there already," said Byfold. "Check the security, would you?"

Overstrand looked out of the window, and noted the position of various towels, shutters, refuse bins and deck-chair loungers.

"Seems all right," he said. "Let's go."

They made their way along the empty passage and into the kitchen. The stove hung suspended in the air.

A pair of steel spectacles gleamed from the darkness of the entrance shaft under it.

"I thought you were never coming," said Goyles. "I've connected up the light. It looks all right from this end. There are twelve bags of sand waiting. We'll have to get them out before digging starts."

All three of them had climbed down the ladder and were standing in the bottom of the twenty-foot vertical entrance shaft. The tunnel itself, rather less than a yard square, ran away from the east side of this shaft. A slight bend hid the working face of the tunnel from a person standing in the shaft.

"I'll go up," said Overstrand. "Give me two minutes and then start checking the pump."

He placed himself face downwards on a small flat trolley which ran on rails up the tunnel and propelled himself forward with his hands. Trolley and man rounded the bend and disappeared.

Goyles looked at his watch.

"Ten to nine," he said. "The shift will be here in ten minutes. Let's have these bags up and get the disposal squad busy."

"Why did God make sand so heavy?" said Byfold. He had tied two sacks together, hung them over his shoulder, and was climbing up the ladder.

Goyles had nothing to say to this and had turned his attention to the pump. He looked at his watch again. Overstrand had said "two minutes" and this was about the time it would take an experienced tunneller to reach the face. A novice would need five.

At eight minutes to nine Goyles started operating the home-made pump. At three minutes to nine he stopped. Byfold had got most of the sacks of sand up and was starting his last trip.

One of the weaknesses of the system, thought Goyles, was that there was no means of communicating with the worker at the face. Even if you shouted, which would have been unwise, your voice, by some trick of acoustics, could not reach him. Something to do, no doubt, with the blanketing qualities of sand. A telephone from the shaft to the face would be a luxury, but might in the end save—

"Hullo," said Byfold, "what's happened to Alec? I've got all the bags clear. The shift's about due."

"Nip up and tell them to wait," said Goyles. "We'll give him a few more minutes. The trolley may have stuck."

As Byfold's stockinged feet disappeared out of the top of the shaft Goyles stared anxiously up the tunnel. If Overstrand really was stuck he would have to go after him and since there was only one trolley he would go on his elbows and knees. This was all right, of course. In fact, during the first fifty feet of the tunnel, before the rail had been laid, it had been the normal method of progress. But it meant an awful waste of time, and every minute that the trap stayed open could be dangerous.

He peered again up the tunnel.

Where there had been a faint glimmer of yellow, it was now completely dark. This did not necessarily mean that the light at the face had failed. Overstrand's body and the trolley between them would blanket it effectively.

He became aware that Byfold was saying something.

"—how long to wait?"

"I don't know," said Goyles. "I think I'll have to go and see— No—hold it. Here he comes."

Two feet appeared in the gloom of the tunnel and they heard the rumbling and creaking of the trolley on its home-made tram-lines.

"How is everything?" asked Goyles.

And then, even in the dim light of the shaft, he saw that Overstrand's face was white.

"What's happened?"

Overstrand climbed off the trolley and stood up. He wiped his hands together, separating his fingers and rubbing them through each other as if to get the sand from between them.

"Part of the roof's fallen in at the top," he said, speaking slowly.

"Has it—?"

"No. It's not right through. There's no daylight showing. I think it's held up by the foundations of the theatre. It's difficult to see. You know we thought we were about under it."

"I see," said Goyles. It didn't sound too alarming. "We'd better get the shoring-up started straight away. I'll call off this shift and we'll have a word with—"

He was aware that Overstrand was staring at him.

"It's not just a collapse," he said. "There's someone in it."

"What's that?"

"There's someone in it. I could see his feet sticking out. I got some of the sand away. I think it's Coutoules. He's dead."

"You're sure of that?"

"Of course I'm sure," said Overstrand. He seemed to be trying to work up a little honest anger to counteract the effect of what he had seen. "You could tell that just from seeing his feet. I dug to his face to find out who it was. What are we going to do?"

It was noticeable that although both Overstrand and Byfold were regular soldiers it was usually Goyles who assumed the command in any real crisis. He did so now.

He wasted no more time on Overstrand but climbed half-way up the ladder and said to Byfold.

"Get this shift away, Roger. Tell them there's a bit of the roof come down and there'll be no digging until we've got it shored up again. Then will you send someone for Doc. Simmonds and—ask Colonel Baird to step along."

Byfold started to say something, took one look at Goyles' face and changed his mind.

II

Colonel Baird was head of the Escape Committee. He was a New Zealander, had commanded an Infantry Battalion and had been acting commander of a Brigade at the time of his capture in the desert. He was a thick, grizzled, slow-speaking man: not a person you took liberties with.

He strolled into the kitchen three minutes later, slashing with his home-made flywhisk.

Both Overstrand and Goyles were up by this time, and standing beside the trap, and he listened to what they had to say.

"It sounds to me like a two-man job," said the Colonel. "You found him, didn't you, Overstrand? Well, that's enough for a bit, I reckon. You go and change. You two—you'll have to get that Greek out. It's not going to be easy. I suggest you push the trolley ahead of you to the face. When you get there you'll have to get either side of it and scrape the sand away with your hands until you can pull the body back on to the trolley. It won't be exactly safe that bit. Do you think you can manage it?"

"I expect so," said Goyles. "The lights still work. Overstrand says that the collapse is pretty well held up by the foundations of the theatre hut—we're underneath that now."

"Stroke of luck," said Baird. "We might be able to save it yet. We don't want to lose *this* one if we can help it. Down you go now. I'll guarantee you ten minutes but don't take longer if you can help it."

Goyles couldn't pretend that he enjoyed that crawl up the tunnel, but by the time he reached the face curiosity had the upper hand.

He had never been in a tunnel fall before. The shift of the previous day had dug about six feet beyond the existing shoring; it would have been the first job for that morning's shift to shore it up with the short lengths of wooden bed board of which a stock was kept in the shaft. Sometime in the night a large neat section had fallen out of the exposed roof. It had not quite filled the tunnel and over the top of it you could see the empty space it had fallen out of, and the bricks and cement which were the foundations of the theatre hut. Underneath the fallen sand, somehow, incredibly was the body.

The actual operation of getting him out proved surprisingly easy, though far from pleasant, with every incautious movement bringing down a fresh trickle of sand from the cavity above.

Somebody—presumably Overstrand in his first effort to identify the body—had already scraped away a lot of the sand on one side. Goyles, lying beside the truck, was able to dig, one-handed, into the pile on the other side. The difficulty was disposing of what he dug, but in the end he simply piled it on the trolley and Byfold, lying behind him, pulled the loaded trolley back and scattered the loose sand up and down the tunnel.

In the end, when the body was nearly clear—it was Coutoules all right—they edged the trolley in under his legs, retreated to the shored-up portion, and pulled. There was a further, alarming, fall of sand, but the body came away with the trolley and the worst was over.

Five minutes later they were back in the kitchen of Hut C. Colonel Baird said: "If my hair's white it's you two who are responsible. Do you know you've been forty minutes?"

"Time stood still, sir," said Goyles impenitently.

The body of Coutoules lay under a blanket in the corner of the room. Overstrand, who had changed and returned, lent them a hand and the four of them lowered the trap.

Up to that moment they had been too busy with the pressing necessities of the moment to give much thought to the problem which the figure under the blanket represented.

The awkward silence was broken by the arrival of the doctor.

"He's over there, Doc," said the Colonel. "It's Coutoules." The doctor turned back the blanket, and then said: "I should like a little more light if I'm going to make a proper examination. Can he be moved?"

"I was thinking the same thing, sir," said Goyles. "We're rather a sitting chicken if anyone should come." The pulleys were still fastened to the stove and there was a good deal of bright, newly excavated sand on the floor, as well as four full bags which they had not yet had time to dispose of.

"All right," said the Colonel. "But have you thought how you're going to move him out of this hut?"

No one had.

"Get him into the nearest bedroom for the moment—that's yours, isn't it, Goyles? Then clear up in here as quickly as you can. I'll fix something up to get him out. We'd better take him into Hut A. Meet us there, would you, Doctor?"

Goyles and Byfold picked up the body. Now that they were out of the tunnel they were beginning to feel glad of the blanket over it. They carried it in and laid it on the floor of their room.

"Get hold of about twelve reliable types," said the Colonel. "People from this hut, if possible. We don't want a lot of coming and going. Tell them to put on some sort of gym kit—and hurry."

The power of Colonel Baird's name was such that in less than five minutes a dozen puzzled but willing gymnasts had been assembled.

Colonel Baird gave them instructions.

Ten minutes later the sentries on the walls were diverted at the sight of seven of their prisoners galloping from the end of Hut C with seven other prisoners mounted on their backs. The procession galloped past Hut B, down the alleyway between Hut B and Hut A, and from there out on to the Sports Ground, where a spirited tourney took place, each pair of riders trying to unseat the other. It did not surprise the sentries because nothing that the British did had power to surprise them. In the general excitement it may have escaped their attention that, whilst seven pairs had started out, only six had arrived at their destination.

The seventh rider was being dismounted from his perspiring horse in the dining-room of Hut A.

"I don't want to do that again in a hurry," said Byfold. "I thought he was going to slip just as we got opposite the sentry platform—and the feel of those arms round my neck—ugh."

"All right," said Colonel Baird. "Put him down on the table, will you? You can do your stuff there all right, Doctor? Byfold, I don't think we need you and Overstrand any more. Fewer people here the better, really. Warn the watchers that something is going on in this hut and we want the longest possible warning if any Italian heads in this direction. Oh, and you might see the Adjutant and ask the S.B.O. if he'll step over here. Warn him not to hurry straight here—the sentries are very quick at picking up things like that—and I don't know whether they've fallen for that bare-back circus act or not. Suggest that he might make his morning round in this direction in about ten minutes. You stop behind, Goyles. I want a word with you."

The Colonel lowered himself on to one of the dining-room chairs—it had been built to Italian barrack specifications and was inadequate to his bulk—and Goyles sat down too, glad that he had his back to the things that were going on on the table behind him.

"Now, boy," said the Colonel, and he said it so kindly that Goyles felt suddenly guilty of nameless crimes, "tell me what happened."

"There's not an awful lot to tell really," said Goyles. "We opened up the tunnel this morning, in the usual way, just after half-past eight. The drill is that three of us go down first."

"Yourself, Overstrand and Byfold."

"Well—not necessarily. Any three out of our room. We happen to be the only three of us there at the moment. The others are in the cooler."

"I see. And you get things ready."

"That's it. We've all been in on this tunnel almost from the beginning and we know our way about it. We check the lighting and the pump and go up on the trolley to see that the shoring is holding up and there haven't been any falls during the night, and we organize the disposal of any sacks of sand that the afternoon shift have left from the day before."

"I see. And this morning—by the way, do you open it yourselves?"

"No. That wouldn't work. It's a four-man job to open or shut the trap, and it might have to be shut in a hurry. The same four chaps always do the opening—they live in the room next to ours—and they have to stand by the whole time the trap's open in case there's a panic."

"I'll have a word with them in a moment," said the Colonel. "What next?"

"I went down first and connected up the light. Then Overstrand and Byfold arrived. Overstrand went up the tunnel and—found Coutoules."

"Just like that," said the Colonel. "Quite simple, quite straight-forward, and plain bloody impossible."

"I agree with you, sir," said Goyles stiffly, "but that's what happened."

"I'm not disbelieving you, boy," said the Colonel. "How was he lying when you found him?"

"I didn't actually find him," said Goyles. "Overstrand did that. He says he tried to unearth him. He scraped the sand away far enough to see who it was, but I don't think he moved the body. When Byfold and I went up to get him he was lying, half on his side, half on his face. His hands were in front of him, as if he was trying to scrape his way out. Enough sand had come down on him to pin him, though. He wouldn't have had a chance. He must have died quite quickly."

"He didn't die all that quickly," said the doctor from behind him. "Take a look at his face."

In life Coutoules had not been a particularly handsome little man. Now, in death, his lips were lifted from his teeth in a grimace of pain and his brown eyes, from which the doctor had carefully wiped the sand, were open and staring.

Footsteps sounded in the passage outside and they all got to their feet as Colonel Lavery came in. In fact, Colonel Baird, being a full colonel, was the senior officer, but Colonel Lavery was, by appointment, Senior British Officer in the camp and formalities of that sort were observed.

"Please sit down," said Colonel Lavery. "What—oh, I see. A tunnelling casualty."

"Yes," said Colonel Baird. "I expect that's right. But it's not quite as straightforward as that. Goyles, would you tell Colonel Lavery what you just told me."

Goyles repeated his story. It took longer this time, because there were a lot of details which he had to explain to Colonel Lavery which Colonel Baird, as head of the Escape Committee, had understood without explanation.

When he had finished, Colonel Lavery turned to the doctor.

"Can you tell us anything now," he said. "It might help to clear things up. At the moment, I can't see—"

"Certainly," said Doctor Simmonds. He was an unexcitable Scot who had left a first-class job in Edinburgh to look after the simple ailments of a Lowland Regiment in the Western Desert. "This man died of asphyxiation. He's been dead, in my opinion, rather less than twelve hours. Certainly nine or ten. I can't be more precise."

Everybody looked at their watches and did sums.

"Ten o'clock now," said Colonel Baird. "That makes it that he died about eleven o'clock or midnight last night."

"The whole thing is impossible," said Colonel Lavery. "Unless there's been a conspiracy of silence in Hut C—" He looked speculatively at Goyles. "As I understand it, it takes four men to open this trap, and four men to lower it. Will someone tell me how Coutoules got into that tunnel. I'm leaving aside altogether the question of how he got into the hut. So far as I know, at lock-up last night, he was in his own room in our Senior Officers' hut—"

No one found anything to say.

"I'm perfectly aware," went on Colonel Lavery steadily, "that Coutoules was not a popular character. It was, in fact, at your suggestion, Baird, that he was removed from Hut C and was segregated in a small room in our hut."

Colonel Baird nodded.

"If I might suggest it," he said bluntly, "we're putting the cart before the horse. There's no doubt *how* Coutoules died. Anyone who wasn't used to tunnelling, blundering along in the dark—particularly not realizing that the last six feet hadn't been shored up—would be more than likely to bring the roof down on top of himself. I should say that the chances were in favour of it. How he got into the tunnel I know no more than anyone else, but the fact is that he *did* get there—and I expect the truth about it will come to light sooner or later. It usually does. So I suggest we stop worrying about what can't be helped and tackle the immediate problem. What are we going to do with the body?"

"We shall have to tell the Italians," said Colonel Lavery sharply. "We can't keep a death quiet for ever—besides, we should be putting ourselves hopelessly in the wrong."

"All right," said Colonel Baird. "We hand over the body, I agree. But do we have to say where we found him?"

Whilst Colonel Lavery was thinking this one out Colonel Baird went on.

"Because if so, I'd like to put it on record that we should be making the enemy a present of the only undiscoverable tunnel in the camp."

"I can quite see we don't want to do that," said Colonel Lavery.

"Let me be quite frank about this," said Colonel Baird, "and strictly I ought to turn these two young men out of the room before I say this, but I expect they can be trusted to keep their mouths shut—"

The doctor grunted, and Goyles nodded.

"I don't really visualize this tunnel being used for an escape—not a normal escape. We all know that the British have taken Pantellaria. The Eighth Army will be in Sicily soon—and Italy after that. Suppose the Italians pack up. Have you thought yet what the Germans are going to do—about us, I mean?"

"I've asked myself the question a dozen times," said Colonel Lavery. "I haven't liked any of the answers either," he added.

"All right," said Colonel Baird. "Let's take the obvious answer. The Germans aren't going to let go the sixty thousand prisoners in Italy that it cost them all that sweat and blood to take—not if they can help it. One morning we're going to wake up and find the Wehrmacht on these walls, and a train in the station getting up steam to take us all to Krautland. Tell me how much you'd pay then to have an absolutely fool-proof tunnel waiting and ready."

"Yes," said Colonel Lavery.

"Not just a rat-hole which a dozen men might squeeze through with luck, but a decent, wooden-lined, three-feet-by three, guaranteed back door. With proper organization we could empty this camp in one night—*and the British lines might be at Naples by then.*"

"Yes," said Colonel Lavery again. "You're absolutely right. What do you suggest?"

"I suggest," said Colonel Baird, "that we dig a hole right here and bury him. Let the Italians look for him."

"And what if they find him," said Colonel Lavery, "as they may very well do. Murder's a civil offence; even in a prisoner-of-war camp. Would there be anything to show that we hadn't suffocated him first and buried him afterwards. They know very well he was unpopular in the Camp. There have been threats. It wouldn't be too pleasant if they started to hang someone for a murder which we knew had never been committed."

"It's nasty either why," said Colonel Baird.

"There's just one thing about that," said the doctor. "If they examine the body properly they can't maintain that he was suffocated and buried afterwards."

"Do you mean the sand in his nose and mouth. There's nothing to show that wasn't put in after death is there?"

"Have you looked at his hands?" said the doctor. "He was alive when he went under that sand all right. He's pulled one of the nails clean off his right hand and the other three nails nearly off, trying to scratch his way out."

There was a short silence.

"If it comes to that," said Colonel Lavery, "I suppose we might have faked even a detail like that, but—"

"Could I make a suggestion, sir," said Goyles.

"Certainly."

"Why don't we bury him in *another* tunnel. There's one started in this hut. It isn't, actually, a very good tunnel. It hasn't gone more than about twelve feet and I think it's been a bit lucky to survive so far—"

"You suggest," said Colonel Lavery, "that we put him in this tunnel, pull down some of the roof on top of him and call in the Italians—pretending it's a normal tunnelling accident."

"Something like that, sir."

"What do you say about that, Baird?"

"I think it's a damned good scheme," said Colonel Baird. "I don't think this other tunnel's got a hope in hell of getting anywhere. The Committee thought twice about letting them start even. The trap's much too obvious for one thing. If we've got to throw away a tunnel, this is the one to discard."

"All right," said Colonel Lavery. "The less I know about it in my official capacity, the better. I'll leave the details to you."

CHAPTER THREE

SECOND INTERMENT

I

THE HUT A TUNNEL STARTED FROM THE BATHROOM. A square of tiles had been taken up, and the tiles had been cemented on to a wooden, tray-shaped frame. The work had been done neatly enough and, in its original state, it had probably made quite a satisfactory cover. Unfortunately it suffered from the frailty of its construction. Daily use had cracked and chipped the edges of the tiles, so that its outline was becoming distressingly apparent to the eye. Also it had developed a slight, but detectable, wobble.

From this and other reasons the tunnel had been allotted low priority by the Escape Committee; in particular very little material had been made available for shoring-up. Things had gone well enough whilst the diggers were actually under the foundations of the hut but now that they were striking out into the sand of the open compound progress was becoming increasingly difficult. That they had got as far as they had was almost entirely due to the enthusiasm of the tunnel's proprietor and only begetter, "Brandy" Duncan of the Black Watch.

There was another reason for its slow progress, and "Brandy" expressed this bluntly to Goyles. "They're such a hopeless crowd in this hut," he said. "No bowels."

"I know what you mean," said Goyles.

"They spend their days sun-bathing, and their evenings filling up their stamp albums and playing roulette and complaining about the food. I ought to be sick at you for collaring this tunnel, but, by God, I'm not. Book a place for me and Andy in your outfit and you can have this tunnel and welcome."

Goyles thanked him and reported back to Colonel Baird. He had known that *morale* in Hut A was low, but hadn't realized how far it had slipped.

Colonel Baird wasted no time.

"We'll want someone to go down the tunnel and do the actual damage. I think it had better be Byfold—he's the nippiest of you. Get him over here with his tunnelling kit. Duncan and Anderson can open the trap for us. Doctor, will you give Goyles a hand and fetch the body along?"

So, in haste and with no rites, the second interment of Coutoules took place. The watchers were alerted round Hut A. "Brandy" Duncan and his friend, Lieutenant Anderson, opened the trap-door in the bathroom floor and helped Byfold down with the body. Laboriously it was handled along to the far end of the tunnel.

To Byfold's eye the whole thing looked shockingly makeshift. To start with, the shaft went down a bare seven feet—as opposed to the twenty feet in their tunnel—so that the roof had very little clearance from the surface. So long as they were under the hut this did not matter, because the concrete foundations of the hut themselves formed a roof to the tunnel. The last six or eight feet were a different matter. It was like going along a rabbit hole.

Alone, it would have been tricky. With Coutoules in tow it looked both dangerous and impossible.

When the body was at last in a position at the end of the tunnel which resembled, as closely as possible, the position in which it had been found, Byfold crawled back to the shaft for further instructions.

He was running with sweat.

"Now you'll have to fake the accident," said Colonel Baird. "One thing, though, you'll have to take care not to open a hole right up to the top. A partial fall is what we want."

"I don't think that's possible," said Byfold. He was irritated and exhausted and his eyes were full of sand.

"If it can't be done," said Colonel Baird patiently, "the scheme's a wash-out. Think, man. If you make a hole that can be seen from the top, a sentry will spot it happening and we'll have Benucci here in five minutes. What do you think he's going to say when his doctors tell him that Coutoules has been dead for twelve hours?"

"Hm," said Byfold. It really hadn't occurred to him before to wonder what the Italians would say. So long as his own tunnel was not in jeopardy he was quite happy.

"I think," said Duncan diffidently, "that it could be managed. If you were to take one of the uprights from the shaft"—these were about nine feet long: they had come out of the rafters of the theatre hut—"I think you could squat down in the safe part of the tunnel and work the end of the wood into the roof. You ought to be able to bring down a good slab that way, without too much danger—"

"Try it that way first," said Baird.

The upright to which Duncan referred was one of four which ran up each corner of the entrance shaft and supported the trap. They were all embedded in the earth at the bottom and screwed into a framework at the top, on which the trap itself rested.

It took a little time to get one out, but they did so in the end, and Byfold grasped it in his hand, lance-like, and crawled once more along the tunnel until he was in sight of Coutoules' boot-heels.

He hoped it was for the last time. He had not loved Coutoules in life; in death, he felt he was seeing a good deal too much of him.

He propped himself on one elbow, made sure that he was himself still under the firm foundations of the hut, and edged forward the piece of wood which he held.

The roof of the tunnel, which had looked only too ready to collapse, proved, of course, tiresomely difficult to dislodge. He thrust his wooden spear lengthways into it and wriggled it about. A thin dusting of sand fell from the roof and the wood came out and fell with a soft thud on Coutoules' rump.

Byfold swore and began all over again. He saw that he would have to dig the roof out in a series of steps.

Jab, jab, jab.

His arm was aching, he was sweating all over, and the sand had got into his eyes again.

Why to God do we ever trouble to shore-up a tunnel, he thought, if it takes all this trouble to bring it down.

He dug the end of the wood in once more and levered downwards. There was a soft, rushing noise, quite unlike anything that had gone before and the air was full of falling sand.

When he raised his head he saw that he had done an almost perfect job. The whole of the roof at the far end of the tunnel had come down. The body was completely buried. There was no daylight showing, but judging by the depth of the fall he guessed that there was very little left between the roof of the cavity and the surface.

He crawled back to the shaft, propped the wooden upright loosely back into position, and climbed out.

Cyriakos Coutoules was reinterred.

II

"I do not understand, Colonel," said Captain Benucci. "You say that this Greek died in the tunnel, but you do not know who was with him."

"I didn't say I didn't know," said Colonel Baird. "I said I wasn't going to tell you."

"And why is it you who reports this, and not Colonel Lavery?"

"As you are well aware," said Colonel Baird, "I am in charge of all escaping enterprises in this Camp. And if you want to make anything out of it," he added, "go ahead."

"It is not I who will want to make anything out of it," said Captain Benucci. "If a man has been killed it is a matter for criminal process."

"What do you mean—*been killed?*"

"Been killed or died—what difference for him? He is dead. In any event I suggest that you, by your own admission, are his murderer."

Colonel Baird slowly turned dark red. Then he said, in a voice which he made not even a superficial effort to control. "Will you explain what you mean by that?"

"I take the words from your own mouth. You are the organizer of these childish enterprises. You encourage men to risk their lives in underground burrows and in suicidal attempts to climb the walls. If they fail, as they must, and men get killed, then you are responsible."

"I see," said Colonel Baird. "I thought for a minute you were being personal."

The two men were standing in the bathroom of Hut A. The trap-door was open. The body of Coutoules had been recovered and removed. The room seemed to be full of the dark blue uniforms of the carabinieri. Behind Captain Benucci was the chief interpreter, Tenente Mordaci, known to the camp as Dracula on account of his gross figure, his large red lips and his habit of wearing a long, silk-lined cloak; with Mordaci was his assistant, Paoli, a youthful, girlish-looking Under-Lieutenant, who was known as "The Boy" and whose alleged relationship with Mordaci was a source of unfailing ribaldry to the prisoners.

Outside, one party of soldiers was beginning to break down the roof of the tunnel and another was roping off the area. Photographs were being taken.

"You tell me, Colonel," went on Captain Benucci, "that the diggers—the nameless diggers—of this tunnel—came to you this morning and reported this matter to you. They say that Coutoules was the last man in the tunnel last night—and must have been pinned down by a fall of sand—unknown to his friends."

"Yes."

"That they became alarmed when they found that Coutoules was missing this morning—reopened the tunnel, and discovered his body."

"Yes," said Colonel Baird again. He felt that the less he said at this juncture the better.

"And Coutoules was a member of this—tunnel-digging gang?"

"Yes, he was."

"Curious. I should not have thought, from what I have observed, that he was of that type."

"Life is full of surprises," said Colonel Baird. "Do you want me any more?"

"Not at the moment," said Captain Benucci.

They hated each other with the instinctive hatred of different sorts of animal.

Colonel Baird walked thoughtfully back to his own quarters. There was something about the way in which the situation was being handled that he did not like at all. It was difficult to put a finger on it. Previously, when an escape attempt had "broken" or had been discovered before it could "break" the Italians had behaved in a different and much more predictable manner. There was a purposefulness about their moves this time, an altogether un-Italian lack of excitement. It almost looked as though what happened had not come as a complete surprise to them.

Colonel Baird liked it not at all.

III

When Byfold and Goyles got back to their room they found Tony Long sitting at the table. "Hugo and Grim are out too," he explained. "We only got seven days this time. Just petty criminals. What on earth have you been up to whilst I've been away?"

Goyles and Byfold told him what had happened.

"Thank God Colonel Baird stuck his toes in over our tunnel," said Long. "It should be through in six weeks—less if we hurry. The other scheme's not unpromising either." He reported the results of his and Baierlein's observations the previous night. "Both cell windows are wide open," he said. "It took two months to do but it's a beautiful job. The stone that holds the bottom of the middle bar has been loosened so that you can slide it right out. The bar then drops away from the top socket and leaves you quite enough room to squeeze through and get out on to the roof. Grim was too hefty, but Hugo and I did it easily. Once up on the roof you need a short wooden ladder. Pick your moment when the gate sentry's in his box, and it would be money for old rope."

"The real difficulty," said Byfold, "would be making sure that we all got put in the cooler at once."

"There's a bigger snag than that," said Goyles. "The first part's all right, but what about the next. We should need all the usual kit—money, food, and so on. How are we going to get it into prison with us?"

Whilst they were thinking that one out, it might be an opportunity to snatch a moment to introduce them.

They formed one of those close, prisoner-of-war friendships which, if analysed, would have been found to be based on community of interests and dissimilarity of character.

Their own accounts of how they came into captivity afford a sufficient commentary.

Roger Byfold was a regular soldier. He had left Sandhurst at about Munich-time to join a Lancer Regiment already under orders for the Middle East. He had been there when war was declared. He was a tankman and a professional soldier, and desert warfare had suited him down to the ground. Indeed, he had done very well at it, as the white-and-purple ribbon on his battle-dress bore witness, until one day everything went wrong. "Just a normal patrol. Can't help thinking it must have been Friday the thirteenth and I never noticed it. First my wireless went dead. Then I broke a track. Told the rest of the troop to complete the *recce* and pick me up on the way back. I heard afterwards they lost their way and were lucky to get back themselves. Got out and mended the track and found we were in a mine-field. First news of this was when we blew the other track off, and half the suspension with it. Nothing much left to do. Waited for the troop all day. When they didn't turn up, we tried to walk back. Got picked up by the Krauts early next morning."

"Bad luck," everyone agreed, "but just the sort of thing one expected in armoured warfare."

Henry Goyles was a schoolmaster, the son of a solicitor. He was a good bit the oldest of the three. When war broke out he joined the ranks of a Gunner Regiment, where his precision of thought and speech, his occasional absence of mind, and his large round steel spectacles had earned him the name of "Cuckoo"—a name which had followed him through the Army and accompanied him into captivity. He must have been quite a good gunner, because in 1941 he got one of the few and much-coveted commissions into a regular Horse Artillery Regiment, and he reached his battery in time for the Auchinleck offensive. If he was frequently frightened in the course of the next three months he managed to conceal it as well as most, particularly when he could devote his mind to a purely technical problem.

This was eventually his undoing.

"It was rather an advanced sort of O.P.," he explained. "We got there before first light, in Bren carriers, and then everybody who had come with us seemed to fade away. I was just thinking that we were rather out in the blue, and perhaps we ought to pull back a bit, when suddenly I saw a most beautiful target—the type of thing you get on the ranges at Larkhill, but never expect to see in real life. It was a German Staff car, which had broken down, just behind a sort of hump. They thought they were hidden, but I could see them all right. A pin-point target, you understand, with flank observation. Really, a fascinating problem. Being out to one side, you could see the effect of the charge zone very clearly. I bracketed for line, and I bracketed for range and I worked out the angle and the factor and then I put over a beauty—I think it landed on the radiator cap. I had noticed someone come up behind me just before

I gave the order to fire, and I turned round and said, 'What about that for a shot?' And," concluded Goyles sadly, "it was a German with a tommy-gun."

"Very bad luck," everyone agreed, "but just the sort of thing which was always happening to forward O.P.s."

Tony Long, the youngest of the three, was a born irregular. He took to any form of special service like a duck to water. To look at him you might have thought that he was one of those serious, polite, hard-working, athletic boys who make the best regimental officers. To a certain extent, this was true. What you would never have guessed was that he was at heart a bandit and a killer. He had arrived at Campo 127 after three years of miscellaneous and improbable enterprises.

"The last one really was rather mad," he said. "I landed on the coast of Sicily with one sergeant and a bag of bombs. I had to blow up two railway bridges. Moreover, I did blow them up. Unfortunately, something went wrong on the last one and we brought down a good deal of bridge on top of ourselves. When I came to I found the sergeant was dead and I had broken an ankle. I got picked up two nights later."

"Extremely bad luck," everybody agreed. "But what else can you expect if you go about behaving in such an unorthodox way?"

IV

"You want to do what?" said Colonel Lavery, surprised for once out of his usual calm.

"Just a precaution, you understand," said Benucci.

"Everybody's finger-prints?"

"We must take everybody's, otherwise the check will not be complete."

"The orderlies too?"

"Everyone," said Benucci firmly.

"I don't think you can do it," said Colonel Lavery. "I don't think the Geneva Convention allows it."

"The Geneva Convention governs the conduct of the captor towards his prisoners of war," agreed Benucci. "In this case it is not a question of prisoners of war. An unexplained death has taken place. Indeed, the matter has ceased to be entirely under my control."

"How do you propose to set about it?"

"It should not take very long. The pads have been prepared and if you will issue the necessary orders, I will have it carried out at roll-call this evening."

"I shall report the whole matter to the Protecting Power," said Colonel Lavery.

v

"Really," said Rupert Rolf-Callender to his friends in Hut A. "I mean to say—finger-prints. What next?"

"If you feel so strongly about it, why didn't you refuse?"

"Really, Terence, I couldn't start a brawl."

"If you want my opinion," said Captain the Honourable Peter Perse, "it's all on account of this stupid tunnel. I always told Duncan it would be discovered, and of course it has been, and now there's going to be nothing but unpleasantness, you see if I'm not right."

"I've never known them behave quite like this before," said Terence Bush. "Usually they strafe the hut a bit when a tunnel's discovered and then forget about it. They haven't done a thing this time except shut up that actual bathroom—they haven't even turned the showers off."

"I don't think they're really worried about the tunnel," said Rolf-Callender. "It was finding that chap in it."

"How did he get there?"

"As a matter of fact I can tell you that," said Bush. "He was put there. I got it from Chris Martin in Hut C. Apparently Colonel Baird got a lot of them to put up a sort of gym display to cover up carrying the body across and Chris was in it. They put Coutoules on Byfold's back and galloped him across."

"Do you mean to say," said the Honourable Peter with some indignation, "that they simply dumped him on us. Why can't Hut C stick to their own rotten bodies. Here we are, cut down to one bathroom between eighty of us—"

"Shocking."

"What can you expect," said Rolf-Callender. "Those cloak-and-dagger types are all the same. It isn't as if they'd got a chance in a million of getting anywhere. If they had, one might do something about it. But no one's ever got out of this country yet and no one's ever going to. All that happens is that they dig these footling holes in the ground, which get discovered, and everyone else is made uncomfortable. If they *do* get out they spend about three nights in the open and then get caught and come back and have thirty days in the cooler and think themselves no end of chaps."

"In any case," said the Honourable Peter, "we've only got to sit tight a few more weeks and the Eighth Army will catch up with us. Is anyone going to spin the wheel to-night?"

"Not to-night," said Rolf-Callender. "Have you forgotten? We're rehearsing to-night. We'll use the dining-room after supper's been cleared away."

"We shall probably find someone starting another tunnel there," said the Honourable Peter bitterly.

VI

Baierlein, Overstrand and Grimsdale were walking round the perimeter of the camp, just inside the trip wire, which guarded a six-foot forbidden zone at the foot of the wall itself. Every fifty yards inside the wire a notice board bore an imaginative piece of English prose which ran "Passage and Demurrage strictly forbidden". If anyone stepped over this wire the sentries had orders to shoot at them.

Baierlein and Grimsdale were busy reporting to Overstrand the result of their recent imprisonment. Their conclusions were much the same as Long's had been.

"It's easy enough," said Baierlein, "provided you're a stock-size person, to get out on to the roof. If Grim's going to do it, it will mean loosening another bar."

"What about the gap between the roof and the wall?"

"Ten feet," said Baierlein. "You'd need a short ladder for that bit, but you could make it out of the double bedsteads in the cell. They're enormous things—the side pieces are over ten feet long. That isn't the real trouble though—"

"It's the kit," said Grimsdale. "What's the use of getting over the wall if you find yourself, dressed in battle-dress, with no food and no money and no papers in the middle of Italy."

"I had wondered," said Baierlein, "if we mightn't arrange to have the stuff brought in to us. I know we shall get thoroughly searched when we go into the cooler, and I agree that it would be unnecessarily risky to try and smuggle much escaping kit in with us. One might get away with money and maps and compasses, but nothing really bulky."

"If we're going cross-country we should want some sort of covering—a blanket, or at least an overcoat, and a knapsack to carry hard rations."

"To say nothing of the rations themselves."

"Exactly," said Baierlein. "Well, my idea was, we take in the small stuff hidden on us, and get the orderlies to smuggle the rest in bit by bit, in the food."

"It would need a bloody big apple pie to hide an overcoat in," said Overstrand.

They paced on for some minutes and had made a complete circuit of the camp before Overstrand spoke again.

"I've been thinking," he said, "that we ought to look for something more immediate."

Neither of the others said anything.

"I've been in nearly two years," went on Overstrand, "and that's one hell of a sight too long. Now we've had this trouble over the Hut C tunnel I don't see it going ahead very fast. They may decide to seal it up altogether for a bit. There are too many snags in this 'cooler' business to make it worth going flat out for—that's my view, anyway. I think we ought to try something more straightforward and less—well, less fiddling."

Baierlein and Grimsdale looked worried. They were both genuinely fond of Overstrand, but they knew that he was apt to be unreliable where his emotions were involved.

"Had you anything particular in mind?" said Baierlein.

"As a matter of fact I had," said Overstrand. "It's something that Desmond Foster is doing—"

"He can't be starting another tunnel already."

"It isn't exactly a tunnel. It's top secret, of course, but he couldn't mind my telling you two. This is how it goes—"

VII

"Should we look in somewhere for a cocktail first," suggested Captain Abercrowther to Captain the McInstalker.

"Not a cocktail," protested the McInstalker. "Geraldo is digging out a 1924 Mouton Rothschild for us. A cocktail would be definitely out of place."

"Perhaps a glass of sherry."

"One glass of brown sherry. We've just time. Let's have it at the Salted Almond. We may run into someone amusing."

A few minutes passed in silence.

"One more."

"One for the road, then."

"Curse. It's beginning to rain—I don't think we'll bother about a cab, though. It's only a hundred yards."

Both gentlemen turned up their coat collars against the light autumn rain and strolled down the Shaftesbury Avenue of 1939.

VIII

"Five women," said Rupert Rolf-Callender, "and twelve men. Thirteen, if you count Flush."

"Was he a man?"

"It says 'Flush—a spaniel'."

"How are we going to manage about Flush?"

"First things first," said Rolf-Callender. "We'll start with the girls. Peter, you'll have to do Elizabeth."

"Must I?"

"Certainly you must. The part's made for you."

"Why do I always have to do girls?"

"To be quite honest," said Rolf-Callender kindly, "I don't know. It isn't as if you were pretty, in any sense of the word, and the trouble we had keeping the backs of your legs shaved for the run of *Bitter Sweet* is a thing I prefer to forget. Nor is your voice precisely virginal. It's something to do with the bones in your face—"

"Who's going to do the father?"

"I think we shall have to ask Abercrowther."

"You can't have a Mr. Barrett with a Scots accent."

"We shall have to put up with it. He's a damned good actor. Do you remember how good he was in the Monty Woolley part in *The Man Who Came to Dinner?*"

"All right, put him down. Where is he, by the way?"

"He's dining out to-night," said Bush. "What are you going to do, Rupert?"

"I rather thought I'd try Robert Browning."

"My God, Rupert, do you mean to say I've got to make love to you *again.*"

"You did it very nicely last time," said Rolf-Callender complacently. "Now all these brothers—Octavius and Septimus and so on. They're really only stooges. We'd better let the Adjutant do one of them, then he'll make no trouble about letting us have the Theatre Hut for rehearsals."

"Whatever happens," said Bush, "we've got one absolutely guaranteed laugh here." He was turning over the pages of the acting edition.

"What's that?"

"At the beginning of Act III. 'Elizabeth (rapturously). "Italy! Oh, it's hard to take in even the bare possibility of going there. My promised land, Doctor, which I never thought to see otherwise than in dreams."'"

"That should bring the house down," agreed Rolf-Callender.

CHAPTER FOUR

THE SCAPEGOAT

I

"DOCTOR SIMMONDS," SAID BENUCCI, "YOU ARE A MAN OF experience?"

"That would depend what you mean by experience."

"Medical experience?"

"I should say so, yes."

"You are not a regular military doctor?"

"Oh, no. Certainly not."

"You are a civilian doctor. You hold the degree of F.R.C.S?"

"It's not exactly a degree," said Doctor Simmonds cautiously. "Anyway, I expect it's in my record somewhere. What's it all about?"

They were in the Camp Commandant's Office. Besides Benucci, the Chief Interpreter and Doctor Simmonds there was a fourth party present. A thin civilian in black coat and striped trousers, with that neat beard which appears to be the hall-mark of professional eminence in Latin countries.

"I must introduce Professor Di Buonavilla of the medical faculty of the University of Florence."

The professor rose to his feet and bowed. Doctor Simmonds half got up, made an indeterminate noise, and sat down again.

"It is because we wish to proceed correctly in this," said Captain Benucci smoothly, "that I have afforded you—Doctor

Simmonds—this opportunity of examining the body of Lieutenant Coutoules. Also because I understood that you were the best qualified in the Camp to make this examination."

"Very good of you," said Doctor Simmonds. He was not quite sure what a professor in the faculty of medicine did. "If this gentleman is a practising doctor, I have no doubt that his conclusions will be the same as my own."

"No doubt," said Benucci. "That is exactly what we wish to establish. I should perhaps have explained that the professor is consultant to the Police Force at Firenze. It is for his experience in this type of work that we have asked him to assist us. He does not speak English himself but I will ask Lieutenant Mordaci to read you a translation of the statement he has prepared. If there are any questions you wish to ask, pray use the services of the interpreter."

Mordaci read from the statement in front of him. It was a long statement. It started with a description of the body of Coutoules as the professor had seen it at two o'clock on the afternoon of its discovery. It contained some sound observations on rigor mortis, post-mortem bruising and the tendency of blood to drain outwards from the centre of a corpse after death. Doctor Simmonds, who had the essential disinterested honesty of the expert, found it hard to disagree with any of its conclusions. These were: that Coutoules had died some time one side or the other of midnight, but not earlier than nine o'clock on the previous evening; that death had been due to asphyxiation; and that the body had been moved and handled after death.

"Have you any comments to make, Doctor?" asked Benucci, when the statement had finished.

For form's sake, Doctor Simmonds asked a few questions and Mordaci translated them, and retranslated the professor's answers.

He asked the professor if he had noticed a bruise on the back of Coutoules' neck. The professor had noticed it. He suggested it might have been made by a stone in the fall of sand. Doctor Simmonds agreed that it might. It was quite clear to him that the professor knew his job—as he would be likely to do if he was, in fact, a police consultant.

"Well, Doctor," said Benucci again, at the end of it, "what are your conclusions?"

"I'm not sure that I follow you."

"It seems plain to you that Coutoules was moved after death?"

"That's a matter of argument and inference. Not a matter of fact."

"If we accept it," said Benucci, "is it not logical to surmise that Coutoules was smothered first, and placed in the tunnel afterwards, in order to conceal the truth about his murder—and his murderers?"

"You mean that you think he was killed in one of the huts and put in the tunnel afterwards?"

"It is not a question of thinking," said Benucci, in an ill-natured parody of the doctor's professional manner. "It is a question of evidence."

"But that's absurd," said Doctor Simmonds. "Did you look at his hands?"

"Not particularly."

"He must have died under the sand. Why, he'd pulled half his nails off trying to claw his way out."

The last few exchanges had been in English. The professor had clearly understood nothing.

"Ask *him*," said Doctor Simmonds.

There was an awkward moment of silence whilst Mordaci looked at his senior officer for guidance.

"Put the question, Lieutenant," said Benucci evenly.

Mordaci said something in Italian.

Doctor Simmonds did not listen to the answer. He was looking at the professor's face. His expression was enlightening. He started to say something, then changed his mind; started a second sentence, and broke off in the middle of it.

Benucci said: "The professor says that he does not attach any particular significance to the state of Coutoules' hands."

II

The Escape Committee met in Colonel Baird's room. Baird sat on the only chair; the other two members of the committee sat on his bed. They were Colonel Stanislaus Shore of the U.S. Air Force and Commander Oxey of the Royal Navy. No one had been able to discover by exactly what administrative muddle these two had been sent to a camp for British Army Officers, but everyone was very glad to have them. Colonel Shore, in particular, was a three-dimensional character in his own right. He was the only prisoner-of-war in Italy who had ever forced an officer of carabinieri to carry his luggage for him to the station. The fact that he was drunk at the time had detracted nothing from the performance.

It was Colonel Shore who was speaking.

"I certainly find it difficult to figure out exactly what they're up to," he said. "They've never made a fuss like this before over a dead body. You remember when they shot Colley and his two friends when they tried to rush the gate—we didn't hear anything more about *them*, did we? They were buried and forgotten inside a week. Forgotten by the Italians, I mean. I reckon someone's got the facts notched up somewhere to sort out after the war's over."

"Or those men who jumped the train—" said Commander Oxey.

"I think this is a little different," said Colonel Baird. "Those others were all killed escaping. For some reason the Italians refuse to be convinced that Coutoules was."

"That doctor from Florence," said Shore, "and the finger-printing and all those photographers they've been taking round the dig. Maybe I've got a suspicious mind, but the whole thing's beginning to look to me like the beginning of a frame up. It has the smell of one. They want to pin the murder on to someone, and I don't believe they're fussy who they choose."

"Who *did* kill Coutoules?" asked Oxey.

This direct, naval question produced a silence.

"I'm damned if I know," said Colonel Baird. "On the face of it, the thing's impossible. The only sort of solution that holds any water is that he was knocked off sometime that evening in Hut C, and dumped in the tunnel."

"If that's so," said Shore, "an awful lot of people are telling an awful lot of lies."

"It might be a good thing to find out," said Oxey. "We don't want the wrong person hanged."

III

"Now, Captain Byfold," said Benucci, "I should strongly advise you to speak the truth."

"I doubt if you'd recognize it if you heard it," said Byfold. Nevertheless, he was neither as comfortable nor as confident as he sounded. He was in the Camp Commandant's Office. The Commandant, Captain Benucci and Lieutenant Mordaci were seated. Since there were only three chairs in the room it followed that the rest of those present—Captain Byfold, Under-Lieutenant Paoli, two camp guards and three or four carabinieri—were standing. They seemed to have been standing for a long time. Byfold wondered what would happen if he suddenly sat down on the floor.

"Were you a member of the party who were engaged in digging a tunnel from the bathroom in Hut A?"

"As I have said a dozen times before, that's not a question I can be made to answer."

"If it was simply a matter of escaping, no. This is a question of murder."

"Who says that it is murder?"

"The facts say so. For the last time, Captain Byfold, did you work in that tunnel?"

"For the last time, I refuse to say."

"Are you aware that your finger-prints—and only yours—have been found in several places on one of the pieces of wood which formed the upright of the framework in the shaft of that tunnel?"

"If you say so."

"I do say so. A piece of wood, Captain Byfold, which formed—I use the past tense—which formed one of the uprights. It had been removed from the framework of the shaft, and very carelessly replaced. It had plainly been put to some use in the tunnel."

"Very possibly," said Byfold wearily. "Woodwork is used in a tunnel you know. It has a variety of uses—"

"A variety of uses." Benucci smiled. It was not a very pleasant smile. "Might I inform you also—I do not wish it to be said at some future time that we have concealed anything from you—might I therefore inform you that photographs taken in the tunnel show a number of marks in the roof—and that these marks have been measured and match exactly the piece of wood to which I refer. What do you deduce from that, Captain Byfold?"

"You tell me."

"I suggest that the wood was used to bring down the tunnel on Coutoules—whilst he was, perhaps, unconscious—"

"That's a perfectly filthy suggestion."

The Commandant said something, and Mordaci translated. Byfold gathered that the Commandant was asking what his answer had been. He therefore said slowly and loudly in his best Italian, "All that has been suggested is quite untrue." The Commandant looked up at him for a moment, but said nothing. He seemed to be almost asleep.

"You still refuse to admit," went on Benucci, "that you were a member of this tunnel gang."

"It's obviously not much use denying it," said Byfold. "You seem to have made up your minds about it. I suppose it hasn't occurred to you that I don't even live in that hut."

"Indeed," said Benucci, "and you never visit it either—after dark?"

Byfold had nothing to say to this. It seemed silly to say that he had visited the hut once only after dark, in order to play a rubber of bridge. Also he had been afforded a sudden glimpse of the care with which the case against him was being constructed—a fractional lifting of the curtain—and it gave him a cold feeling in the pit of his stomach.

"You must not imagine we are blind, Captain," went on Benucci. "Because we do not always take action, it does not mean that our sentries have not got eyes—and tongues."

The Commandant asked a question and Mordaci translated.

"The Commandant asks if you were a friend of Coutoules."

"No. Certainly not. I hardly knew him."

"Then you disliked him?"

"I didn't dislike him—I hadn't much time for him." Mordaci did his best with this idiom and the Commandant nodded, and asked another question.

"Why was Coutoules disliked?"

Byfold, who had seen this one coming, answered it more or less truthfully. "It was thought that he had been giving away information about the prisoners to the authorities—to you." Mordaci again translated and Byfold was interested to see that the Commandant looked genuinely surprised. Benucci remained impassive. Either the suggestion was not news to him or, possibly, he had a better command of his face.

"Thank you," he said, "that is all, Captain Byfold." He motioned with his hand and one of the carabinieri threw open the door. As the two guards hustled him out Byfold saw Benucci lean across and say something to the Commandant. He seemed to be pleased with himself. The Commandant had relapsed into a stupor.

IV

Colonel Lavery refrained from saying "I told you so" when Colonel Baird reported to him that evening.

"They seem to be making a dead set at Byfold," he said. "It's easy to be wise after the event, but if I'd thought they were going to push the case so hard I'd have taken some elementary precautions."

"I don't think it's just Byfold," said Colonel Lavery. "I think the truth of the matter is that they want a scapegoat—"

Baird said, with unusual bitterness, "Since when have they become so fussy about a death. And I don't only mean escaping.

You remember last winter when the Red Cross parcels didn't arrive for two months and we had to live on a minus quantity of Italian rations. How many prisoners did we lose then, from starvation and near-starvation? And young Collingwood, with blood-poisoning, that they wouldn't even let a doctor look at until it was too late. If they want to investigate anything let them start on that."

"I expect that the approach of the British Army is making them progressively more tender-hearted," said Colonel Lavery. "What are you proposing to do now?"

"I suggest we wait and see if the case against Byfold comes to anything. It may be just bluff. Something for the record, as you suggest. Meanwhile, we push on as fast as possible with Tunnel C."

Colonel Lavery looked anxiously at the home-made calendar on the wall. It said "July 5th".

"How soon do you think you can be ready?"

"It isn't just a question of digging," said Baird. "If that's all it was we'd have non-stop shifts and be out inside a week. It's the shoring-up of the tunnel, and, above all, the old, old problem of getting rid of the sand. I've got an idea about that. If it comes off we might be out in just over three weeks—say twenty-five days."

"I hope you're right," said Colonel Lavery, "because if my reading of the situation is correct, that could be all the time we are going to get."

V

"Life," said Rupert Rolf-Callender, "is getting perfectly intolerable."

"Grim," agreed Terence Bush.

"They'll be asking us for another bed board soon."

"It'll be a nice change if they ask for it," said Rolf-Callender. "Last time they just took it. I can't lie on my bed now without bits of me sagging through the boards. I feel like a lot of shopping in a string bag."

"You look perfectly disgusting," agreed the Honourable Peter Perse who slept underneath him. "There's another of those damned penguins."

Through the open door of their room in Hut A they watched in disapproving silence as a large subaltern—a stranger, from Hut C—waddled down the passage. Waddled is the exact description of his gait, since he seemed to find his legs unnaturally heavy, and lifted them one after the other with just the tentative deliberation of a young penguin learning to walk. The ends of his long drill trousers were tied tightly round his ankles, and the calves of his legs seemed to be suffering from a form of shifting elephantiasis.

"Where does he put the sand?" asked Bush, when this remarkable figure had passed out of sight.

"In *our* tunnel," said Rolf-Callender.

"What?"

"It's a fact. The Eyeties have posted a sentry on the outside end, but they just sealed down the bathroom end and left it. The bright boys have got the trap open again and are filling the tunnel up from this end."

"Do you mean to say," said Bush, "that those types from Hut C are digging sand out of *their* tunnel and putting it into *our* tunnel?"

"It's all very well talking about *our* tunnel," said the Honourable Peter, who was a fair-minded man, and also enjoyed provoking people. "I can't remember you doing much about it when it was actually being dug."

"Maybe not," said Bush, "but if this caper is discovered—God, there's another of those penguins"—he got up and shut the door pointedly—"if it is discovered, it's this hut that's going to suffer. With Benucci in his present frame of mind I can see him shutting off the water *and* the electric light."

The others agreed that this was highly possible.

VI

"We're definitely interested," said Overstrand to Desmond Foster, "but we'd like to know a little more about it first."

"Particularly that bit about the lights," said Baierlein.

"All right. You know Tim Meynell?"

"The sewer-rat?"

"That's him—" They referred to an enthusiast from the Royal Engineers who had dug a way for himself from the camp latrine into the main sewer and had propelled himself along it on an inflated rubber mattress in a number of indescribable journeys of exploration. He had never succeeded in reaching the open and the only result so far of his pioneer work had been that his friends ostentatiously walked up-wind of him.

"Well, he went down last week to have another look at the main pipe—he's got an idea of forcing a grating inside the Italian quarters—and he reckons he was just about here"—Foster demonstrated on a plan of the camp which he had drawn—"when he suddenly ran into this new electric cable."

"New?"

"Oh, definitely. He'd been that way two months before, and it wasn't the sort of thing you could miss seeing. A great insulated cable, obviously new."

"That sounds very interesting," said Overstrand. "You think—"

"Well, it's pretty obvious, isn't it? Between the time he was down before, and that time, those four chaps got away over the wall by fusing the lights. You know how it was done."

"They cut the overhead wire with a pair of shears on a stick, didn't they?"

"Yes. And it's hard to guard against that sort of thing. There are too many places where you can get at the overhead wire—from the roof of the theatre for one, or anywhere along the south wall, if you're prepared to take a bit of a chance on it—or from the cooler. Obviously, if they wanted to prevent it happening again, either they had to change all the overhead wiring or else—"

"Or else," said Overstrand bitterly, "or else, like the triple bastards they are, they might instal an alternative *underground* wiring to all the sentry boxes, so that the next lot who tried to fuse the lights and rush the wall would only fuse *one* of the systems—the other would come into operation, and the results would be sticky."

"Just the sort of clever, slightly sadistic thing Benucci would think up," agreed Baierlein. "It's got his signature all over it."

"And you think that this cable is the alternative system?"

"It looks like it, doesn't it?" said Foster. "It was put in a few weeks after the last attempts, and you can see from its direction"— he demonstrated again on the plan—"it runs out from the main towards the outer wall. I don't see what else it can be."

Overstrand and Baierlein turned this over for some time in silence. They were walking with Desmond Foster round the perimeter, since this offered the only chance of complete privacy to conspirators.

"The idea being, I take it," said Overstrand, "to cut *both* systems at the vital moment."

"Yes."

"I think it sounds rather hopeful," said Baierlein. "It's got just that element of the unlikely that brings a scheme off. Have you thought about the ladders yet?"

Foster looked the least bit embarrassed.

"As a matter of fact we have," he said, "only you must most solemnly promise not to say a word about it to anyone. There's going to be a certain amount of feeling about this, when it's found out, but I don't see what we could have done. There simply wasn't another piece of wood in the camp of the right length."

"Of course we won't say anything," said Baierlein. "What's it all about? You sound as if you've robbed a church."

"Well, it's not quite as bad as that," said Foster. "I'll tell you."

VII

"Are you coming out for a kickabout this afternoon," said "Tag" Burchnall, "we thought we might start with a scrum practice and have a pick-up game afterwards."

"I hope there's not going to be any nonsense about allowing baseball on the rugger pitch," said Rollo Betts-Hanger. "I hear the Sports Committee have been approached."

"Baseball. Surely we haven't sunk to that!"

"I don't know," said Betts-Hanger. "It's quite an interesting game when you look into it. People in America get quite keen on it, I believe."

"I've no objection to them playing baseball, as long as they don't do it on the rugger pitch."

"Someone was arguing," said Billy Moxhay, "that July wasn't the right month for rugger. Perfect nonsense, I thought. Rugger's an all-the-year-round game. As I pointed out, the only reason chaps don't play rugger during the summer in England is because the ground's too hard. Here the ground's hard all the time, so it makes no difference."

"Quite right," said Burchnall. "Has anyone seen Gerry?"

At this moment the door burst open and Gerry Parsons arrived at a gallop. His face was red and he appeared to have lost his voice. His friends stared at him in amazement.

"I say," he said at last. "Do you know what?"

"End of the war?"

"Revolution in Italy?"

"Extra issue of Red Cross parcels?"

"No, I say, this is serious," said Parsons. "They've simply gone and pinched them—"

"Pinched what?"

"The rugger posts."

A horror-struck silence was broken by Burchnall.

"This is the final, ultimate limit," he said. "They can't do it. I've a good mind to go straight to the S.B.O."

VIII

At about five o'clock that afternoon—the 5th of July—a garment of comparative peace lay over the camp. The sun still held much of its noon power and most of the prisoners were lying on their beds in their huts or toasting themselves quietly in the open.

A jazz band was practising in the Theatre Hut, and a lethargic class was being lectured to, in the open space between Huts D and E, on the Logistic Problems involved in Hannibal's campaigns.

Even the sentries seemed to feel the weight of the afternoon and they were dozing as openly as they dared on their platforms.

The history don was lying back in his deck-chair, and wishing that he could have been spending the afternoon in a punt on the Cherwell. He was watching, with half his attention, a large covered lorry of the Italian Army type, which had stopped in the road outside the main gate and was now manœuvring backwards and forwards in an apparent endeavour to turn in the narrowest part of the road.

It had got half-way round now and was facing directly towards the outer gate.

It started to move.

The sentries on both gates ran forward and threw the gates open. The van accelerated.

A towel whisked out of a window. The professor jumped to his feet and dropped his book.

The van was inside the camp now, and coming on fast.

In one of the end rooms in Hut C a bell rang three times urgently. Four men left their bunks with a jump and disappeared through the door. As the last of them reached the kitchen they could hear the Italian Army lorry squealing to a stop outside, and a high-pitched scream of orders as the hidden carabinieri leapt from the back of it.

"They'll have to take their chance," said the leader of the four, and as he spoke the stove was already on its way down.

There was a thumping of feet outside the hut and the passage door burst open.

The stove was back in position now and one of the men was doing some quick work with a broom.

"We shan't be able to get out of here," said the leader. "Pretend to be hanging up clothes—and for God's sake, Peter, push that wire further down inside your shirt. I can see the end of it from here."

There was a second of silence, followed by a mutter of Italian voices, among them Benucci's.

"They're in Goyles' room."

"Don't whisper," said the leader, "and try to look as if you really are hanging that shirt up to dry. At the moment you look as if you were auctioning it."

There was another silence, and they heard Byfold's voice.

"I demand to be taken to Colonel Lavery."

"I fear that Colonel Lavery has no jurisdiction in this case."

"Then I protest."

"You may make your protest to the criminal court that tries your case." Benucci's voice had lost a lot of its suavity. He sounded vindictive and triumphant.

There was a further stamping of feet. The hut door slammed and the lorry drove away.

CHAPTER FIVE

GOYLES IS GIVEN A JOB

At ten o'clock on the morning following Byfold's arrest Goyles knocked on the door of Colonel Baird's room and was asked to come in. When he saw that Colonel Shore and Commander Oxey were there, he apologized and prepared to back out.

"Come right in," said Colonel Baird. "This isn't a committee meeting. Have you got some news for us?"

"That's what I wanted to ask you, sir," said Goyles. "Have you heard anything more about Byfold?"

"Not a thing. Just a typical Italian trick." He slapped angrily at a fat black fly on the wall. "They might have been kidnapping him, not arresting him, the way they went about it."

"I expect they thought there would be a riot if they walked in and took him," suggested Commander Oxey.

"Might have been, at that," said Colonel Shore.

"What's the worst they can do to him," asked Goyles, putting into words for the first time something that had been worrying him all night. "They can't try him, can they—he's a prisoner of war?"

"I wouldn't be too sure about that," said Baird. "I remember a case in one of our camps—it happened in the prison cage at Asmara, when I was temporarily in charge of it—a lot of real, dyed-in-the-wool, last-ditch Nazis got the idea that one of the other prisoners was a traitor. I don't know if he really was, or if it was just that he didn't say 'Heil Hitler' smartly enough when spoken to—anyway, they ganged up on him, and one night, after lights-out, they held a set-piece trial and found him guilty, and strung him up. They didn't even pretend to be sorry about it—told everybody what they'd done."

"What happened to them?"

"The three ring-leaders were shot," said Baird shortly.

"I see," said Goyles. A sudden, quite terrifying idea had occurred to him which he took a good deal of pains to suppress.

"I'm afraid," went on Baird, "if they convince themselves that they've got a good case, there's no doubt they could—well, they could make things very sticky for Byfold."

"Even though they know he didn't do it."

"*We* know he didn't," said Baird. "And if the worst comes to the worst we could tell them the truth. But why should they believe us even then? We might have been making the whole thing up to save Byfold's skin."

"Yes," said Goyles. "And, of course, we'd lose the tunnel—"

"It wasn't only the tunnel I was thinking of," said Baird. "I think it's a good tunnel, and it might be a very useful tunnel. But if it came to a direct showdown—tunnel or Byfold—I guess I know which way we'd vote. But it isn't. We could lose both of them, quite easily, if we played this wrong."

"There's only one possible thing to do," said Commander Oxey. "To my mind, it's clear as day. We've got to find out what actually happened, who killed Coutoules, and why and where—and how his body got in that tunnel."

Colonel Baird turned to Goyles.

"Would you like to take that on?" he asked.

Goyles looked considerably startled.

"The Committee would back you, of course. It's not the sort of thing they could very well undertake officially. You're a friend of Byfold. It would be quite a reasonable assignment for you. We'll give it out that anyone who's got any information about Coutoules—where they saw him last—whether they noticed anything suspicious—that sort of thing—is to contact you."

"Yes—but," said Goyles. He was trying hard to see himself in the role of special investigator. "Of course, I'll do anything I can," he added, "only don't hope for too much. Have you got any general idea about it at all—I mean, it seems quite crazy."

"On the face of it," said Colonel Shore, "it *is* crazy. That's what ought to make it easy to solve. If it was ordinary, there might be half a dozen solutions, and you could never be sure that you'd get hold of the right one. With a crazy problem like this, if you can find *any solution at all*, it must be the right one."

"Something in that," said Commander Oxey. He had a deep respect for the American's intellect—a respect based subconsciously on the fact that Colonel Shore looked like Gary Cooper, who was the only American film star of whom the Commander approved.

"We were talking about it when you came in," said Baird. "We hadn't got very far, but for what it's worth you can have it. We thought that the general idea—the shape of the thing—was that Coutoules was an Italian informer. We thought that either there were people in the camp who knew a lot more about this than we did, or else—it would amount to the same thing in the end—who *thought* they knew a lot more than we did. They get together—it must have been four of them at least and kill Coutoules quietly—by tying a wet towel over his face, or holding his head in a pillow or something of that sort. Then they do more or less what we did in the other tunnel—open it up, drag him down, and pull a bit of the roof down on top of him—having first filled his mouth with sand."

"What about what the doctor said—about him having been alive under the sand, and trying to scratch his way out?"

"It's not a pretty idea at all," said Baird. "But having gone that far is there any reason they shouldn't have gone a bit further, and faked that detail too, after he was dead?"

"I suppose not," said Goyles doubtfully. "I take it this means they must have been people out of our hut."

"Not necessarily. They must have known how the tunnel worked, but they needn't necessarily have been from the hut itself. People wander in and out of each other's huts pretty freely, don't they, till lock-up time?"

"Do you know," said Goyles, diffidently but firmly, "I don't believe it."

Colonel Baird and Commander Oxey looked quietly up at him and Colonel Shore said, "No? Tell us why, then."

"It just doesn't seem to me to be the sort of thing that could have happened, sir. I don't believe that any group of people could have got Coutoules off somewhere, and killed him, and taken him into Hut C, and put him down the tunnel, and—and done all the other things you mentioned, sir—without *someone* knowing about it. Why, you can't blow your nose in this camp without at least three people coming along in the course of the day and saying how sorry they are to hear you've got a cold. As for murdering someone and hiding the body—it's just not on."

"Right," said Baird. He didn't sound annoyed, only interested. "What's your idea?"

"I haven't got an idea yet," said Goyles, "but I've got a question that I think wants answering. It seems to have escaped notice in the general excitement, but it's just this. Why wasn't Coutoules missed on roll-call that morning?"

This took a moment or two to sink in. Then Colonel Shore slapped his leg softly and said, "That's quite a point, isn't it?"

"Yes," said Commander Oxey. "Why wasn't he missed? What happened on roll-call that morning in our hut? You've got the room next to him, Baird."

"I'm trying to think," said Baird. "So far as I can remember it was an ordinary morning roll-call. They must have been a little late, because I remember I was up and dressed and I don't get out of my bed a minute before a quarter-past eight."

"I think they were a bit late, that morning," agreed Commander Oxey. "I'd just finished my daily dozen—as often as not they open the door when I'm in the middle of them."

"I'm always asleep anyway," said Colonel Shore. "So I can't help you."

"Well, say they arrived at twenty-to-nine. It was the little boy—Paoli—who was taking roll-call. He looked in my room, said 'Good morning' or something like that—he had a carib with him, I think, but the carib didn't come in. Then—by God, you're absolutely right—*they didn't go into Coutoules' room at all*, I didn't consciously notice it at the time, but I'm sure you're right. They just turned about and marched off down the passage."

"Coutoules had the room next door, didn't he," said Goyles, "that's the last one in the passage?"

"That's right. We two were always the last two to be inspected."

"It's funny either way," said Colonel Shore. "If your recollection's right, it's odd enough that they didn't look in his room on that one particular morning—"

"They might have skipped it because they were late—"

"Well, they might. On the other hand if Baird is wrong—it's some days ago, and he might have been thinking of some different morning—well, it's funnier still. If they deliberately refrained from looking into Coutoules' room that one morning, then either they did the thing themselves, or they were in the know about it being done. It's quite a thought, isn't it? Suppose Coutoules *was* an informer, but his bosses were finished with him. He wouldn't be much use to them after he'd been spotted. And suppose there was another reason for them not persevering with Coutoules—because they'd got a second, *unsuspected* informer in the camp. So what happens? A party of prisoners decide that it's time Coutoules was liquidated for his treachery. The second informer tells the Italians. The Italians say, 'Splendid. Suits us. So far as we're concerned he's safer dead.' So they just sit back and let it happen. The only detail they forgot was that they weren't supposed to know about it at roll-call next morning. It was quite an easy thing to forget. None of us remembered it until a minute ago."

"Yes," said Baird. "Yes. But do you see what it means? It means that the Italians must know all about the Hut C tunnel."

The three men looked at the New Zealander. It was Goyles who spoke first.

"Not necessarily, sir. If Colonel Shore is right, they might have known that Coutoules was going to be killed that night, but they might not have known where he was going to be put."

"Take it a step further," said Commander Oxey. "They might even have known that he was going to be put into *a* tunnel, without their informer knowing which tunnel, or exactly where the tunnel was, or how it worked."

"That does explain one thing," said Baird. "I always thought they were being unnaturally smart about the way they tackled the Hut A tunnel. It wasn't like them at all. All that photographing and finger-printing. But if they knew Coutoules was going to be murdered and planted in some tunnel or other for them to find, it makes much better sense. They'd have had the whole procedure worked out in advance."

"Duns Scotus and the Medieval Schoolmen," observed Colonel Shore unexpectedly, "used to devote many hours to arguing the question of how many angels could balance on the point of a needle. As they were unable to decide either on the size of the needle or on the amount of parking space required by an angel, no very exact conclusion was ever arrived at."

"Moral appreciated," said Baird. "If you're willing to take this thing on, Goyles, the first thing you'll have to do is to ferret about and find out who saw Coutoules last that evening. Anything else that might be helpful, too, of course."

"I can take what steps I like?"

"You've got *carte blanche*, so far as we're concerned. And we'll give you any help we can. The first thing, I suggest, is that we'll put it round the grape-vine that anyone with information should see you. There's one other thing. If you should chance on any-thing"—Colonel Baird paused, and looked at his two committee men—"particularly anything that affects the security of the escape arrangements, we should like to know about it first."

"Not the S.B.O.?"

"We shall pass it all on to Colonel Lavery, of course," said Baird. "We'd just like to have first cut at it, that's all."

Goyles went straight back to his own room, which was empty, and lay down on his bunk with a pillow behind his shoulders, an attitude which he normally found helpful to thought.

He had quite a lot to think about.

He realized that he was in a position which, as a reader of detective novels, he had often imagined himself occupying without ever really expecting to do so. He had been invited to investigate a murder.

The position was, in many ways, a remarkable one.

His suspects, although numerous, were closely gathered together, within the walls of one small piece of the earth's surface, measuring not more than two hundred yards in any direction.

It was a community, moreover, which was relatively without privacy. What he had said to the Escape Committee on this point had been exaggerated, but not greatly. The inmates of a camp like this really did know everything about everybody else: partly because they came of a class which is trained to be observant and partly because they had plenty of spare time in which to observe. One result of this he had encountered already. The most closely guarded escape plans had a disconcerting habit of becoming common property overnight.

Again, it was an investigation with no possibility of competition from the regular police force. Any official action which there might be would be likely to prove unhelpful, if not actually hostile.

Lastly, and above all, Goyles was aware that he was now deputy of the most powerful authority in the camp. It was true that Colonel Lavery, as S.B.O., was the administrative head, and his régime in normal matters was accepted without undue demur.

On the other hand, the twenty-five or thirty per cent of the prisoners who were actively engaged in escaping owed a strong, almost a fanatical allegiance to their own elected committee. It was powerful because it was practical. Even its sanctions were practical. There had been a prisoner who had voiced too loudly and too often his dissatisfaction at having to give up a bed board for the lining of a tunnel. One day he had found himself without any bed at all. His protests had been quite unavailing and he had slept on the floor for a week, until space could be found for him in a new room.

Goyles was sure, therefore, that any help he might require would be forthcoming to the limit of human endeavour.

Nevertheless, he was far from sure as to what exactly his first move ought to be. He lay on his bunk and devoted his quite considerable mental powers to the problem. He imagined that the soundest plan was to begin at the beginning. Accordingly he turned his thoughts to the evening of July 1st, and ran through in detail, first his own movements, then the movements of everyone whom he had encountered: lastly anything that he had heard of the movements of others.

He meditated until the lunch bugle blew.

It was that evening that his first informant appeared. He was a subaltern in the Royal Engineers; his name was Tim Meynell, and his subterranean activities, as has already been mentioned, had gained him the unkind nickname of the Sewer Rat. He was a thin, stringy, serious person, with the faraway look in his eyes of one who works with blind forces and knows that the cube root of the function of a power of seven may make all the difference between inertia and oblivion.

"I say," he said. "I believe you are the person who wants to know about anything out of the way which anyone has seen or heard. Is that right?"

"Well," said Goyles, "in a way I suppose it is. Come for a walk."

They started on a circuit of the camp.

"I don't know if this is going to be any good to you—?"

"Any detail, however small," said Goyles, feeling like all the detectives of fiction rolled in one body.

"It isn't anything really to do with the evening Coutoules disappeared, but it was so funny, I thought you might like to hear it. It was about four weeks ago. I was down the main drain—it goes along about ten yards this side of that path there"—he pointed to the path which bisected the camp and ran out at the main gate—"I must have got a good way along it—further than the dividing wire, I should think—"

"You must have been almost under the carabinieri quarters."

"Yes, I think I must have been. I was under some sort of living quarters—you could see the inlet pipes and so on—"

"If you're right about where the drain runs, it must have been the Italian huts," said Goyles. "It's just playing fields this side of the wire."

"Yes, well, that's what made it so funny."

"What was funny?"

"I could hear voices—you can, sometimes, you know, quite a long way underground. They carry along the pipes—"

"What was funny about that?"

"One of them was speaking English."

"It might have been Benucci," suggested Goyles.

"Oh, no, it wasn't Benucci's sort of voice at all. You can always tell an Italian speaking English, however good he is. This was quite different."

"Might it have been Coutoules?"

"Well, that did occur to me, but I don't think so. As a matter of fact, although I couldn't hear the words, the sort of general rhythm of them and the accent was quite plain."

"Well?" said Goyles.

Meynell looked unhappy.

"I thought," he said, "that it sounded like a colonial. Either that or an American."

"I see," said Goyles thoughtfully. "Well, thanks for telling me."

Later that evening Baierlein found time for a word with him.

"I can't tell you much," he said, "about what actually happened on that night, because, as you know, I was in jail, with Grim and Tony, for my sins. But there's one thing which did strike me—I may be making a mountain out of a molehill."

"Let's have it," said Goyles.

"It was the wireless. I've never heard it before that night, and I've never really heard it since, but that night it was terrific."

"What wireless?"

"The wireless in the Carabinieri Block. Some band or other. It really was making a terrific shindy. It almost blew us out of our beds. Tony remarked on it, too. He found it very helpful when he was scrambling up on to the roof. About five minutes later it stopped altogether."

"What was your idea about that?" said Goyles. He knew Baierlein was no fool.

"It did occur to me to wonder whether it had been turned on loud to hide some other noise."

"I suppose it might," said Goyles. "But wasn't it a bit late? I mean, the camp was all shut up by then. The Italians could hardly have got in and kidnapped Coutoules at that hour of the night without attracting some attention."

"I suppose not," said Baierlein. "It was just a thought."

Goyles hesitated for a moment. He very much wanted to discuss with someone what Meynell had told him. He supposed, however, that it was the duty of an investigator to listen to everybody and confide in nobody.

As soon as Baierlein had left a further thought struck him.

Was it not highly probable that the two pieces of information which he had received, intriguing though each of them was, might cancel each other out? The more he thought about it the more likely it seemed. What Meynell had heard from underground had been a wireless set. One of the Italians had been secretly listening to an American station—that, of course, would account for the accent.

Goyles dismissed all thoughts of the problem from his mind and stumped off angrily down the passage to keep a bridge date. He was an enthusiastic if over-scientific player.

Next morning, after breakfast, he sought out the Camp Quartermaster, Captain Porter, a wily old regular soldier, on the whole sympathetic to escapers, but inclined to stand on his dignity.

"You have most to do with the Italians of anyone here," said Goyles. "You see them every day about parcels and that sort of thing, don't you?"

"I suppose I do really," said Porter cautiously. "If it's Red Cross boxes you want you're out of luck. I gave the last lot to the Sports Committee."

"I don't really want anything," said Goyles. "Except information. I was wondering if you could find out for me which sentries were on certain posts on certain nights."

"I expect I might," said Captain Porter. He knew the power of a tin of Red Cross butter in fat-starved Italy. "Which one had you particularly in mind?"

"I wanted to know who was on duty on the north-east guard platform round about midnight on July 1st."

Captain Porter looked out of the corner of his eye at Goyles and said, "That would be the night—"

"Yes," said Goyles. "That was the night when Coutoules bought it."

"Funny thing that," said Captain Porter. "I'll see what I can do. Come back and see me after lunch."

After lunch, however, the Quartermaster's room was empty, and Goyles was lying on his bunk before tea when Porter came in. "It's a damn funny thing," he said, "I've never known them so sticky. Usually a little thing like that you can get for the asking. Someone's been scaring the pants off them. I had to blow a whole Red Cross parcel and fifty cigarettes. I hope it was worth while. The two you want are Private Biancelli and the carib who was with him was called Marzotto."

Goyles wrote down both names, and said, "Do you think you could possibly get Biancelli into the camp?"

"I can't get him into the camp if he doesn't want to come. What I can do is give you the tip when he next shows up. There's a big fatigue coming in to-morrow after tea with new beds for Hut E. If he isn't actually on guard he might be on that."

Goyles thought for a moment.

"If he is on the fatigue," he said, "could you get him away from it for five minutes, to the cook-house, say?"

"It'll be as much as my job's worth if I'm caught tampering with an Italian detail," said Captain Porter. "However, I'll do what I can. I suppose you know what you're up to."

"I hope so," said Goyles. "I'm not doing it just for my own amusement, if that's what you mean."

"So I understand," said Captain Porter. "I had the tip from Colonel Baird this morning. I'll do what I can."

A message at five o'clock the following afternoon told Goyles that the Quartermaster had been as good as his word. He accordingly made his way to the cook-house and was waiting when Biancelli came in. He was escorting two British orderlies who were carrying rations, but as soon as the door was closed the orderlies made themselves scarce and Goyles was left alone with his man. He recognized him as one of the sentries who had often stared down from the walls at him; a small, duck-like person with a sallow face and an ill-fitting uniform.

"Please sit down," said Goyles, in passable Italian. "Have a cigarette." He passed over a whole packet, which Biancelli pocketed unopened and without comment.

Goyles tried one or two of the normal conversational opening: the hardness of the war; the shortness of food; the separation from family and children. None of these evoked any response at all and Goyles found this, in itself, curious. Always before when he had made the opportunity to talk alone with Italian soldiers he had found them sympathetic—almost child-like in their anxiety to please. Why, he wondered, was Biancelli suddenly acting the strong, silent man. Was he trying to put the price up? He did not look naturally strong or silent.

He found the answer suddenly.

Far away across the barrack square Captain Benucci's voice was raised in anger.

Biancelli shot to his feet, and scuttled towards the door.

Goyles got in front of him.

"Look here," he said urgently, "there's nothing to be frightened about. Do you want to earn a hundred pounds—"

"I cannot say anything," said Biancelli. Nevertheless he had stopped moving and his eyes looked interested.

"You know as well as I do," said Goyles, "that Italy will be out of the war before many months are passed. The carabinieri and all Fascists will be in hiding for their lives and honest people will come into their own."

"*Speriamo*," said Biancelli.

"It is not a hope. It is a certainty."

"You mentioned one hundred—"

"One hundred pounds in British gold." He wondered as he said it where on earth he was going to get it from. "We cannot talk here and now, but I have an idea. Can you arrange it so that you are one of the guard on the walk to-morrow?"

"Yes. That could be done."

"I will get myself put on the walk. I will be in the last file. There should be plenty of opportunity to talk at the halts, if we are careful."

"It shall be arranged."

"To-morrow then. And death to all Fascists."

"May they dine together for eternity on their grandmothers' tripes," agreed Biancelli.

Goyles was on his way back to his hut when he stopped because he noticed that something out of the ordinary was happening.

A crowd of prisoners had gathered in the middle of the sports field, and all the hut windows looking on to the main gate were crowded with faces.

Goyles found Baierlein standing by himself.

"New prisoners," said Baierlein.

"What's the excitement?"

"I don't know," said Baierlein. "There's something up though. Have you ever seen prisoners arriving here in that state? This isn't a reception camp."

The little group of prisoners in the forecourt showed even at that distance a battered and disreputable look. Their clothes hung from them, they were carrying practically no kit, and they looked as if they had spent the last three nights in a coal truck.

"You're absolutely right," said Goyles. "They're straight from the front line."

The excitement in the crowd was growing. If new prisoners were being brought direct to a camp as far north as 127, the implications were obvious.

"Looks as if the guards are expecting trouble," said Baierlein.

A third man had appeared on each of the guard platforms and a line of carabinieri had stationed themselves on the inner wire between the forecourt and the main camp. In the forecourt Benucci and the Commandant were talking together, and eyeing the growing crowd of British officers on the playing field.

"I don't believe they're going to let those chaps in here at all," said Baierlein. "They're putting them in one of the Italian blocks."

As the little group of new prisoners started to move an officer on the sports field cupped his hands to his mouth and shouted, "Where are you from?"

Benucci screamed out an order and two of the machine guns on the wall turned quietly in the direction of the crowd.

Goyles suddenly went hot and cold.

"I hope no one starts anything," he whispered to Baierlein.

"Get flat on your face if there's anyone starts shooting," said Baierlein. "Whatever else you do, don't run for it."

The little file of prisoners was moving off now. Then something rather exciting happened. There was a moment when the last of them, a small dark man, was out of sight of the guards on the head of the file. He jumped round towards the group in the camp, his back against the wall of the guard hut.

His arms rose and fell about a dozen times, quickly.

Goyles was unable to read it, but more than one of the prisoners was expert enough in semaphore to take the message.

"Sicily invaded."

CHAPTER SIX

COLONEL LAVERY MAKES A SPEECH AND
GOYLES PRACTISES VENTRILOQUISM

I

"I HAVE CALLED YOU TOGETHER, GENTLEMEN," SAID COLONEL Lavery, "because, in my view, this may be the last opportunity we shall have to think matters over calmly, and to plan, so far as we are able to plan, our own future actions. Things should start moving fairly soon."

He looked down at his audience of four hundred officers gathered in the Theatre Hut. He was well aware that they were four hundred individualists, and that his authority over them was tenuous. He sometimes thought that the only real reason that any of them obeyed his orders was that they came, most of them, from a people to whom order and discipline were as natural as breathing. A people, moreover, who had learned, in the hard school of history, that in a crisis it pays to hand over authority to one man and to follow his orders. As he looked at the faces in front of him, Colonel Lavery felt all this, without perhaps precisely thinking it out; and he chose his words very carefully.

"It's no news to you that the Eighth Army is in Sicily. That fact, which was first passed across to us by one of the new prisoners, has been confirmed from other sources. I can't suppose that they intend to stop at Sicily. The Straits of Messina are no great obstacle.

It is quite certain that they will land, rather sooner than later, in Italy. When that happens, so far as I can see, one of three things may happen—or perhaps a mixture of them.

"The Italians may go on with the fight. Or they may give it up, in a straightforward and orderly way, doing the best they can by their present allies: in which case one of the things they will be sure to do is to hand us over intact to the Germans. Or they may chuck in the sponge at a moment's notice, without consulting the Germans at all, in which case a pretty fair period of chaos is liable to ensue. I imagine a lot will depend on Mussolini. I understand, from guarded references which our 'I' people in camp here have deciphered from the daily press, that the two ends of the axis may not be revolving at quite the same speed just now.

"However, please let no one deceive himself. Whichever of those three things happen, our course is not going to be easy or straightforward.

"If there is chaos, then we will take what advantage of it we can. If, on the other hand, it seems that we are going to be moved further north, under Italian control, or handed over lock, stock and barrel to the Germans, then a very awkward decision may face us. I don't want to make too much of it, because it may never happen. But in such circumstances, we might have to face the fact that it would be our duty to rush these walls regardless of cost."

Colonel Lavery paused for a moment and looked round at his audience, which had fallen strangely silent. He himself was thinking of Benucci's words to him a week before—on the night, in fact, that Coutoules had disappeared.

He repeated, "Regardless of cost. If the British Army was in Italy and advancing towards us fast, through a friendly or at any rate a neutral countryside, then it might be our plain duty to go over those walls on the calculation that if sixty or seventy per cent of us got clear we should have taken a justifiable chance. As I said before, I am not stressing this, because we are working now on certain alternative methods which may be available when they are required.

"Meanwhile, I intend that the whole camp—I include the orderlies—they are not here at the moment but they will be told later—the whole camp will be organized on an infantry basis into companies and platoons, so that a proper chain of command will exist, anything which has to be done can be done promptly and efficiently. Details will be given out later, by Hut Commanders. Two or three other things. I have noticed that army boots, of which a fair number have been issued lately, are being cut down and made into walking shoes. This will cease. All boots will be carefully preserved, also all Army clothing, particularly overcoats, raincoats and mackintoshes. Everyone should see that he is equipped to the best of his ability for a long, hard, cross-country march. Secondly, the issue of additional Red Cross food parcels, which has been possible lately from our accumulated stocks, will stop. I have instructed the Quartermaster to save all possible food. Lastly, since it is particularly his province, I have asked Colonel Baird to have a word with you about security."

Colonel Baird was a less practised speaker than Colonel Lavery, but he made up in directness what he lacked in flourish. He said, "Things have been happening in this camp in the last few days that we don't like, and that we can't explain. Most of you know, and if you don't it's time you did, that the body of Lieutenant Coutoules was found about ten days ago in very suspicious circumstances. Captain Byfold has been arrested by the Italians on having had a hand in his death. We happen to know that this is nonsense. A lot of people thought Coutoules was an informer—I mean, that he told the Italians about escape plans and so on. I don't suppose we shall ever know the truth of that now. But something else more unpleasant has grown out of it."

Colonel Baird paused here, not for oratorical effect, but simply because he wanted to be very careful about what he said next. The silence in the hut was painful.

"Certain facts have led us to believe that there may still be an informer among us. I can't say any more at the moment. I asked that the orderlies should not be here to-day. I don't want this information passed to them."

Colonel Baird paused again, almost as if he had finished. Then it seemed to occur to him that some explanation of his closing remarks might be required.

"I don't want you to think," he said, "that we suspect any particular orderly. We don't. It's just that their backgrounds are more difficult to check than yours are. Most of you chaps come from a very small number of regiments and schools, and businesses and families. We've done a certain amount of work on you already. I hope you won't take it the wrong way, but we're going through the whole business again to see if we haven't missed someone. It may mean asking you a lot of silly questions, but it can't be avoided."

He turned to Colonel Lavery to indicate that he had finished.

"Very well," said Colonel Lavery. "That's all."

II

"Just picture me," said Rupert Rolf-Callender, "trudging through the Italian countryside, dressed in some or all of these clothes." He had laid his spare wardrobe out on his bed. It consisted of two very thin Italian cotton shirts, a pair of bathing trunks, three pairs of sunglasses and a pair of sandals.

"You shouldn't have flogged all your issue stuff for cigarettes," said the Honourable Peter Perse. "Now you'll have to get it back again. It's going to be a buyers' market, too."

"It just shows you," said Tag Burchnall virtuously to his friends. "What did I say all along? Don't worry about footling escape schemes, just keep absolutely fit and let the Army think for you. Can anybody lend me some dubbin?"

Overstrand said to his friends in Room 10. "My God, that shook them. Were you looking at their faces when the S.B.O. talked about storming the walls?"

"They didn't look too happy," admitted Tony Long. "I'm not sure that I exactly welcome the prospect myself, not in broad daylight. It would be an awfully long way up that wall with a couple of machine guns firing at you."

"It was the first time that half of them have faced up to the fact that the war isn't finished," said Overstrand. His voice sounded bitter. "They've spent a year, lying in their beds in winter and on them in summer, and physically and morally they're as hard as a school of baby jellyfish."

"I didn't quite get what Baird meant about security," said Baierlein. "What's the connection between security and Coutoules?"

This question was obviously aimed principally at Goyles who weighed for a moment the claims of professional integrity against friendship and decided that a limited amount of indiscretion could do no harm.

"They think," he said, "that the Italians knew that Coutoules was going to be killed and dumped in a tunnel."

"In our tunnel?"

"No. In some tunnel; when we produced him in the Hut A tunnel they naturally assumed that that was where the interment had taken place."

"So they knew all along that it was a fake," said Baierlein. "I thought they got on to poor old Roger rather smartly."

"Yes, but look here," said Overstrand, his face getting red, as it usually did when he was excited, "that means there's another informer in the camp."

"That's Baird's idea," said Goyles patiently.

"But was it this other informer and his pals who killed Coutoules?"

"Not necessarily. They just told the Italians it was going to happen."

"Then who did kill him?"

"That's the thing we've got to find out. There are really two enquiries going on, you see. One's a sort of security check to spot the informer. The other's a criminal investigation—who was doing what, where and with whom the evening of July 1st—that sort of thing."

"Well, Tony and you and I were all right," said Grimsdale a little tactlessly. "We were all in jug. What about you three?"

"It can't be Goyles," said Baierlein, "he's the detective in the story. And Byfold has been arrested for the crime by the Italians, so by all the canons of detective fiction he can't be guilty. It must have been Overstrand—"

"Plenty of motive," said Grimsdale, "we all know he hated Coutoules."

"I don't see," said Overstrand angrily. "Why has it necessarily got to be one of us six?"

"Don't be a goat," said Baierlein. "Grim was only pulling your leg."

"One good thing," said Goyles, adroitly changing the subject. "We've got the word to push on with the tunnel double shifts. They want us to have it ready by the end of this month."

"All very well to talk about pushing on," said Baierlein. "It's true that we've cleared the fall, but we can't go ahead without putting a proper roof across that cavity. It's a bloody big hole. You can't do it with fiddling little pieces of bed board. I was down there yesterday to measure it. If you stay the four corners as close as possible to the fall, you're still going to need a huge sheet of plywood, or something of the sort. At least four feet by six."

"I doubt if there's such a thing in the camp," said Goyles.

"My God, but there is," said Overstrand. "And you shall have it."

III

"Good morning, Tenente Mordaci," said Tony Long affably, as he leant from his window.

"Good morning," said Mordaci. He hitched his cloak over his shoulders and creased his face into an amiable smile. He was not averse to paternal conversations with blond young English lieutenants. Nevertheless, he was never quite certain that Tenente Long was really as respectful or as ingenuous as he liked to appear. Indeed, the respect of the prisoners for their jailers seemed to be getting distressingly smaller every day. There was an undercurrent of feeling. Even Mordaci, who was not the most sensitive of men, had noticed it.

"And how are *i nostri?*"

"Our gallant troops are everywhere in good heart."

"As at El Alamein?"

"At El Alamein we were grossly betrayed and deserted."

"And at Tripoli?"

"The greater part of our troops were safely evacuated from Tripoli."

"And at Pantellaria?"

"An unimportant outpost."

"And now in Sicilia?"

"In Sicilia great victories are daily being gained."

"And soon in Italia?"

"Italia—never." Mordaci waggled a fat forefinger reprovingly at his young interrogator. "Never shall foreigner defile the sacred soil of Italy."

He hitched his cloak once more round his massive shoulders and rolled off across the compound with the satisfied smile of one who has dealt firmly with a tiresome interrogator. It may be that had he known that Tony had spoken to him simply because it was part of his duty to detain him for as long as he could—or had he even guessed that, somewhere beneath his feet as he stood talking, the sacred soil of Italy was being excavated at the rate of more than a square yard a day—it is possible that had he known all this his smile might have been less complacent.

IV

That afternoon the new prisoners were allowed to join the rest. Since the news of the invasion of Sicily was by now general, and had in fact appeared, suitably garbled, in such Italian newspapers as were allowed into the camp, there seemed no point in keeping them in the already overcrowded Italian Staff Quarters.

Normally, new prisoners were welcomed immediately into the living huts, where they found themselves the centre of a gratifying amount of attention. They personified the outside world. They *were* the latest news. On this occasion, however, Colonel Baird's hand was over them from the moment they entered the camp, and they were taken immediately to the Senior Officers' Quarters, where they were brought, one at a time, before the Escape Committee, in session in Colonel Baird's room. The interrogation was friendly, but thorough.

The first of them happened to be the little dark subaltern who had semaphored the news of the fall of Sicily. His name turned out to be Potter.

"Now, Potter, perhaps you could give us a few details, Regiment and Division and so on. I see you were in the Signals."

"Yes, sir. I was signals officer in the 15th R.H.A."

"What Division was that?"

"Eighth Armoured—that's their Divisional Flash I'm wearing."

"So it is, I hadn't spotted that. Who commands them now?"

"Colonel Williams."

"Is that Chubby Williams?"

"No, sir. It's his brother. Chubby commands the Ninth."

"Of course. By the way, where did you say you were at school?"

"Shelton."

"Oh, yes. Which house?"

"School House."

"Let me see. You're just twenty-two. I suppose you would have left there in '39."

"'38 actually, sir. I left early to start my articles."

And so on.

At the end of about fifteen minutes the officer concerned, feeling that he had been very carefully and skilfully taken to pieces and put together again, was allowed to join his hut.

Where, of course, the questions started all over again.

"You were in the 15th were you? Oh, Tag—here's a chap who was with the 15th in Sicily. He says Mike has got a Battery."

"If Mike's got a Battery," said Burchnall, "all I can say is, it's a damn shame I was ever captured. I should have been a Brigadier by now."

v

Next day Goyles' plans suffered a set-back. He heard about it after breakfast from Long.

"I say," said Long, "have you heard the latest."

"Nobody ever says that, in that particular tone of voice," said Goyles, "unless it's bad news, so out with it."

"I'm not sure whether it's bad news or not," said Long. "Rather a sign of the times, really. Benucci has stopped all walks."

"Curse," said Goyles.

"If you ask me, it's not because he's worried about people escaping. It's simply because he's afraid that the populace will begin to show too much sympathy with us. They haven't been exactly hostile as it is. With the Eighth Army in Sicily they'll begin to pelt us with flowers."

"It isn't that," said Goyles. "I'm not all that keen on walks. It's just that—look here, you'll have to keep your mouth shut about this."

"This detection business is ruining your faith in human nature," said Tony coldly. "Of course I'll keep my mouth shut. What is it?"

Goyles explained about the arrangement he had made with Biancelli.

"I see," said Tony. "Yes. That is a bit awkward, isn't it? What exactly were you hoping to get out of him?"

"Coutoules had the end room in the S.B.O.'s hut. The northeast sentry platform is the only one that overlooked his window. If Coutoules was in his room at lock-up, almost the only way he could have been got out was through the window."

"Why? They don't lock the hut door at night."

"I know. But think of the risk. Even if Coutoules was dead when they got him out of his room, it would have meant carrying the body past half a dozen doors. Anyone might have looked out. If he'd still been alive and kicking the risk would have been greater still."

"I don't believe you could kidnap anybody out of one of these huts without everybody knowing about it," said Tony thoughtfully. "But that's not the point. I agree that if anything was to be seen Biancelli probably saw it. I don't imagine you could have got much out of him on a walk, though. The sentries nearly always walk in pairs. There's only one place in this camp where you can rely on an hour's undisturbed conversation with a sentry. Do you think you can get a message to Biancelli?"

"I expect so. The Quartermaster seems to be able to get hold of them."

"Then ask him when he's next going to be on guard in the cooler."

"Tony," said Goyles, "that's brilliant."

"It's the fish diet," said Long modestly.

VI

"I say," said Baierlein, "have you heard what's happened?"

Goyles turned over on his bed and groaned. "Yes," he said, "they've stopped all walks."

"No doubt," said Baierlein, "but that wasn't what I meant. They've removed Potter."

"Which Potter?"

"He wasn't in the camp long enough for us to get on Christian name terms," said Baierlein. "Young Potter—the chap in the Royal Corps of Signals who came in with the last bunch."

"The one who did the semaphoring?"

"That's the chap."

Goyles sat up slowly, to consider the new development. On the face of it, it didn't seem to make a great deal of sense.

"What actually happened?"

"They didn't make any palaver about it. Nothing like they did about Roger. Paoli came in after lunch, and told him to get packed, as he was going on somewhere else. Not that he'd got much to pack, poor chap. The people in his hut had a quick whip-round for him and got together some food and a set of battle-dress."

"Did Paoli stay with him whilst he was packing?"

"Yes," said Baierlein. "Why?"

"I don't know," said Goyles, "it just occurred to me that they might have wanted to stop him talking. Supposing he had a bit of information they particularly didn't want him to pass on. If he suddenly heard he was going to be moved to another camp, his natural reaction would be to try to tell it to someone. If Paoli was standing over him, he couldn't. That's all."

"It's possible," said Baierlein. "But don't forget he'd been in the camp nearly twenty-four hours. The Escape Committee and the 'I' people had already had a go at him. To say nothing of the people in the hut. The poor chap hardly stopped answering questions from the moment he got into the camp, till he was removed. If there was anything, surely he'd have spilled it already."

"Always supposing," said Goyles thoughtfully, "that he knew exactly what it was that he knew that the Italians didn't want us to know."

"This detecting business is going to your head," said Baierlein.

VII

"It's all very well to talk about getting yourself arrested," said Goyles, "but it isn't so damned easy, just at the moment."

"There's ingratitude for you," said Tony.

"I'm not ungrateful," said Goyles. "I still think it was a brilliant idea. And I've been in touch with Biancelli. He says he will be on the cooler guard to-morrow night. It's a twenty-four-hour guard—two hours on and four off. All I want is a few days solitary, starting to-morrow, and everything in the garden would be beautiful."

"Forget to salute the Commandant."

"He never comes into the camp nowadays."

"Be rude to Benucci."

"That's the trouble. Benucci's such a tricky customer. If you say something perfectly outrageous to him, he just grins like a cat, and you feel a fool. I suppose you could go a step further and trip him up and kick him in the stomach or something. Then he'd probably pull out his toy revolver and shoot you."

"Hmph," said Long.

"The trouble is everybody's in such an awkward frame of mind at the moment. It's going to be damned tricky—"

"You just leave it to me," said Long. "Everything shall be arranged. You want the best prisons. We have them. Tactful insults a speciality."

VIII

"Well, I call the whole thing a lot of nonsense," said Rolf-Callender. "Ever since the S.B.O.'s speech people have done nothing but form threes and slope arms and talk the most ropey old nonsense about attack in depth and where they're going to site the 'B' Echelon. I suppose one can't prevent them making fools of themselves, but when it comes to suggesting that we give up the play—"

"Has anyone actually suggested that we drop it?"

"Not in so many words, but I can tell from the way Uncle Percy looks at me" (he referred to his Hut Commander, an elderly regular Major in Indian Cavalry) "that he thinks we're just fiddling whilst Rome burns. Personally I can't see it at all. Didn't the Duchess of Thingummy give a ball on the eve of Waterloo?"

"If she hadn't," suggested Peter Perse, who never missed an opportunity of provoking Rolf-Callender, "Wellington mightn't have come so jolly near to losing the battle."

"I can't see it," said Bush. "It isn't as if we were using anything that anyone else would want if we did have to escape—unless you suggest that Peter tries to get to Rome dressed as Elizabeth Barrett Browning. I agree that the general get-up is smashing, but I'm afraid the skirt would date him."

"Exactly," said Rolf-Callender. "Just because they want to play at soldiers, is that any reason to stop us playing at theatricals? When it comes to the big night, I expect our performance will be far more amusing than theirs. And I shall tell Uncle Percy so next time he wants me to join one of his TEWTS."

"If that's all agreed," said Bush, "what are we waiting for. On with the rehearsals."

"There's one thing," observed Captain Abercrowther, who was trying on a formidable pair of side-whiskers. "I haven't haird yet how you propose to deal with that wee dug."

"Flush," said Rolf-Callender thoughtfully. "Yes. He is going to be a bit of a problem. I suppose that if the worst came to the worst we could cut—"

"Shame," said Bush. "The Barretts without Flush! It would be like *Hamlet* without the First Grave-digger."

"I know, but—"

"I had an idea about that," said Captain Abercrowther. "Has that fellow Paoli not got a wee dug—"

"But it's not a spaniel."

"Not precisely a spaniel, no. But it's a plain, white, podgy little creature and seems tolerably placid. Could not some of our make-up artists—"

"Liver and white markings," cried Rolf-Callender.

"A pair of false ears!" suggested Bush.

"And a nubby little tail!"

"Mac," said Peter Perse, "it's the idea of the century. I can plainly see that this performance is going to be a riot."

IX

The next morning, making his rounds of the camp, Tenente Mordaci suddenly stopped.

He stopped because he fancied he heard his name.

Not only his surname, which would have been interesting, but his Christian name, too.

More interesting still.

He looked round him. He was standing in the open space

between Hut B and Hut C and it was from a window in Hut C that the voices seemed to come.

He knew well that Hut C was notorious for containing a high percentage of evil characters, maniacs who could not see that they were well off out of the war, but must ever be plotting and scheming and disturbing the peace of mind of those lawfully placed in authority over them.

It was clearly his duty to investigate. His presence did not seem to be suspected. Hitching his cloak round his shoulders—a subconscious gesture, in moments of crisis—he tiptoed to the outer wall of the hut and sidled along towards the window.

What he saw transfixed him with astonishment.

Seated on a bed, surrounded by a grinning group of prisoners, was a most extraordinary figure. Padded into gross obesity with many pillows, the lips puffed and reddened with make-up, a doll on his knee, a blanket thrown cloak-wise round his shoulders, and an absurd travesty of a carabinier's cocked hat on his head, it took Mordaci a few seconds to recognize the usually sedate Goyles.

It had never occurred to him that Goyles was an actor. It now appeared that he was a very competent ventriloquist also.

Mordaci peered closely at the doll.

It appeared, from its dress, to be a lady of doubtful taste and non-existent virtue.

Since nobody was looking towards the window he was able to study this edifying scene for some minutes.

"But Ercolo," said the doll, "your suggestions fill me with alarm and suspicion."

"Come, come now," said Goyles, in a revolting imitation of Mordaci's unctuous bass. "You are a woman of the world."

"It is because I am a woman of the world that I hesitate."

"Then hesitate no longer. It is I, Ercolo Mordaci of the Carabinieri Reali, who speaks—"

"It is I indeed who speak," said Mordaci.

All heads in the room swung towards the window in gratifying unison.

"It is I who speak, and I say that you will cease this imposture and accompany me to the office—"

"But, Tenente—"

"At once."

"It's only a play I was rehearsing."

"And its name?"

"Oh—we hadn't thought of a name."

"Beauty and the beast," suggested someone from the crowd.

"Enough," said Mordaci. "This vileness will bring its own reward. For seven days at least you shall not pollute the camp with your presence."

"There you are," said Tony Long, five minutes later, "absolutely painless. I'll help you carry your kit as far as the guard house."

X

The Punishment Block, or the cooler, stood, as has been already explained, in the outer section of the camp. In this area, between the inner wire and the north wall, lay the guard quarters, the carabinieri offices, the Italian administrative huts, and the prisoners' food and clothing store.

Surrounded as it was on all sides by Italians, the cooler itself was not particularly well or systematically guarded. It comprised a small, brick block, divided by a central corridor, with two cells on either side. Those on the north (or outer) side were traditionally reserved for British prisoners, those on the other side for Italian soldiers who had been found guilty of derelictions of duty. On one side, at the end, was an ablution room. At this point the corridor turned through a right angle, so that the actual entrance door was out of sight of the cells themselves.

In this entrance door a sentry was posted. It was his duty to make a periodical turn up the passage and inspect such cells as were occupied, by glancing through the inspection slit in the door.

Since the sentry wore heavy, studded boots and the floor of the corridor was tiled, his arrival on a tour of inspection never really took anyone by surprise.

The possibilities of this arrangement had been quickly appreciated, and a succession of self-condemned prisoners, suitably equipped, had already rendered the barred windows of the two British cells rather more ornamental than useful. Long and Baierlein had also proved that a rough dummy in the bed was sufficient to satisfy a sentry, particularly one who was looking from a lighted passage into an unlighted cell.

The whole arrangement was so scandalously careless, Goyles reflected as he sat on his bed that evening with his phrase book of modern Greek, that it would be criminal not to take some advantage of it. There seemed no reasonable doubt that four prisoners, if only they could get into prison suitably equipped could get out of the window, on to the roof, and over the wall, with a minimum of difficulty.

The loose bar and brick could be replaced from the outside, as Tony Long had already demonstrated, and if dummies were left in the beds they would not be missed until reveille.

Suitably equipped—that was the snag. Even in Italy during the summer, you needed, for a cross-country journey, food and warm clothes and maps, and a host of other things: you could scarcely hope to smuggle them past the very thorough search which took place before you were jugged.

Even so, there might be a solution that—

At this moment the lights went out and Goyles glanced at his watch. It was ten o'clock.

Biancelli, he knew, was not due on guard until eleven.

He got up on to his bed, covered himself with a blanket, and prepared to wait. To prevent himself from nodding off altogether, he forced himself to think about the death of Coutoules. In his mind he went over and over every fact that he knew, and then again, remorselessly.

He realized that he had very few facts to build on. But equally, as Colonel Shore had said, the whole problem was so crazy that any feasible solution must surely be the right one.

Might Biancelli be bringing him just that one little *extra fact* which would make all the difference—the twist which would unlock the whole puzzle.

It was very quiet in the cell.

There was no Italian wireless blaring to-night. In the silence Goyles could hear a murmur of voices from the Carabinieri Block next door. He could almost make out individuals—the deep bellow of Mordaci, the thin pipe of Paoli, the incisive tones of Captain Benucci.

When he looked at his watch again, it was eleven o'clock. He swung his feet over the edge of the bed and sat up. His bed was alongside the door and on a level with the peephole, so that he had a clear view of the passage as far as the turn. He could hear the sentry, who had not stirred for the last hour, moving about, no doubt in preparation for his relief.

Suddenly there came a snap and a double stamp as the sentry sprang to attention.

There was a noise of feet, and a few words were spoken, which he could not catch.

Then the light threw a long shadow down the corridor and Captain Benucci appeared. He walked right up to the door and stood outside, for a moment, looking at the darkened peephole. His face was not more than twenty inches from Goyles, who could smell the peculiar pomade which he used.

"Captain Goyles."

"Yes," said Goyles cautiously.

"Ah—you are awake. I wondered. I have a message for you. I have to tell you that Private Biancelli will *not* be on duty to-night. He shot himself this evening. He was cleaning his rifle. It was an accident."

Goyles had nothing to say. He saw Captain Benucci turn and he watched his back disappear down the passageway and heard the clock as the guard came to attention, and the sound of Benucci's feet clattering away down the path.

CHAPTER SEVEN

FRACAS

I

"I DON'T LIKE THIS POTTER BUSINESS A BIT," SAID COLONEL
Baird.

"Stinks," agreed Commander Oxey.

"Why do you think they did it? They can't have got on to that
semaphoring stunt—even if they did—"

"Even if they did," said Commander Oxey, "it would be stupid
to take any notice of it days after the event, when everybody knew
about Sicily anyway."

"Then why pick on him? They haven't tried to shift any of the
other newcomers?"

"Not that I know of."

"He seemed a perfectly genuine and harmless little man. He
knew a lot of the officers in 15 R.H.A.—"

"By name?"

"Certainly. Why? What are you getting at?"

"Well," said Commander Oxey slowly, "I've been digging round
among the gunner officers here—we've got one or two from that
Regiment, and others who were in the same Division. They all
agree that Potter seemed perfectly genuine. He knew the right
answers. He'd heard of all the right people. He knew them by their
names—even by their army nicknames—only—"

"Only what?"

"Only they none of them remember meeting him."

"That's quite reasonable. He was a replacement signal officer. He was straight out from England and he only joined the Regiment a few days before the actual Sicily show—"

"Quite," said Commander Oxey. "Then how did he come to know all those other people? He must have done some remarkably intensive visiting round the Division in those few days, to pick up all that gossip. I'm not too well up in army matters, but I should have thought that if he'd only been a few days with his Regiment he might have known one or two of the officers—the ones he actually messed with and worked under—but he'd still be a bit vague about the rest of the Regiment, wouldn't he? Let alone the Division."

"There's something in that," said Baird. "What's your idea?"

"I haven't really got an idea yet—but I asked Lieutenant Long to come and have a few words. I think he might be able to help us."

"Tony Long," said Baird. "What makes you think that? He's not a gunner—and he was in Special Service most of his time."

"Not all his life," said Commander Oxey with a smile. "That sounds like him now. Come in, Long. I was just talking about you to Colonel Baird. So far as I can see from our records you're our only Sheltonian in the camp. At least the only one of the right age."

"The right age, sir?"

"Young enough, I mean. You were there in 1936 weren't you—in School House?"

"Yes. I went in winter '33 and left in '37."

"Then you'll remember Potter?"

"Potter," said Tony slowly. "Was Potter at Shelton?"

"That's what we're asking you," said Colonel Baird sharply.

"I can't say I remember anyone called Potter. When was he supposed to have come?"

Colonel Baird referred to his notes—"New boy in 1935."

"Oh, well, that would make him two years younger than me. It's quite possible I wouldn't know him. After all, there were six hundred boys there, in a dozen different houses. If he was in another house—"

"That's just it," said Commander Oxey. "He was in School House."

"Well, that settles it," said Long. "He wasn't. You're sure he said School House."

"Certain."

"Then he's a liar."

"I thought he might be," said Commander Oxey. "I just wanted to be sure. Thank you very much."

When the door had closed behind him Colonel Baird said, "Well, what do you make of that?"

"It's obvious, isn't it?" said Commander Oxey. "Somebody killed off their former stool-pigeon. They waste precious little time over installing a new one."

"No doubt. But why remove him before he's had a chance to do any stooling?"

"Perhaps," said Commander Oxey with a grin, "they heard of the precautions we were taking. They wouldn't want him to go the same way as the first one, would they?"

II

"We're to go ahead with the tunnel at full speed," said Hugo Baierlein. "I saw Baird this morning and he approved most of my suggestions. It's a pity that both Roger and 'Cuckoo' should be out of circulation just now, because they both know the ropes. We're going to work three shifts instead of two—the first from nine to one, the afternoon shift from two to six, and a short evening shift from six till just before lock-up. First, we're going to take some steps to speed things up. We're only going to half-shore the tunnel. We'll put in complete box sections of wood every other foot, and only a few thin pieces across the interval to form a ceiling—"

"That's all right as far as it goes," said Overstrand, "but it doesn't solve the main problem. It's the disposal of the sand that's holding us up. Even using the A tunnel—which is very nearly full now—we're getting out more than we can dispose of."

"I was coming to that," said Baierlein. "The order there is that everything goes. You can put it on flower beds, paths, the playing fields, underneath huts. You can store it in boxes round the cook-house. The Escape Committee have come to the conclusion that the Italians know very well that there's a tunnel being dug. They just don't know where it starts from. If they find fresh sand it won't tell them anything they don't know already."

"Provided people aren't spotted coming away from this hut with it."

"Yes. That's vital. Well then"—Baierlein turned to Duncan and Anderson—"I take it you're on."

"You may take it so," said Duncan, "and we can probably raise a complete working shift from our hut. Tunnelling stock has gone up a point or two after the S.B.O.'s speech."

"Right," said Baierlein. "Will you collect your people now and dribble them across? We'll have the tunnel mouth open and show you the way around. You can start proper work this evening."

"By the way," said Duncan, "have you roofed over the fall yet?"

"Surely," said Overstrand. There was a degree of malice in his smile. "We've found a perfect roof for it."

When their visitors had gone Baierlein and Overstrand walked along to the kitchen.

"No hurry," said Baierlein. "We shall have to wait for them anyway, to help us up with the lid."

"As a matter of fact," said Overstrand, "it's perfectly possible for two people to do it if you take it slowly. Grim and I did it the other day."

"Did you now?" said Baierlein. "Well, I'm not Grim. We'll wait till the others turn up if you don't mind, and do it properly."

III

"Come in," said Colonel Lavery. "The Adjutant tells me you want a word with me."

"If I could," said Rolf-Callender. He was looking pink but determined and his rather girlish mouth had tighter lines round it than usual.

"It's about some property of ours, sir, that's been stolen."

"Stolen? That's a horrible word to hear in a prisoner-of-war camp. Are you certain?"

"Absolutely, sir. In fact I don't think the thief is even troubling to deny it."

"I see." A wary look came into Colonel Lavery's eye. "You said 'our' property. It's not just your private stuff?"

"No, sir. It's a roulette board. It belongs to Captain Perse and Lieutenant Bush and myself. We bought some of the stuff from the Italians, and got the rest from the Quartermaster. We made it ourselves."

"I see. You're quite sure you haven't just lost it?"

"I don't think that's really possible, sir. It was a huge thing. It was hinged in the middle, but when it was flat it was about six feet by three."

"Yes—"

"Besides, we all know who's got it. They've practically boasted about it. It's Overstrand and his friends—we know—at least we're practically certain"—Rolf-Callender almost gobbled over this final indignity—"they're using it to roof a tunnel."

"I see."

"And that's not all, sir. They—or some of the other escaping people—stole the rugger posts. I don't know if it was a tunnel—it was something to do with escaping—and people are getting pretty fed up about it."

"Yes," said Colonel Lavery.

"It's not only me—you could ask anyone in our hut. We're all for live and let live, and when it comes to the point—I mean, what you said in your speech—I hope we'd do our bit like anyone else, but it's these cloak-and-dagger types—why *should* they go round pinching other people's stuff and behaving as if they owned the place? Why should they have special privileges?"

"What do you want me to do?"

Rolf-Callender became aware that he might have been saying a little more than he had started out to do. He pulled himself up and said, "We'd like our board back, sir."

"There's one practical difficulty to that," said Colonel Lavery with a smile. "I don't even know where their tunnel is—"

"Well—I expect Colonel Baird does."

"Do you want me to ask him?"

This suggestion made even Rolf-Callender hesitate. He was as conscious as anyone of Colonel Baird's personality. He therefore hedged.

"Am I to take it, sir, that escaping activities have official priority over any other forms of activity?"

Colonel Lavery felt tempted to tell the petulant young man that he could take what he liked and do what he liked with it, but he restrained himself in time. Though badly put, the grievance was, he knew, a real one in the minds of many people.

"I can't give any general ruling," he said. "You know that it's your military duty to take every reasonable chance of escape."

"Every reasonable chance, yes, sir."

"Quite. Well, all that means is that every case must be judged on its merits. In this case, since you put it to me, I do think that that particular piece of wood is serving a better purpose where it is now. I know enough about this tunnel to know that it's a good and careful one, and has a very fair chance of success. And if it does come through it may be very useful. I think that the people concerned should have asked you openly for the board—you might even have felt it your duty to give it to them."

"Hmph!" said Rolf-Callender.

"But now that it's been done, I don't think I can possibly order it to be given back again."

"I see, sir."

Rolf-Callender saluted insubordinately and withdrew.

Colonel Lavery sighed.

IV

It was certainly unfortunate that on his return to Hut A the first person that Rolf-Callender met should have been Overstrand.

Overstrand had come across to the hut to work out with Anderson and Brandy Duncan the last details of the new digging teams. For various reasons they were anxious, if possible, that one complete shift should come from Hut A. They wanted eight men at least and had been finding last choices a bit difficult despite the fact that, as Duncan said, digging stock was temporarily on the rise. For the truth of the matter was that digging tunnels was a very specialized pursuit, in which experience counted for a good deal more than enthusiasm.

The three of them were standing in the passage when Rolf-Callender arrived.

Rolf-Callender pushed past the little group, trod on Overstrand's foot, apologized unconvincingly, and made for the door of his room.

"Been playing much roulette lately?" enquired Overstrand genially.

Rolf-Callender stopped in his tracks, turned round slowly, and said, "Just because you stole some of our property and got away with it doesn't give you any right to be funny about it."

"Sorry if I've said something to amuse you," said Overstrand. "Now perhaps if you told me what on earth you were talking about—"

"You know damned well what I'm talking about."

"And what exactly do you mean by 'got away with it'?"

Rolf-Callender said nothing. His face was white and he was breathing heavily.

"So that's why you wanted to see the S.B.O.," continued Overstrand, suddenly enlightened. "Sneaking again! And the S.B.O. told you to go and chase yourself, did he? Good for him."

"Half the trouble in this camp," said Rolf-Callender, "is that you escaping people think you're a race apart. You're above the law." His mouth was working so that he found it hard to shape the words. "Some of the things you do would get you kicked out of any decent regiment—"

"I'll take your word for it," said Overstrand, who was as red as Rolf-Callender was white. "I can never remember whether that flash on your battle-dress represents the R.A.S.C. or the Army Pay Corps—"

"Acting at cowboys and Indians all over the camp. If you didn't interfere so much with everyone else's comfort you'd just be a joke—"

"If I'm as funny as all that, possibly you could find a part for me in your forthcoming production—"

"But when it comes to stealing property and murdering a harmless little creature like Coutoules—"

"Why, you little twerp," said Overstrand.

"You thought you'd got away with it, didn't you—"

Overstrand slapped Rolf-Callender hard, with his open hand, on the side of the face.

Rolf-Callender hit out, and caught Overstrand, without any force, on the point of the nose.

Overstrand took two paces forward and hit Rolf-Callender under the heart. The three blows were as quick and as pat as in some well-rehearsed music-hall turn, only there was nothing funny about their intention or their effect. Rolf-Callender fell forward on to his knees, stayed there for a moment, fighting for breath, then, with sudden energy, seized Overstrand round the knees, heaved with his shoulders, and toppled him to the ground. Then he threw himself on to him and started to claw. As the two of them rolled round in a threshing, dusty cloud, doors began to open along the passage.

Overstrand was a great deal bigger and heavier than Rolf-Callender and about three times as strong. As soon as he was on top the fight was over. He had Rolf-Callender's throat in his hands and was banging his head on the floor.

"This has got to stop," said Duncan. He was well aware that what was happening was one of the things which simply must not be allowed to happen—anyway not in a prisoner-of-war camp, where nerves were constantly frayed by proximity and boredom. It was the ultimate indecency.

He and Anderson got hold of Overstrand and dragged him off his opponent, and somebody helped Rolf-Callender into a sitting position, with his back against the passage wall.

"Look here," said Duncan. "You'd both better apologize and call it a day. I think there were faults on both sides."

"All right," said Overstrand. He was still red and breathing hard; but it is easier for the victor in these affairs to be magnanimous. "Let's forget it."

"I expect you hope so," said Rolf-Callender. His face was covered with blood and dirt, and his mouth looked like a mean little slit in a dishevelled mask. "I suppose if all these people hadn't been here I should have been finished off the same way as Coutoules."

Overstrand looked down at him for a moment. Then Duncan touched him on the arm and the two of them walked out of the hut, which had suddenly grown silent.

v

"How on earth did it start?" said Baierlein.

"Why get angry with a little blot like that?" said Grimsdale. "He's not worth powder and shot."

"I suppose he wanted his roulette board back," said Long.

"Yes, that's what started it."

"How did he know we'd got it?"

"I don't know—I think it must have been something I said." Overstrand sounded uncomfortable. "Anyway, he went to the S.B.O. and complained. I gather he didn't get much change out of him, though."

"Serve him right," said Long, "but in that case what was all the fuss about? Was it just his usual anti-escape moan?"

"Yes, that sort of thing."

"Why-did-we-go-on-trying-when-no-one-had-ever-got-out-of-the-country?"

"No—he didn't get as far as that. He said that pinching property was one of the things that wasn't done in the best regiments."

"What does he know about the best regiments?"

"When I was in the 60th," said Grimsdale, "we hardly ever stopped pinching things—"

"Doesn't seem much to fight about," said Long.

"He also as good as accused me of murdering Coutoules."

"Well, you didn't, did you," said Baierlein, "so why worry?"

VI

"Have we got time to dress to-night?" enquired Captain the McInstalker.

"'Fraid not," said Captain Abercrowther. "I've got a rehearsal later on."

"Pity." The McInstalker looked at his watch. "Now that we've got our clean shirts we never have a chance to use them."

"We're going to the Café Royal to-morrow night."

"Does one dress for the Café Royal?"

"I should say that it was optional. Suppose we have a quick pub-crawl to-night round the Covent Garden area—start at the Final in William IV Street and work our way along to the Pillars of Hercules."

"All right—if you've got enough time. It's a great mistake to hurry a pub crawl. What are you doing in this play, by the way?"

"I'm Barrett."

"Who's he?"

"A chap who bullied his children."

"Good idea, really," said the McInstalker. "I was always bullied when I was a child. Look at me now."

"I see what you mean."

"Talking of dress shirts, do you know, I always thought it was rather odd."

"What was odd?"

"You remember that night what's-his-name was killed—that Greek."

"The one they found in a tunnel?"

"Yes. You remember we were waiting for our clean shirts then—we wanted them badly for Lady Pat's party—when I saw the laundry van come in I reckoned we should get them."

"We didn't though, did we?"

"No. The van didn't actually come to any of our huts at all. I didn't see it delivering any laundry. I don't believe it collected any either."

"Come to think of it, I believe you're right. What do you think it was up to?"

"I think you ought to tell Goyles about it."

"He's in the cooler at the moment. I must remember to tell him when he comes out."

VII

"I love you," said Rolf-Callender.

"I should have refused to see you again after our first meeting," said Peter Perse. "For I loved you then, though I would have denied it—even to myself... Oh, Robert, I think Eve must have felt as I did when her first dawn broke over Paradise—the terror, the wonder, the glory of it—"

"No, no," said Rolf-Callender. "You mustn't look at me like that, Peter, really you mustn't. The book says 'with restrained *spiritual* passion'. 'Spiritual', please. You're looking at me like a greedy little parlour-maid with her first date."

"It's all very well," said Perse, stretching his legs as comfortably as he could on a couch made up of two packing cases, "but how can you expect me to be spiritual about someone with a big black eye and a plummy nose."

"If you were really concentrating on your part," said Rolf-Callender stiffly, "you wouldn't notice my appearance."

"How can I help noticing it when you drip blood over me?"

"Come, come," said Captain Abercrowther—he had on an excellent pair of side-whiskers and contrived to sound, despite a Scots accent, every inch the Victorian parent. "We'll never get anywhere at this rate. I suggest we take the scene again from 'Forgive me, I won't be silent any longer', and will you boys please remember that you're in love."

VIII

"I told you I'd give you the word when we were ready," said Overstrand to Desmond Foster. "I think we can make it in about two days' time."

"You and Hugo and Grim."

"Yes. We've been quite lucky with our kits. We haven't lost anything in the last searches. Either the Italians are losing their touch or their minds are not on the job."

"All right. I'll tell Tim. I hope he can cut the underground cable without killing himself."

"He's a Sapper—he ought to know what he's doing."

"Rather him than me. However, if you're sure you want to try it. I think everything's set."

"Certainly we want to try it," said Overstrand. "You're not backing out are you?"

"I'm not backing out," said Foster. "I just thought that as your tunnel was so far on—"

"I don't think," said Overstrand slowly, "that the tunnel is ever going to come to anything."

"What makes you so certain?"

The two of them were walking round the perimeter path, and they had gone almost a hundred yards before Overstrand replied.

Then he said, "You mustn't repeat this to anyone, Desmond, because I can't prove it—at least, not in a way that anyone would believe—but I think the Italians know all about the tunnel."

IX

"Come in, Pat," said Colonel Lavery to his Adjutant. "Shut the door. Take a seat on the bed. It's more comfortable than the chair. Have a fig?"

"Thank you very much, sir."

"Now, what's all this about Overstrand and Rolf-Callender?"

"They had a scrap, sir, this afternoon, in Hut A."

"Not a very level fight, I should have thought."

"No, sir. More of a massacre."

"Any idea what it was about?"

"I thought at first it was just an ordinary escaper versus non-escaper row. They've been spoiling for it for a long time—"

"Yes. I had Rolf-Callender in here after lunch. He seemed to think that Overstrand had pinched some of his property. I suppose he went straight back to his hut and happened to run into Overstrand and—"

"Yes, sir. I thought it was that at first. But I was having a word with Terence Bush, who didn't see the fight but came out after it was over and heard what was being said, and he got the impression that Rolf-Callender had accused Overstrand of murdering Coutoules."

"He said that, did he?" Colonel Lavery looked more interested than surprised. "Any reasons given?"

"No. Just a general accusation."

"I wonder," said Colonel Lavery. "He couldn't have done it alone—I think that's pretty well established. It takes four people to open the trap."

"I'm not so sure about that either," said the Adjutant. "I've been talking to one or two people about it myself, and Grimsdale apparently told someone that *if* you understood the trap, and if you were strong enough, two of you could manage it. He said that he and Overstrand had done it once or twice when the regular team wasn't available."

"Did he now?" said Colonel Lavery. He sat for a few moments, picking the fig seeds out of his teeth and considering the possibilities opened up by this new information. "I take it that it's not just *any* two people who could do it. You've got to have the knack of the thing, and you've both got to be hefty sort of chaps."

"Yes, sir. And I don't imagine that one person could do it, however strong he was. To start with, it would be impossible for one man to pull his weight on all four ropes at the same time."

"Yes. Even so I don't quite see—I suppose the idea is that Overstrand and—well—let's say one other person in Hut C—might have come to the conclusion that Coutoules was overdue for dispatch, might have taken him apart somewhere, finished him off, and hidden him—then dropped him down the tunnel later that night."

"Yes, sir. But, of course—"

"There are a million difficulties," said Colonel Lavery. "Where did they kill him? Where did they hide him? How could two people do all that without being seen a dozen times over?"

"Quite so, sir."

"I've come to the regretful conclusion that there's only one body of men in this camp with the means and the space and the organization to pull off a job like that—"

"Who's that, sir?"

"The Escape Committee," said Colonel Lavery.

Evening had been drawing in as they were talking and in the uncertain light Captain Armstrong found it very difficult to decide whether Colonel Lavery was smiling or not.

CHAPTER EIGHT

VIEWED FROM OFF-STAGE

I

THERE WAS ONE THING TO BE SAID FOR SOLITARY CONFINE-
ment: it gave you plenty of time to think. Goyles, who had
never been so fond of the company of his fellows that he felt lost
without it, lay in his favourite position on his bunk with the pillow
under his shoulders. It was three hours since the orderly had
brought him his breakfast. In another hour he would doubtless
bring in his lunch. He let his thoughts drift.

First he considered the disappointment of the night before last.
He could find no explanation for it at all. Or rather, the obvious
explanation did not seem to lead anywhere.

Clearly the unfortunate Biancelli had been indiscreet. He must
have revealed to one of his fellow guards that he had a secret to
sell; he might even have been rash enough to explain the arrangements he had made with Goyles. The person to whom he had
spoken had reported him to Benucci. That was the sort of rotten
thing that people did in Fascist countries. Whether Biancelli had
actually been shot seemed doubtful. Such a step would have been
drastic, even for Benucci. No doubt, however, he had been removed
to another camp.

That Benucci should have taken the trouble to come along
himself that night, at exactly the time when Biancelli was due to
come on guard, was, thought Goyles, entirely in character.

There was no doubt about it: Captain Benucci was a four letter man.

So far his real, inner, beastliness had been cloaked to a certain extent by the necessary minimum civilities of an officers' prisoner-of-war camp, regulated technically by the General Protocol and watched over by the Protecting Power. Goyles wondered how long all that was going to last. When the pinch came, which of the two Benuccis was going to take charge? The suave, capable, formal Latin, or the German-trained sadist? Goyles had met many Italians, both of the old and of the new régime; but he had never met anyone quite like Benucci. He hardly seemed of the native stock at all, or if of native origin, warped from it by alien forces.

The strange thing was that out of these rambling thoughts an idea began to grow.

It had no definite beginning and no very logical thesis, but it centred around an expression which he had heard Hugo Baierlein use some weeks before.

"War Criminals."

At the time the idea had been quite new to him. If he had considered the matter at all he had thought of war as a sort of football match. When the final whistle blew you went back into the pavilion and changed into your ordinary clothes and became friends again.

Now it seemed that this was not the invariable rule; that there were people whose crimes were so full-blown that they would be tried for them after the war; tried in a court of law, and duly punished with death or lesser penalties.

If there were going to be any war criminals in Italy, thought Goyles, Benucci must be well up on the short list. Consider the cases which he knew about himself. There had been Lieutenant

Colley. Goyles had not been in the camp at the time but he had heard all about it. Colley, who was an excellent linguist and a professional actor, had disguised himself as an Italian officer, and with two friends dressed as Italian soldiers had bluffed his way out of the main gate. The security precautions in those early days had not been so strict. The trio were actually passing through the outer of the two gates when Benucci had happened to come out of the office building. He had recognized them as impostors at once. What happened next was not entirely clear, but all eye-witnesses were agreed that Colley and his friends had from that moment no chance of escaping. There were groups of Italian soldiers in the road itself and in the square at the end of the road. Benucci had, without hesitation, ordered the sentries to shoot. All three escapers had been shot down at point-blank range.

The case of Major McFadden had been a good deal worse. There had been a faint cloak of military necessity about the killing of Colley and his friends. The McFadden case, if what was suspected was true, was unvarnished murder.

Major McFadden of the Ulster Rifles, an intemperate but likeable Irishman, and a declared enemy of Benucci, had been Colonel Baird's predecessor as head of the Escape Committee. In this capacity he had been a constant thorn in Benucci's flesh. After a number of undignified brushes with authority he had been dispatched to Campo 5, the Punishment Camp, in the fortress of Gavi, in North Italy. Benucci and one sergeant of carabinieri had gone with him as escort.

The party, however, did not arrive at Gavi.

McFadden, as Benucci had reported on his return, had been shot whilst trying to escape. The carabinieri sergeant had been posted elsewhere. At all events, no one had seen him again.

Very well, then, thought Goyles, assume for a moment that all these suspicions were correct. Assume that Benucci might be a man with a dirty past and a sticky future. How did that tie in with Coutoules?

He began to see how it might very well tie in.

Coutoules, it seemed certain, had been a creature of Benucci's. He had been introduced into the camp by him, for his own purposes. They must have been, to a limited extent, in each other's confidence.

With the immediate approach of the Allied Armies, and, over the horizon, the ending of the war itself, two things might have happened. First, and most probably, Coutoules might have tried a little gentle blackmail. He was well placed for it. With a foot in both camps, the chances were that he not only knew about Benucci's war crimes, but might be in a position to prove them to a disinterested authority.

As he lay on his bunk in the sunlight and thought of these things Goyles experienced that faint electric current, the water diviner's touch, which every investigator feels when, for the first time, he forces his way down from the surface of things as they seem, into the opaque depths of things as they might be.

It was at least a solution which put motives and actors in their proper perspective. He had felt all along, when he was considering the matter generally, that the killing of Coutoules had been an affair of organization. It was no sketchy improvisation. He was far from seeing how it had been done—how the body had been spirited from a room in one hut to a tunnel under a different one—but if the Italians had done it themselves it did, at least, open up certain fields of possibility.

It also produced the distasteful corollary that the Italians—or Benucci at least—must know all about the Hut C tunnel.

There was, however, a second and in a way an even less pleasant line of thought. The Escape Committee, as the Intelligence Authorities of the camp, would certainly have questioned Coutoules once his position was known. Supposing their questioning had been—well, a little more rigorous than they had intended and Coutoules had collapsed. Would they not have been well equipped to dispose of him in a tunnel? On the other hand there was a good deal against this idea. Had not the Committee themselves been the prime objectors to disclosing the body to the Italians? Had they not, in fact, organized its removal to the other tunnel, and thus unwittingly implicated Roger Byfold in the design? Had they not, lastly but by no means least, employed him, Goyles, to investigate the matter for them? And yet—the beginnings of a third and perfectly horrible theory came into Goyles' mind.

He was so overcome by its nightmare possibilities that he did not hear the footsteps in the passage outside, and he nearly fell off his bed when the key grated in the lock and the door swung open.

He glimpsed a figure in British Orderly's uniform.

"Oh, it's lunch already, is it?" he said. Then he looked more closely and saw that it was Tony Long. "What the devil are you doing in that rig? Glad to see you, anyway."

Tony put the lunch tray carefully down on the table, and walked back to the cell door, took a quick look down the passage, and pulled the door shut. Then he turned to Goyles and said, "Cuckoo, you've got to do something."

Goyles was shaken by the unmistakable note of panic in his voice.

"What is it?" he said. "What's up?"

"It's that ass Overstrand. If it was only his blood on his own head I wouldn't mind so much, but he's dragging in Hugo and Grim as well."

"Just start at the beginning," said Goyles.

"They've been pretty hush-hush about it—and I only heard to-day, rather by accident, from Hugo. They've been working on a wall-jumping scheme. It's Desmond Foster's scheme really. They've made ladders—there was rather a rumpus about that"—Long managed to smile in spite of his anxieties—"they pinched the rugger posts. They're going to fuse the overhead lights at half-past twelve to-night, and get over the east wall between the theatre block and the showers."

"They'll never catch them napping twice," said Goyles. "You remember what we all said after the last show—they'd be bound to put in an alternative system of wiring—probably underground."

"That's just it. They think they have." He told Goyles about Tim Meynell and his discoveries.

"Sounds just feasible," agreed Goyles. "What's worrying you particularly?"

"I don't know," said Long. He looked sick. "I've got a feeling about it, that's all. I don't believe that they can be certain of fusing all the lights—it seems too easy to be true—and if they *don't* succeed in fusing them—well—in the present state of nerves it's going to be an execution."

"Why is Alec so set on this scheme anyway? If he sits tight for a week or so the tunnel will be through, or the Italians will have packed up and let us out."

"That's what I said to Hugo. Apparently they don't think it's going to work out like that. To start with, they've got an idea—it's Alec's idea really—that the Italians know about the Hut C tunnel—"

Goyles looked up sharply, but said nothing.

"Then, again, they don't believe that the Italians are going to let us out if there is an armistice. They think that this is the

best time there's ever going to be for a break. I'm not at all sure
there mightn't be some truth in this part. They say that all one
has got to do is to get out and go south and sit tight. The theory
is that when the British do land in Italy, the Germans are going
to form a line somewhere—but obviously it won't be right at
the toe of Italy—probably somewhere about Naples—or even
further north—"

Goyles nodded. It was what he thought himself.

"If you can get out now, and get south of this line and lie
up, you're safe as houses. When the landing comes, you'll be
picked up by your own side. On the other hand, if you're north
of the defence line it's going to be a very different proposition—
to say nothing of the fact that you may never get started at all.
The Italians may simply bundle us up and hand us over to the
Germans. It's all very well for the S.B.O. to talk about making a
rush. Supposing one morning Benucci lines the walls with soldiers and says 'Pack up your kit, gentlemen. There's a German
column waiting outside to escort you'—do you think anyone's
going to commit suicide?"

"Something in that," said Goyles. "Was that their only reason?"

"No," said Long slowly. "There's something else too. Something
you haven't heard about. It happened yesterday, and I haven't
quite sorted it out yet, but Alec had a scrap with Rolf-Callender.
It started over something quite silly, but the upshot of it was that
Rolf-Callender accused Alec of murdering Coutoules."

"He did *what?*"

"Just that. And what's more, Alec didn't deny it. Not directly,
anyway. He just went very pink and haughty, and intimated to
Hugo and Grim that if that was the sort of thing people were
saying about him, the sooner he got out of this camp the better—"

"That's crazy."

"The whole thing's crazy. Look here, Cuckoo. If Alec really is sure that the Italians know about this tunnel, he must have some information that we haven't got. He must tell us what it is."

"Ten to one it's nothing at all, or he's just imagining things."

"Then if he's wrong, he ought to call the stunt off to-night. It isn't just himself. If he wants to earn a V.C. and clear his good name one wouldn't mind him doing a crazy stunt like this—but he's dragging Grim and Hugo into it too. I got the impression Desmond himself would have called off, if Alec hadn't been so keen."

"What do you want me to do about it?" said Goyles.

"I thought—look here, you've got more influence with Alec than any of us—couldn't you have a word with him?"

"From here?"

"I thought—it might work—couldn't you change into this kit and walk out with the tray. We're about the same height and shape. Even if they noticed in the end, you'd have time for a word with Alec."

"There's one very good reason against that," said Goyles. "And that is that the sentry, who's not such a fool as you took him for, has been standing outside the door looking through the spy hole for the last two minutes."

II

The afternoon light had gone out of the sky. At seven o'clock Goyles' evening meal had arrived. It was a genuine orderly this time—Corporal Pearce, a young, black-haired Irishman who worked in Hut C. He had nothing to report. He said the camp seemed very quiet.

At eight o'clock the lights in the cell had been turned on, and at ten they had gone off again.

Goyles lay on his bed. There was no chance of sleep. His own thoughts, mingled with what Tony Long had told him, had thrown a long shadow of foreboding over his mind. He wondered if it would, in fact, have made any difference if he had been able to have a word with Overstrand. He had managed to talk sense to him on previous occasions. Could there be anything behind this idea that Overstrand had killed Coutoules?

It seemed on the face of it, the most arrant nonsense. Where had Overstrand been between nine o'clock and lock-up that evening? He himself had been taking his regular evening walk round the perimeter with Roger Byfold. Their room had been empty when they got back to it. Alec had come in at half-past ten. He hadn't told them where he had been—why should he? You didn't go round explaining to people where you'd come from last.

Looking at his watch Goyles saw that the time was near.

He pulled the table up to the window, put a chair on it, and climbed up.

Without shifting the centre bar he could look out far enough to see the north-west sentry platform and the line of overhead lights. The searchlight on the platform, which came on every few minutes, was almost blue, so intense that it paled the overhead lights to a dull yellow.

Everything remained quiet.

Goyles looked at his watch again. It was almost a quarter to one. A tiny flicker of hope sprung up, that the attempt might have been abandoned.

As he was in the act of looking up again, all the lights went out. First the overhead lights flickered and disappeared: then, in mid-sweep, the searchlights dimmed and faded.

They've done it, said Goyles.

Then something happened which made his stomach turn right over. The searchlights glowed and came on again.

A second later he heard the machine guns start. They went on and on.

CHAPTER NINE

CAPTAIN BENUCCI REMOVES THE MASK

I

GOYLES SLEPT VERY LITTLE AND WOKE EARLY. HE WAS LYING on his bed, fully dressed, when Corporal Pearce brought in the breakfast coffee and bread.

"You know what happened last night, sir?" said Pearce.

"I heard it happening," said Goyles. "Put down the tray on the table, would you?" It took a momentary courage even to frame the question. "What was the result?"

"Major Grimsdale and Captain Overstrand, sir—killed. Captain Foster and Captain Baierlein were wounded. They don't think Captain Foster has got much chance."

"What about Baierlein?"

"They don't think he's too bad. He fell right up against the wall, and they couldn't get a machine gun on to him. He got some in the legs."

"I see," said Goyles. It was a tiny little bit better than he had dared to hope. In his own mind he had written them all off. Poor old Grim—

"—all over the camp, sir," said Corporal Pearce.

"I'm sorry," said Goyles. "I didn't hear what you were saying."

"I was just saying, sir, that there's a funny sort of feeling in the camp this morning, if you know what I mean."

"Yes, I do," said Goyles. He had seen it, and noted it before: the after-effects of successful violence. He remembered a train journey before he had come to that camp. One of the prisoners, a young Air Force officer, had tried to jump from the train in broad daylight and had been filled full of buckshot by an excited sentry. Then other guards on the train, who up to that moment had been behaving quite reasonably, had become hysterical and arrogant. The prisoners had gone sullen. It had not been a pleasant journey and but for the tact of a senior officer might have ended in a massacre in the station waiting-room at their destination.

"Does anyone know how it happened?" he asked.

"They say that the searchlights have all got spare power-units now, sir. They run on the mains for most of the time, but if anything happens to the mains, they can run on their own juice for a bit."

It seemed a likely enough explanation.

"Would you like me to wait and carry your things out for you?"

Goyles looked surprised.

"You've miscounted," he said. "I've got about three more days to do."

"I was having a word with the sentry when I was coming in," said Corporal Pearce. "So far as I could make out they're clearing you out this morning. I reckon they think they're going to need all the cells they've got before long."

"I see," said Goyles. "As bad as all that, is it?"

"All the chaps are talking about stringing up Benucci next time he shows his face in the camp, and the Eyeties have put double lots of sentries on the walls and they're all talking monkey-talk and cleaning up their guns."

"If they're as trigger happy as that," said Goyles, "I'd better wait for a formal order of release. Thank you very much all the same."

After Corporal Pearce had gone he went over to the window and stood looking out of it. He stayed there for a long time whilst his coffee grew cold and his bread lay untasted.

He was getting used to the thought that two people he had known so well should be dead.

II

"I'm very sorry," said Colonel Baird flatly. "It was a feasible scheme—a good deal more feasible than many—and it failed, because we were without one piece of information."

"I'm not quite clear about that," said Colonel Lavery.

He and his Adjutant were seated at one side of his table, the three members of the Escape Committee were on the other side. The atmosphere was formal.

"On the previous occasion," said Colonel Baird, "it was established that a single set of overhead power-lines carried the current for the perimeter lights and the searchlights on the sentry platforms, and, as you know, we succeeded in fusing these with secateurs mounted on poles. We had always anticipated that the Italians would guard against this by putting in alternative, underground, wiring. Well, we found this underground line and we arranged to have it cut, too. What we didn't know was that there was a *third* source of supply, a self-contained emergency power-unit for each searchlight. The sort of thing they have in operating theatres."

"I see," said Colonel Lavery. "You were satisfied that if the lights had been put out properly there was a fair chance of success?"

"Certainly. Once the four of them were up on the wall in a direct line between sentry platforms, the sentries daren't fire in the dark for fear of hitting each other. All the escapers had to do then was to drop from the wall and disappear down the hillside."

"On the face of it, then," said Colonel Lavery, "it doesn't seem to have been anyone's fault." He paused. "It does bring me to my next point though. Up to now I've agreed—and I've been very happy to agree—that all escaping activities should be run by your committee. I haven't asked to be told about them. I felt that knowing nothing about them has strengthened my hand in dealing with the Italians. I'm afraid that's got to stop."

"Stop?" said Colonel Baird.

"I mean," said Colonel Lavery, "that from now on I want to know about any attempted escape before it takes place."

"Know about it, or approve of it?"

"Know about it and approve of it."

The line of Colonel Baird's jaw had become a fraction more prominent. Commander Oxey was unsmiling but neutral. Colonel Shore seemed to be secretly amused.

"It worked very well before," said Baird. "I'd like to understand why it's got to be changed."

"It worked in normal times," said Colonel Lavery patiently, "but these times aren't normal. We're sitting on the edge of a land-mine which is going to go up at any moment. The whole situation is all of a piece. Anything one party does affects everyone else. If I'd known about last night's attempt—however much chance of success I thought it had—I'd have stopped it."

"Could you tell us why you would have done that, sir?" asked Commander Oxey formally.

"Have you looked at the sentries this morning? Have you ever watched a cat the first time it tastes blood? Sooner or later—it may be weeks, it may only be days—we're going to have to deal with these gentry. I'm going to have to deal with their Commanding Officer. I'm sure you won't misunderstand me if I say that all our lives may depend on the sort of attitude we have towards them and they have towards us. Well, last night wasn't helpful."

"I can't see how us stopping trying to escape is going to make the Italians any more respectful," said Colonel Baird.

"This morning," said Colonel Lavery, ignoring this, "I had a message that I was to go and see Captain Benucci at his office at midday. I was to go and see *him*. Formerly, when he has had anything to say he has come to see me. It's a small thing, but it's an example of what I mean."

"Do I take it," said Colonel Baird, "that you want to know all the details of escape activities—or do you just reserve the right to veto them?"

"I want full co-operation," said Colonel Lavery.

There was an awkward silence which was broken from an unexpected quarter. Colonel Shore said, "If I might be allowed to say so, I think you're plumb right. This isn't a situation where it's going to help to have people pulling in two directions."

"Oh, quite," said Commander Oxey hastily.

"I'm not disagreeing," said Colonel Baird. "I'll do what I'm told, of course. It's only that—well, just because we got a poke in the eye last night, it doesn't seem logical to suspend all escaping activity."

"Far from it," said Colonel Lavery. If he breathed a sigh of relief he was too experienced a tactician to do so openly. "If there's one thing that stands out above everything else it is that that tunnel's got to be finished. I believe that it doesn't even matter now if they guess what's going on—provided, of course, they just don't know where the tunnel starts. Suppose they do catch people dumping sand? What does it prove that they didn't know already?"

"It might even be helpful," said Colonel Shore. "You know what you were saying about moral ascendancy. It's a thing I've noticed about these Italians myself. If you shout at them and insult them, it just raises their morale. They're like a troop of monkeys. They're bucked to think you're taking so much notice of them. But if you laugh at them they're lost."

"All foreigners are like that," agreed Commander Oxey.

III

Tenente Mordaci had been in two minds about coming into the camp at all that morning.

In the end, being in receipt of a direct order from his superior officer, he had belted on a large Biretta pistol under his cloak, and had started out cautiously on his morning round.

The routine of the camp seemed to be proceeding normally. A dusty game of basket-ball was in progress on the sports ground. The Dry Fly Club was holding a casting competition behind Hut B. A row of builders of the body beautiful were busy adding another layer of tan to their already over-cooked torsos.

None of these groups made any hostile demonstration as Tenente Mordaci walked past them, clutching his Biretta moistly beneath his cloak. Nobody spoke to him at all.

The whole camp seemed unnaturally quiet.

Between Huts E and F he came upon Lieutenant Long. Lieutenant Long was raking thoughtfully over a rose bed. It was, in many ways, rather a curious rose bed. When it had first been dug, many months before, its surface had been level with, or even sunk below, the surrounding soil. Now, with successive loads of sand from the Hut C tunnel, it had grown upwards in an ever more and more voluptuous curve until it threatened with extinction the row of struggling rose bushes which were by now barely managing to keep their heads above the surrounding surge.

"A lovely morning, Tenente," said Long, as Mordaci came up.

"I am surprised you can say so," said Mordaci solemnly.

"Why, what's wrong with it?"

"Can it be that you have not heard of the events of last night? Two killed, two wounded. Useless stupidity—"

Tony suspended his raking and looked up at him. "Good gracious me," he said, "surely you don't believe that stuff—"

"Believe! I myself have seen."

"I thought everybody knew by now that it was a fake. Surely those dummies didn't deceive you?"

"Deceive me! What fantasy is this?"

"The truth of the matter is that the only people who got hurt were the two sentries who shot each other in the confusion."

"Is that so?" said Mordaci. "Then perhaps you will explain how—"

"The trouble with you Fascists," said Long, "is that you've been propaganding people for so long that you can no longer recognize the difference between truth and untruth—I'm sorry I can't stop and gossip. I've got a date with a girl—"

IV

At five minutes to twelve Colonel Lavery, accompanied by his Adjutant, walked across to the main gate and asked to be taken to Captain Benucci.

There were two sentries on the inner gate, and one of them pointed his short rifle in the direction of the S.B.O. whilst the other went to the telephone.

Colonel Lavery was aware that this was only a gesture, but he felt happier when the second man returned and started opening the gate.

"You only," said the sentry who had telephoned, "not the other officer."

Captain Armstrong hesitated for a moment.

"That's all right, Pat," said Colonel Lavery, "don't let's start an argument. I expect it's only something about the rations."

The Adjutant saluted, and walked back to the camp. Colonel Lavery, followed by the second sentry, made his way to the carabinieri quarters, which lay beyond the Punishment Block. This was arranged, like the Punishment Block, with an L-shaped passage, only it contained more and smaller rooms: three on each side, and one at the end. Benucci's office was at the far end, on the left, and Colonel Lavery had taken two steps towards it when he was stopped by a soft whistle. He looked round, and saw, at a slit in the nearest door, the anxious eyes of Roger Byfold.

"Nice to see a friendly face, sir," said Roger.

"Good heavens, Roger! How are they treating you?"

"*E vietato*—" began the sentry in an anxious squeak.

"A bit short on exercise," said Byfold. "Otherwise all right."

"Anything I can do for you?"

"*E asolutamente vietato*—" said the sentry.

"You go and boil yourself," said Byfold.

The sentry, despite the fact that he was still holding his rifle contrived the child-like, outward-turning gesture with both hands which an Italian makes when a situation is beyond him. Then he said, "*Eh—ma—*", and bolted down the passage towards Benucci's office.

"We've got a second before they turn the dogs loose," said Colonel Lavery. "Are you sure you're all right? They haven't been—"

"Not a single rubber truncheon," said Byfold. His face was white but his grin was unimpaired.

"Has there been any sort of court proceeding?"

"If anything's been done," said Byfold, "it's been done behind my back. Nor have I yet been induced to sign the traditional confession. Ah—here comes Torquemada."

"I regret," said Benucci, "that talking to the prisoner is forbidden." His voice was polite but his eyes had a cold, enquiring look in them. "Will you come to my office, please?"

In the office there was a silence which Colonel Lavery was determined not to be the first to break. In the end Benucci said, "I expect you are wondering why I have sent for you?"

"Since, in the past, you have always come into the camp to see me, I imagined it must be something out of the ordinary."

"Yes," said Benucci. "I think you will think so. I sent for you to tell you that Captain Byfold is to be shot."

The satisfaction was so apparent, the animal was so near the surface, that the spectacle turned Colonel Lavery's stomach. Also it steadied him.

Without taking his eyes off the Italian, and keeping his voice at a careful, conversational level, he said, "Oh. When?"

"The execution will take place at dawn the day after to-morrow."

"On what authority?"

"The sentence has been confirmed by the Headquarters of this District."

"No doubt," said Colonel Lavery, "but whose sentence?"

"The sentence of the Military Tribunal convened by the Commandant of this camp."

"Is it customary in Italy for a prisoner to be tried on a capital charge in his absence?"

"Depositions were read from all witnesses, including the prisoner himself. All possible evidence was considered by the tribunal."

"Yes," said Colonel Lavery. "Did you give evidence?"

"My deposition was read also."

"And no doubt you stated in it that you knew perfectly well that Captain Byfold had nothing to do with the death of Coutoules?"

There was a sudden gleam of white as Benucci showed his teeth. Then he got up from his chair, came to the front of his desk, within a few feet of Colonel Lavery, sat on the edge of it and crossed one neatly booted leg over the other.

"I answered the questions that were put to me," he said.

"I see."

"If you consider that an injustice is being done, you must comfort yourself with the consideration that, in war, injustices are common. Particularly in prison camps. Both in ours, and, no doubt, also in yours."

Colonel Lavery considered this for a moment and then said:

"Were you thinking of any particular instance of injustice?"

"No. Not of any particular instance. I was speaking generally."

"And is that all you had to tell me?"

"That is all."

Colonel Lavery hesitated. He knew quite well that he only had one possible card in his hand, and it was a matter of life and death that it be played properly. Not too soon, and not too late.

He turned as though to leave the room, then, over his shoulder, he said, "I suppose you realize that you will be held responsible for this when the British Army takes over."

"When they do," agreed Benucci.

"Personally responsible, I mean. You can't hide behind a tribunal which hasn't even been given a chance of hearing the prisoner."

Benucci stifled a yawn.

"There is an English saying," he observed, "about crossing a bridge when you come to it. No doubt you are right. *If* this camp was taken over by the British Military Authorities and *if* I was still in the camp at the time, some form of reprisal could no doubt be exacted."

Colonel Lavery left the room without another word. In fact he had nothing left so say.

When he got back to his room he found the Escape Committee waiting for him.

"They're out for blood, all right," he said.

"You don't think it's possible that Benucci was trying to frighten you?" asked Baird. "It would be well in character."

"No, I don't. He's thought it all out and he means to do it. At one time, something he said gave me the impression that he might be getting a sort of personal satisfaction out of it all. It occurred to me to wonder—still, that doesn't matter now. The thing is, what do we do?"

"I can't understand it," said Commander Oxey. "He must know that his German pals are taking a beating in Sicily and he must guess that the British Army will be in Italy soon. He can't hope to shut all our mouths."

"I put the point to him," said Colonel Lavery. "But it didn't ring the bell at all."

"That's not healthy," said Baird.

"So I thought. To my mind it can only mean that the Fascists are going to make a fight for it. Italy's a damned long prickly country, full of defensive positions, and we're about four hundred miles up it as the crow flies. If the Italians stick by the Germans and keep their heads it's going to take the Army months to reach us. By the time they get here, we'll all be in Germany, Benucci included. Or that's what he's reckoning on, anyway."

"Might be a sea-borne landing," suggested Commander Oxey. He didn't say it very hopefully. All four men were thinking the same thing.

"There could be," said Colonel Lavery. "Hardly as far north as this, I should have thought."

There was another silence.

"If we told them everything," said Baird, "where we found Coutoules and how and everything. Made a clean breast of it. Do you think it would be any use?"

"I think they'd laugh in our faces," said Colonel Lavery. "They'd appropriate the tunnel, say thank you very much, and carry on with Byfold's execution, as planned."

"Then what do we do?" said Baird. "Sit and wait for it, and hope for a miracle?"

"If I might make a suggestion," said Colonel Shore. "Stop me if I say anything you don't agree with, but isn't there one pos-sible solution we've been overlooking. It's a golden rule, when you've got two dangers, to see if you can't set them to cancelling each other out. The Italians have taken Byfold, and they're forc-ing our hands by threatening to shoot him—with just enough colour of legality to make them feel good about it. The only possible way we can save him, and it isn't a very certain way at that, is by giving up our last trump card—the Hut C tunnel. All right. Now we know where Byfold is. Colonel Lavery saw him this morning. He's in the Carabinieri Block, next to the cooler. That's right, isn't it?"

"Yes," said Colonel Lavery.

"And the cooler's empty at the moment, waiting for an expected influx of prisoners. And the cooler is next door to the Carabinieri Block. Do you see?"

"Not at the moment," said Colonel Lavery, "but please go on."

"Why don't we stage a nice little riot this evening, and get half a dozen of the right types put in the cooler? There are officers in this camp who can pick a lock with their eyes shut. They break out some time to-night, quietly remove the sentry in the doorway of the cooler, move across to the Carabinieri Block, let out Byfold, and then—"

"Yes. Then what?" said Baird.

"And then," said Colonel Shore, "they simply *come back into the camp*. That part shouldn't be difficult. There's only one gate sentry at night—and he's in his box on the outer gate. Provided the guards on the platform don't spot what's happening—and remember, they are concentrating on the camp, not on the Italian quarters—then the whole gang should be back in the huts before the alarm is raised."

"They might," said Baird. "I agree. It's so mad, and so unexpected, that it might work. But how are we any better off? We can't keep Byfold if they want him. That would simply lead to a pitched battle that we should be bound to lose."

"Surely," said Colonel Shore. "That wasn't my idea at all. I suggest that once Byfold is safely in the camp, *we put him down the Hut C tunnel*."

It was Colonel Lavery who eventually broke the respectful silence which greeted this suggestion.

"Pure genius," he said. "No other word for it. It puts them in a cleft stick, of course. Once they've searched the camp and failed to find Byfold, they must guess that he's in the tunnel, because that's the only considerable hiding place they have so far failed to discover. If they *do* know about it, they'll have to show their hand. If they don't they've got to give up Byfold."

"What about the other six?" said Baird. "They'll know who they are and they'll be certain to take it out of them—or do you suggest we put them down the tunnel too?"

"I should hardly say that was necessary," said Shore. "I don't think even Benucci could shoot them out of hand—they'd need some form of hearing if only to protect themselves—and that's all going to take time—"

"Provided they don't kill the sentry, I don't see that there could be any question of shooting them. The most they would get would be a term of imprisonment—"

"All right," said Baird. "The first thing is, who's going to do it? We haven't got much time. Goyles and Long are obvious choices. If they're willing, we'd better let them pick the rest of the team. I'll have a word with Goyles now. What do you say, sir?"

Colonel Lavery took his time over answering. Before he did so he looked at the calendar on his wall. July 19th.

"I wish it was a week later," he said. "Yes, I agree. It's almost the only thing to do. It may come off. It's better than sitting back and waiting."

V

"I wonder if I could have a word with you," said "Tag" Burchnall.

"Of course," said Goyles. "Come in. If it's about those rugger posts," he added, "I can only say how sorry—"

"No, nothing like that. It's just that we heard—it may be quite wrong, but you know how things get about in this camp—we heard there was some scheme on foot for getting Byfold out of clink—"

"That's right."

"From what I heard, it sounded rather a sporting thing altogether. I wondered if you wanted any help—Gerry Parsons is quite useful if it comes to a rough-house, and Rollo isn't such a fool as he looks—"

Goyles made very little effort to conceal his surprise or his pleasure.

"You'd be very welcome," he said. "We'd got four already. Anderson and Duncan are helping, but we needed two more. Come for a stroll round the camp and I'll give you the details—"

VI

Goyles was on the final tunnelling shift, and after tea he changed slowly into his digging kit, and made his way to the kitchen. He had done it all so many times before that most of his actions were mechanical, and only a quarter of his mind was on his job.

He had a lot to think about at that moment. It was as if two enormous kaleidoscopes were being shaken before his eyes, forming and reforming their incomprehensible patterns; or two wheels rotating and two films unrolling simultaneously. Sometimes the pictures coincided, but more often they were different. On the one side was Captain Benucci and the Fascist machinery of their captors, and beyond him the ranked Fascist hegemony of Italy itself, with the Duce at the summit, all revolving, in some quite inexplicable way, around the person of Roger Byfold, who was sitting in his cell, waiting for what the day after to-morrow might bring. On the other side was the microcosm, the little world of the camp itself, the cell-like organization through which its four hundred inhabitants crawled and swarmed. Those who knew you and those who didn't. Your friends and your enemies—and it was becoming difficult after his surprising conversation with Burchnall that morning to be quite sure which was which. And just as the one pattern seemed to centre itself round the figure of Roger Byfold, so was the other concentrated on the awkward, unlikeable, unforgettable figure of Cyriakos Coutoules who, in that very tunnel, only eighteen days before—

"Wake up, Cuckoo," said Long. "You're number one to-night."

"All right," said Goyles. "Let's go. Who's doing number two?"

"Andy's two, I'm three. I'll start the pump going when you reach the bend."

Goyles lowered himself on to the truck and started, with the expertness of long practice, to propel himself forward up the tunnel. Anderson crawled more slowly behind him, holding in his hand a rope attached to the truck. It was Goyles' job, as number one, to do the actual excavating. The sand which he dug was placed in cardboard boxes, six of which fitted on to the trolley. Anderson, from an excavation at the half-way mark, would pull the trolley back, and load the boxes into two sacks. Long, at number three, would then make two journeys to fetch the sacks back to the shaft. It was also his job to keep the pump going. Now that the tunnel was more than a hundred and fifty feet long this system saved time and meant that the man at the face could dig almost uninterruptedly.

The tunnel was no longer quite the comfortable, all-enclosed affair that it had been. The effect of the half-timbering which the Escape Committee had ordered in the interests of speed was already apparent. To move at all in the last thirty feet was an agonizing performance. It was all right as long as you were on the truck itself, but moving on hands and knees was like making your way across a series of diabolical railway sleepers, and the sides of the tunnel, which were naked in every alternate revetment, dribbled a small but increasing shower of sand on to you as you moved.

Goyles hardly noticed any of this. He scooped and dug mechanically, filling all six boxes once, and then again. The end of his forty minutes' turn at the face was nearly up. Whilst he waited for the jerk on the cord attached to his foot which would indicate that the truck was ready for hauling back from the half-way house, his mind reverted once again to its pressing problems.

The cord jerked.

Goyles half-turned on his elbow, his leg caught the woodwork of the last revetment, and the next moment he was lying, flat on his face, in pitch darkness. He was pinned to the ground, like a slug under a lawn roller, by the weight of the sand which had fallen on him.

It was a few seconds before he actually realized that he was unable to breathe.

But even in that agonizing moment, as he arched his back and strained his muscles in a futile effort to raise himself, as the red lights started to flare and wheel behind his eyes, and his heart came bursting outwards from his lungs, even at that moment, in his mind, curiously detached from the agony of his body, a tiny but decisive piece of the puzzle fell into place.

CHAPTER TEN

THE PUT-UP JOB

I

GOYLES OWED HIS LIFE TO THE FACT THAT LONG AND Anderson were both old hands at tunnelling; to the fluke that they happened to be together, at the half-way post, unloading the last lot of sand, when the fall occurred; and to the fortunate chance that the lights did not fail.

If any of these things had fallen out differently he would certainly have died.

"Start the pump," said Long. "I'll dig him out. You'd better use the trolley to get you back to the shaft." Almost before he had finished speaking he was himself moving at reckless speed, towards the face of the tunnel.

As he moved he calculated the chances.

The airline of the pump was a series of jointed tins, and it ran in a shallow trench, on one side of the tunnel. It was the first rule of tunnelling that you extended this line scrupulously, tin by tin, as you went, and he prayed that Goyles had not forgotten to do so. Even in a heavy fall the digger's body might come down across the end of the airline and protect the outlet from the sand, and in such cases experience had shown that enough air could be pumped into the fall to keep the victim alive during the period of his unearthing. The chief danger was that, so long as he was conscious, his struggles to assist might block the airline altogether.

It was a big fall, and it was obvious to Long as soon as he saw it why it had occurred. The tunnel had run into the footing of the outer camp wall. The soil having already been disturbed from above would be the more likely to collapse when excavated from below.

Long lay on one side, his head almost on Goyles' stockinged feet and started to shovel the sand past his own body like a fox-terrier at a rabbit hole. He could hear the wheeze of air under pressure coming out somewhere in the mass ahead of him. He hoped that all the sand which was going to come down had done so already.

Goyles was showing no signs of life.

"Probably better if he stays that way for the moment," thought Long. He himself was sweating all over and the tips of his fingers were already raw. There was no time for finesse. He simply worked his way in until he could get his hands hooked into Goyles' belt. Then he braced his knees against the last intact frame of the tunnel, humped his back and heaved with all the unexpected strength that was in his slight body.

The frame shifted ominously.

The sweat on Long's body seemed to turn cold all at once. He stopped pulling and resettled himself. Then he took a deep breath, and pulled again, less violently, but as strongly. Under this pressure Goyles' body started to move. Tony pulled him back steadily, shifted his own position again, and pulled again. Now he had him clear. He disengaged one hand, felt down to the side of the tunnel, and tore open one of the joints in the air pipe.

The fresh air poured out over both of them, cool and sweet.

He was lying there, trying to think coherently, and aware that he had gone dangerously near the limit, both mentally and physically, when he felt a hand on his heel.

Help had arrived in the form of "Brandy" Duncan.

"I've brought the trolley up with me," said Duncan. "Better get him on it. We can't try any first aid here. There isn't room. Are you all right?"

Long was almost as white as the unconscious Goyles.

"I shall be O.K.," he said. "Let's get him moving."

Back in the Hut C kitchen they found Doctor Simmonds who, like the stormy petrel, could smell trouble from afar. Under his direction they laid Goyles on the floor and started to work. His glasses had been broken in the fall and in the rescue operations a splinter of lens had dug a long furrow down the side of his nose. This was now bleeding.

"Very healthy sign," said Doctor Simmonds. "He'll be round in a minute."

"We'd better clear up," said Duncan. "Give us a hand and we'll get the trap down. And we'd better get some of that sand swept up."

At this moment Goyles opened his eyes. He lay for a moment looking at the ceiling and then said, in a conversational tone of voice, "You can't move your hands, you know."

"That's all right," said Doctor Simmonds, "take it easy. You'd better carry him along to his room."

"But you can't move them," repeated Goyles. "It's not true. You can't move them at all."

"Get him under the legs," said Duncan. "You take his head, Tony."

"I'll be along in a minute," said Doctor Simmonds. "I'll mix him a sedative. He'd better stay in bed for twenty-four hours."

After they had gone the doctor stood for a moment, a puzzled look on his face. He had just realized what Goyles was talking about.

II

Hands. Dozens of hands. Singly and in pairs. A hand, larger than life, dragging itself, like a maimed octopus across the sand.

Curious, thought Goyles, that he had never before realized how significant was the human hand. It was in its shape that its true secret lay. The broad river of the palm, flowing out to the delta of the fingers. Four fingers, each one with a life and character of its own, four tapering, aristocratic, fingers and a gross plebeian thumb, a bastard connection, sprung from its own root back in the wrist. A distant and disowned collateral to the four beautiful sister fingers. Each one with its sensitive tip and its sheath of horn.

A man could live with his hands, by his hands and through his hands, thought Goyles. And, conversely, he could be more truly hurt in them, than in any other part of his body. The stout Elizabethan, John Stubbs, punning at the scaffold when his hand was to be struck off: "Pray for me, now my calamity is at hand." Gestapo torturers, with delicate precision, plucking off nail after nail from the living flesh, like shells off a ripe filbert.

It was in the hands of Cyriakos Coutoules that the answer to all the mystery was contained. With the clarity that sometimes comes in a nightmare and disappears within a few seconds of awakening, so that it must be caught instantly or lost for ever, Goyles glimpsed the naked logic behind the mysteries that had puzzled him and it shocked him, so that he cried out, and woke up to find an anxious Tony Long shaking him by the arm.

"It's all right," he said, "just a nightmare."

"You've been talking to yourself for hours," said Long. "I could put up with that, but when you started screaming—"

"I shall be all right now," said Goyles.

When he next opened his eyes, it was late morning, and his head was clear. There was no one in the room.

He groped for his spare pair of glasses and put them on. They rested awkwardly on the thick strip of sticking plaster down the side of his nose. They were a pair which had been issued to him, many years before, in England, for use inside a respirator, and this was the first time he had ever worn them. He took them off, bent them into a more comfortable shape, and put them on again, as the door opened and Corporal Pearce came in with a cup of coffee.

"Thanks very much," said Goyles. "I'm afraid I'm a fraud, really."

"Doctor's orders," said Corporal Pearce. "I hear you were in a bit of a turn-up yesterday evening."

"Roughly speaking, yes. Very good coffee, this. By the way, who told you about it?"

"These things get round," said Corporal Pearce. He started to brush diligently under the beds.

Goyles watched him for a bit. Then he said, "Stop that for a moment, would you, and come and talk. There's something I wanted to ask you."

Corporal Pearce obediently propped the broom against the bedpost and sat down on the end of the bed. He was a good-looking boy, of about twenty, with the dark black hair and deep blue eyes that sometimes come together in the Celt or the Spaniard.

"How many orderlies are there in this camp?"

"There's about forty of us now, sir. Used to be more."

"They sent a lot of you off about a fortnight ago, didn't they—to do farm work?"

"That's right, sir."

"How did they choose the party?"

"There wasn't any choosing, sir. They just took the first twenty in the queue."

"Everybody wanted to go, did they?"

"Almost everybody. It was more food, you see, and more freedom, and the chance of seeing a few *signorinas*—"

"Did you volunteer?"

"No, sir, I didn't."

"Why not? Aren't you fond of food and freedom and *signorinas*?"

Corporal Pearce grinned and said, "Well—you had to give your *parole*—I didn't fancy that—particularly not just now."

"Are you hoping to escape, then?"

"You never know, sir. There's sure to be a chance—when things pack up—"

"I'm not arguing with you," said Goyles, "I just wanted to know. Would that be the general view among the orderlies—or is it just your own idea?"

"One or two of the lads think like I do. It's difficult to say, really."

Goyles pondered for a moment.

"Look here," he said. "This is something that perhaps I oughtn't to ask—and you mustn't pass it on. You say that some of you—you and a few of your friends—are keen to escape. The others, I take it, don't mind one way or the other. They're glad the fighting's over—and as long as they get enough to eat and don't get pushed around, then they're happy enough."

"That's about it, sir."

"All right. But does it go any further than that? Would any of them actually help the Italians—if a suitable reward was pushed in their direction?"

Corporal Pearce looked unhappy.

"They're a mixed crowd," he said. "Some of those South Africans are very rough characters—don't even speak English, some of them—jabber, jabber, jabber, in a lingo of their own, sounds just like German to me—"

"But you don't know of anyone in particular?"

"Oh, no, sir. It's just that you can't answer for them, not knowing them."

"If any of you wanted to get a word to the Italians it wouldn't be difficult for you."

"Easy as falling down. We're in and out all day—fatigues, Red Cross carrying parties—odd jobs—like that time I was bringing you your meals in the Punishment Block, remember?"

"Yes," said Goyles, "that's rather what I thought. Well, forget all this, will you—"

An hour later he had another visitor. Colonel Baird came to see him.

"I thought you'd like to know," he said, "that the tunnel is all right. We had an inspection party down this morning. What fell on you was practically all the sand under the foundations of the outer wall."

"It felt like quite a lot of sand," agreed Goyles.

"We're not even going to roof it over. There's no need. In fact we'll probably develop it into a sort of second 'half-way house'. I reckon it pays to have a few sitting-out places in a tunnel of that length. You can get some traffic-control installed when the time comes—"

Goyles agreed, but absent-mindedly. His interest in the tunnel, at that moment, came second to more urgent problems.

"Any news of Roger, sir?"

"Nothing reliable."

"Do you think they mean business—or are they only bluffing. It would be just like Benucci."

"Very like," agreed Baird. "I don't know. One can't rely on it being one thing or the other. We're going ahead with this evening's show, anyway. That was one of the things I wanted to talk about. I don't think, in your present state, you could quite pull your weight in a show of that sort—".

"But I'm as fit as a fiddle, sir—really—"

"Well, there are plenty of others who can do it. Besides, we needed one more lock expert, so that both cell doors could be opened at once—"

"But really, sir—I'm not—"

"Look," said Baird, kindly but firmly, "this is just one of those rare cases in this God-damned camp where an order is an order. You're not going. Now relax."

Which was all very well, thought Goyles, as he lay on his bed at six o'clock that evening and looked out of the window.

He knew that, as originally organized, the riot was due to take place somewhere on the playing field and at about that time. It might, of course, have been changed. No one would have told him anything.

He could see the usual evening sports programme getting under way. There were games on both of the basket-ball pitches and a small group of experts were pitching a baseball in one corner, but the chief attraction that evening was the rugger game. The Old Hirburnians appeared to be playing a Scottish team. Goyles could see nothing out of the ordinary, except that Tony Long (neither a Scotsman nor, incidentally, a rugby enthusiast) had apparently been co-opted into the Scottish scrum in which Anderson and Duncan were also performing. He noticed both Burchnall and Parsons in the Hirburnian scrum.

The Italians, as usual, were suspicious of the whole performance. Ever since an enterprising escaper, under cover of a reconstruction of the rugger pitch, had caused himself to be buried in a shallow trench from which he hoped to emerge after dark, the orders had been that sentries were to exercise an active vigilance during all such games. When it did happen, everything happened very quickly.

At one moment a small sentry, his rifle slung over his shoulder, was pacing importantly across the half-way line. The next moment the ball had appeared from nowhere and struck him on the chest. He had barely time to utter a single, indignant bleat before the scrum had caught him, and he disappeared under a cataract of arms and legs.

The sentries on the walls were plainly in two minds. Outrages were being committed in front of their eyes, but they were unable to shoot. They relieved their feelings by screaming. The gates opened and a file of carabinieri doubled on headed by Paoli. The scrimmage subsided and the sentry reappeared. He had lost his rifle and bayonet and, as became horribly apparent when he tried to stand up, his braces as well.

Goyles held his breath.

It was always touch and go at moments like this whether the Italian sense of humour or sense of dignity was going to come to the top. It was with mixed feelings that he saw that Captain Benucci had arrived and appeared to be taking command of the situation.

The groups separated and the dust settled.

To his surprise it became apparent that most of Captain Benucci's wrath was concentrated against the sentry. His admonitory remarks practically reached the hut. The sentry, holding his rifle in reverse in one hand, and the top of his trousers with the other, scuttled off.

The game restarted.

Half an hour later a dishevelled and despondent Tony Long arrived and perched on Goyles' bed.

"You saw it?" he said. "Seemed to go pretty well, didn't it? Well, it was an absolute flop." He sat for a moment swinging his legs, and then said, "Wouldn't you have thought it a safe bet that they'd have arrested the lot of us? We were all there, all six of us, as arranged, holding little bits of that sentry's clothes and gear, all utterly arrestable. I had his hat and bayonet scabbard. If ever you could have betted you were on to a safe thing, I should have thought that was it. I was only scared they were going to machine gun the lot of us. Then Benucci arrived—"

"I saw him," said Goyles. "What happened?"

"What happened?" said Long. "He laughed."

"I see."

"I'll do him this much justice," said Long. "He behaved exactly as an English officer would have behaved in the same circumstances. He tore the sentry off an awful strip—so far as I could follow what he was saying—for getting in the way of the game. He then told him to get back to barracks and get dressed. Then he gave everybody a sort of paternal tick-off. 'Boys will be boys—don't get carried away'—that sort of thing, and sauntered off."

"With the honours of war—"

"Oh, Lord, yes," said Long. "With every honour that was going. I've never seen a bluff called more competently."

"You don't have to be a good poker player," said Goyles, "to call a bluff when you know exactly what cards all your opponents are holding."

"Say that again."

"Look here," said Goyles, "either I'm mad or everyone else in this camp is blind. But isn't it perfectly obvious that everything we do and say *goes straight back to Benucci*."

Long suspended his undressing and stood for a moment, with his head on one side, looking anxiously at Goyles.

"You're not still delirious, are you?" he said.

"I've never been clearer headed in my life. You remember that first morning—when the Italians found Coutoules' body in the Hut A tunnel. All that finger-printing and photographing and measuring marks in the roof of the tunnel. It stuck out a mile that they knew perfectly well that they were being offered a put-up job. I don't go so far as to say that they knew where or how Coutoules was killed, but they knew that he had been put in that tunnel for them to find. That stuck out so far that even the Escape Committee noticed it."

"All right," said Long. "When else?"

"Well, you remember my fiasco in the cooler. I thought at the time that poor little Biancelli might have blown his mouth off and got nabbed for indiscretion. Now I'm not so sure. And this business to-night makes me even less sure. You said yourself that it was unnatural. It was more than unnatural. It was plain bloody incredible."

"You realize what you're saying, I suppose," said Long slowly. "Take those three cases alone. If Benucci got hold of them as quickly as you say he did, he's got to have an informer who's well in the swim. Not just anybody. I don't suppose that more than a dozen people knew about any of them."

"I agree," said Goyles. "And it means a good deal more than that, too. Benucci's not a fool. He must know that we're capable of working this out. Why should he practically go out of his way to give us the information? Why should he come and rub my nose in it, as he did over that Biancelli job?"

"You tell me," said Long.

"I'll tell you what I think," said Goyles. "I don't think he cares a brass farthing for the safety and well-being of his informer in this camp. Any more than he did for his other stooge, Coutoules. And I'm beginning to think—and hope—that the reason for this is simply that he realizes, better than we do, that time is running out. We can't see the line running off the end of the reel, but he can."

"Hang on to that," said Long soberly. "It's almost the only hope left for Roger that I can see."

III

Very late that night Colonel Baird was sitting in Colonel Lavery's room. They had been talking for a long time. Neither of them felt much desire for bed.

Breaking the silence, Baird said, "I don't believe he'll do it. I don't believe anyone in his position would risk it."

Colonel Lavery had no need to ask him who he was talking about. "Anyone but Benucci, no."

"He's a tough character," agreed Baird.

Another silence.

"Do you remember once telling me," said Colonel Lavery, "about the time when you had a German prison camp under your command in the Delta? About the Nazis who ganged up on one of the prisoners and tried him and executed him? You had the ring-leaders shot—very properly, in my opinion—you can't allow mob law like that in a prison camp—or anywhere else."

"Certainly I remember it," said Baird.

"Did it ever occur to you that Benucci—who's a pure Nazi, if I'm any judge—might be taking a sort of back-handed swipe at you for that incident? It's got all the usual Nazi trimmings. You manacle ten of our prisoners, we manacle twenty of yours. That sort of thing."

"You mean," said Baird slowly, "that because I have three men shot who *are* murderers, self-confessed murderers—he's going to shoot an innocent man?"

"That's about it. With all suitable display of justice and wash-ing of hands, but that's about what it boils down to. I got the idea from something Benucci said when he broke the news to me about Byfold. 'Injustices are apt to happen in prison camps. They happen in your camps and in ours.'"

"If you're right about that," said Baird, "we shouldn't kid our-selves that there's much hope, should we?"

"The only glimmer I can see is in a report I had this evening from our 'I' people. I can't make very much of it, but apparently the Fascist Supreme Council had an emergency meeting yesterday afternoon. It seems to have lasted until after midnight."

"Another of Musso's gags?"

"I suppose so. The only thing is that one usually reliable source says that the meeting wasn't called by Mussolini at all. Some people think it was Roatta. There's another school of thought that it was Graziano."

"One Eyetie's very like another to me," said Baird. He sat for a few minutes puffing at his empty pipe. "I'm inclined to fall back on the old infantry motto: 'When in doubt, dig.' It may be a waste of time, but we've got so far with that tunnel I think we ought to bring it through."

"I hear you had some trouble."

"Yes. Some sand came away under the outer wall. It's always apt to fall if it's been disturbed from above. We've got it all under control again now."

"How far are you going?"

"That may depend on the time element. I want to go at least another fifty feet. We're twenty feet below the surface now. If we go straight on for fifty feet we shall hit the slope of the hill over the crest and out of sight of the wall. It should make a very snug exit."

"Provided it doesn't collapse again," said Colonel Lavery. "I take it you'd thought of that. It'll be more vulnerable as it comes nearer the surface."

"It will be, and we had thought of it. From now on every inch of that tunnel's going to be revetted, if it means using every last bed board in the camp. Let 'em sleep on the floor. It'll harden them up for what's ahead of them."

Colonel Baird got to his feet, and added, à propos of nothing at all that had gone before.

"I'm sorry if we haven't seen eye to eye in the past. That's all over now. I'm on your side."

He was gone before Colonel Lavery could frame any suitable reply.

CHAPTER ELEVEN

COLONEL LAVERY TAKES OVER

I

GOYLES WAS LYING PROPPED UP ON ONE ELBOW, ON HIS bunk. He was looking out of the window. It was six o'clock in the morning and it was as quiet and peaceful as the beginning of time.

The sun had come up from behind the eastern wall and was sucking the dregs of the early morning mist. Everything in camp was silent. Only faintly from outside came the sounds of the little village at the foot of the hill as it woke. An occasional car went past on the lower road. A woman could be heard shouting something in a high-pitched voice. The bells of two churches were wrangling for an early service.

Goyles sensed that Tony Long was awake, too.

"They can't do it," he said, without turning his head. "Not on a morning like this."

Tony said nothing.

There was a shuffle of steps in the passage and the door opened. It was Doctor Simmonds. He was fully dressed.

"Would you come along here," he said, "and see what you make of this."

"Make of what?"

"I may be imagining things. Come and see."

Goyles and Long both pulled on some clothes and followed the doctor along the passage to the small room at the other end of the hut which he shared with the *padre*.

From this room you could see most of the northern wall of the camp.

"What's up?" said Goyles. "The sentries seem very pleased with themselves."

"That's not all of it," said Doctor Simmonds. "Where are the caribs?"

"You're right," said Long. "There's not one in sight."

The sentry on the platform nearest to them caught sight of the faces at the window and a wide grin split his face. He put down his rifle, extended his left arm, and executed that indescribable Italian gesture which is made by chopping the forearm with the palm of the right hand.

"What does he mean?" said Long.

"It's usually a sign that someone's bought it," said Goyles grimly. "You don't think the little bastard means—?"

"He's pointing at the camp gate—what the devil's up?"

"We can see the gate from our room," said Goyles. "Come on."

The three of them raced back.

When they got to the window of their own room they saw that something unusual was, indeed, happening. Normally, no Italian ever came near the camp before eight o'clock. Now there was a small crowd in the compound and the inner gate was being thrown open.

"My God," said Goyles. "My God, it's Roger."

A small procession had entered the camp. There were two figures in front, one of whom was undoubtedly Roger Byfold. The other looked like Colonel Aletti.

"I'm going out," said Goyles suddenly.

Before anyone could stop him he opened the top of the window level with his bunk, pushed his long legs through and slid to the ground.

The sentry on the near platform must have seen him, but he made no move.

Trying to look as if it was the most natural thing in the world to break out of your hut in broad daylight, Goyles strolled across to the next line of huts, walked along the side of Hut D, and peered round.

The deputation had passed him and had reached the Senior Officers' Hut. Colonel Baird, Colonel Lavery and the Adjutant had all come out to meet it.

Goyles, realizing that nobody was worrying about him at all, sidled up and attached himself to the group. Everybody was talking at once. Roger Byfold caught Goyles' eye and grinned, and at that moment Colonel Lavery turned round and saw him.

"Please, sir," said Goyles, "what's happened?"

"What's happened?" said Colonel Lavery. "Mussolini's fallen. Graziano's taken over. The Fascists are out."

II

"It doesn't mean that they're going to open the gates, you know, and let us all go," said Colonel Baird.

"I suppose not," said Byfold. He had eaten an enormous breakfast, and apart from a tendency to grin at everyone who spoke to him, was showing little outward signs of what had passed. "I suppose," he added, "that life should be a bit easier."

"In a way," said Colonel Baird.

"All the really top-line thugs have gone, sir. They melted last night. Benucci and Mordaci and that horrible little Marie-scalo Butsi—the one we called the Butcher."

"When did you hear about it?"

"Late yesterday evening. I was lying on my bunk practically composing my own funeral oration—"

"You knew what was going to happen to you?"

"Oh, yes. Benucci told me yesterday morning. In detail."

"I see," said Colonel Baird. "Please go on."

"Well, about nine o'clock last night I think it must have been, there was a lot of coming and going. I take it that was Benucci and Co. packing up. About an hour later, the Commandant arrived and after a good deal of huffing and blowing said that the dawn firing party had been postponed. I said that was all right so far as I was concerned."

"He didn't tell you about Mussolini?"

"No. But a bit later I noticed that I'd got a new sentry—an ordinary Eyetie—not a carib. He was bursting with the news. Didn't need any prompting. He told me the whole thing. I gathered from him, incidentally, that he wasn't really a Fascist at heart. Just an ordinary citizen who did what the brutal Fascisti told him to."

"I expect we shall meet a lot of those," said Baird dryly. "When you said that all the top-line thugs had gone, what exactly did you mean? Have all the carabinieri cleared out?"

"Oh, no, sir. At least, I don't think so. Paoli's still here—he was looking a bit sea-sick last time I saw him—and the ordinary carib is just running round looking for someone to give him orders."

"I see," said Baird. "As I said before, this doesn't mean that we're all going to be set loose. It's bound to make a difference though. Everybody must know, now, that Italy's going to pack up their piece of the war. That's bound to affect their attitude towards us."

"They'll be ever so tender-hearted," agreed Byfold.

"Another thing. You realize that the gentry who cleared out last night were all the real anti-escape experts. That's going to make life a bit easier."

"There's something I meant to say about that," said Byfold. "I got the impression that Benucci knew about the Hut C tunnel—"

"You're not the first person who's thought that," said Baird. "How did you get the idea?"

"Something he said—I can't remember exactly what it was—not in so many words. But I remember thinking that he did know about the tunnel, and that it was just like him to tell me that he knew, when he imagined I was going to be—well, when he thought I couldn't do anything about it."

"I see."

"Then, when I was thinking it over last night, I couldn't help thinking what a joke it would be if Benucci and his own particular buddies *did* know about the tunnel, but in the general excitement they had pulled out and had forgotten to pass the information on to anyone else."

"Either forgotten, or not bothered," said Baird. "I don't suppose there was much love lost between the two gangs. Was there anything else you picked up that might be useful?"

"Well—no. Nothing in particular." For a moment Byfold looked almost embarrassed.

"Certain?"

"Yes. Quite certain. If I do think of anything I'll let you know."

"All right. The S.B.O. wants a word with you before you go back to your hut. You might go and see him now. I think he's in his room." Colonel Baird paused. He felt that the occasion demanded something. "I'm glad they didn't shoot you," he said.

III

"All I really wanted to see you about," said Colonel Lavery, "—do sit on the bed, it's much more comfortable than the chair—is to get your ideas on the present set-up on the other side of the wire. You're probably in a better position than any of us to judge it. In particular I'd like to know what you make of our Commandant. He's going to be the important factor now that Benucci's gone."

"I didn't see a great deal of Colonel Aletti," said Byfold. "I was kept to the carib quarters. He presided at both of my official examinations—if you can call them that, they were hardly trials—more like a Court of Enquiry in the Army. He never said much and left most of the talking to Benucci. I don't know whether he knew what was in the offing, but I think he was quite glad to put most of the responsibility on to Benucci's shoulders."

"I expect he feels that now," agreed Colonel Lavery. "What I was really getting at was, what sort of person you thought he was?"

Byfold considered this. He realized that a compliment was being paid to his judgment and he did his best. "I think," he said, "that he's like any weak man when he's forced into a position of responsibility. He'll be pleasant as far as he can, so long as it doesn't put *him* on the spot. But if any higher authority threatens him, he'll go back on us without any compunction."

"And if the Germans say one thing and his Italian bosses say something different—?"

"It would depend which was in a position to kick him hardest."

"That's much as I thought," said Colonel Lavery. "But I'm glad to have your confirmation. Did you pick up anything else that might be useful whilst you were over the other side?"

"No, sir. Nothing startling."

If there was, once again, a certain hesitancy in Byfold's manner, Colonel Lavery apparently did not notice it.

IV

"Come in," said Colonel Lavery. "Who is it? Oh, it's you, John. Sit on the bed—it's more comfortable than the chair. What's up? You look as if you've had some bad news."

"Not bad news, just news," said Major Gibb—he was the tall major in the I Corps who has already been noticed coordinating security arrangements for the Hut C tunnel—"I'm trying to make out what it means."

"How did it come?"

"The usual way," said Major Gibb. "I think there's no doubt it's a War Office instruction all right." He produced a sheet of paper on which he had himself transcribed the following message:

> In the event of an Allied Invasion of Italy, Officers Commanding prison camps will ensure that prisoners of war remain within camp. Authority is granted to all officers commanding to take necessary disciplinary action to prevent individual prisoners attempting to rejoin their own units.

Colonel Lavery read it through carefully once and then again. He seemed to be weighing the value of every word.

"How long do these messages take to come in?" he asked.

"It's difficult to say, sir. It's not a quick system, you know. That message might have originated two or three months ago."

"That's rather what I thought. I take it that no one else knows about this?"

"Actually two of my chaps got it independently. I've shut both their mouths, I hope. I'm the only other person in camp who knows about it."

"It had better stay that way for a bit," said Colonel Lavery. His eyes again sought the calendar on his wall. July 21st.

v

"Come in," said Colonel Lavery. "Oh, yes. The Adjutant told me you wanted to see me. Do you think you could make it after lunch, I'm a bit rushed—"

"It won't take a minute, sir," said Rolf-Callender.

"All right, then." Colonel Lavery repressed an inner sigh. It was soon apparent, however, that Rolf-Callender was not in an aggressive mood. On the contrary he appeared to find it difficult to start.

In the end he said, rather abruptly, "I wanted to clear up a bit of a misunderstanding."

"Yes."

"It's about Overstrand, sir. Some time ago—you may have heard—we had a bit of a row. It wasn't anything much, just one of those things that happen."

"I did hear something about it," admitted Colonel Lavery.

"Well, I lost my temper, and—among a lot of other nonsense—I hinted that he knew something—that he had something to do with killing Coutoules."

Colonel Lavery looked up sharply, but said nothing.

"I thought I ought to tell you, sir, that it was nonsense. It was just one of the stupid things people say when they're in a temper. There was nothing to it at all. In view of what happened—"

"If it's any comfort to you," said Colonel Lavery, arriving with some skill at the real heart of Rolf-Callender's discomfort, "I can assure you that Overstrand's attempt to escape had nothing to do with your accusation. We're pretty sure now that he could have had nothing to do with Coutoules' death and presumably he knew that he himself was innocent."

"Thank you, sir."

"In fact," said Colonel Lavery. "If anyone was to blame for his death, in the last analysis it was probably me."

VI

"Come in, all of you," said Colonel Lavery. "There's one chair, but I expect some of you can get on the bed—it's a bit of a squash, but I won't keep you long."

Besides the Colonel there were seven men in the room: the five hut commanders, Colonel Baird and the Adjutant.

"I expect," he went on, "that you've all heard what's happened. It's a bit difficult to straighten out, but I gather that Mussolini's out of office, and his personal gang are on the run. General Graziano has taken over, nominally still under orders from the Fascist Grand Council. I imagine, however, that there's no doubt about his real position. He's only got one brief—and that is to get Italy out of the war, by hook or by crook."

"How soon, do you think, sir?"

"As soon as he can—but I don't imagine it's a thing that can be done in a matter of days. Getting out of a war is a two-sided business. They've got to get in touch with our military headquarters, and fix up some sort of terms, and I don't imagine that the Germans are going to sit by and watch that happening—it'll all have to be done very carefully under cover."

"How long do you think, sir?"

"I give it a month. But that may be two weeks wrong in either direction. It's that interval we've got to use to the best advantage. We've got to get on with the tricky business of ousting the Italians and taking the real control into our own hands. We can't go the whole hog yet"—Colonel Lavery grinned—"but it will be instructive to see how far they do let us go. First of all, I intend to make the evening parade for roll-call a British parade rather than an Italian one. You all know how it's run at the moment—people slope on to parade just in time to have their names called and get away as soon as they are allowed to. As from to-morrow that's going to be changed. Huts will parade, as companies, under their Company Commanders, five minutes *before* the time fixed by the Italians for the roll-call. Moreover, no one will dismiss until I give the word."

Of the five hut commanders, four made no attempt to conceal their satisfaction at these rather startling orders. The fifth, a small major from a Heavy Anti-aircraft Regiment, looked so upset that Colonel Lavery made a mental note that he would have to be replaced immediately.

"We don't want to run before we can walk," he went on, "so I'm not going to risk a full-dress inspection at once. I'll give you ample warning when it is going to come off, and by that time"—he allowed himself another fleeting smile—"I don't want to see *any beards*. That's as far as I've got at the moment. Has anyone else got any suggestion?"

"Are we going to adopt any sort of uniform dress?"

"I think not—not yet, anyway. It would attract attention, and would be asking for trouble. You might make sure that everybody has one serviceable outfit for an emergency."

"Can't we introduce some proper system for requests and complaints. At the moment anyone who wants anything comes straight up and starts blowing his head off."

"I entirely agree," said Colonel Lavery, remembering his encounters with Rolf-Callender. "We'll have the army system put into force—complaints to be put forward through the usual channels."

"Security," suggested Baird.

"I was coming to that," said Colonel Lavery. "I think that for the next few days you can chance your arm to almost any extent—I mean, over sand disposal and that sort of thing. They're bound to be disorganized, with Benucci and his trained thugs gone, and it's going to take them time to sort themselves out."

"I was thinking the same thing myself," said Baird.

VII

"It is my destiny," said Roger Byfold, "to do the right thing at the wrong time. I am told that I grinned fatuously whilst I was being christened, and I broke into loud howls during my wedding. No doubt at my funeral—"

"What's all this about?" said Goyles.

"I was referring to my recent incarceration. Normally a period in the condemned cell will set a man up for life. He can sell his life story to the *Daily Yell* and his love story to the *Daily Smell*. Serial rights alone should be enough to keep him in modest comfort for the rest of his life—or his widow, should his appeal fail—but look at me!"

"If you insist," said Long agreeably.

"What sort of rake-off have I got from my harrowing ordeal? When I was coming back to the hut this morning I met Dopey

Gibbon. He had almost got past me when he stopped, came back, and said, 'Weren't you going to be shot this morning, or something?' 'They've postponed it,' I said. 'Oh, good,' he said, 'it just occurred to me to wonder if you had any spare *vino* tickets. You won't have been able to use yours lately, I suppose?'"

"Never mind," said Goyles. "Tony and I are glad to see you back."

"Did you pick up any ideas about what's going to happen to us—all of us, I mean?"

"I've no doubt in my own mind at all," said Byfold, speaking, for him, fairly solemnly. "This country's heading for one great big typical Italian shambles, with everybody screaming and waving their hands and shooting their best friends, and it's going to be up to us to take the best advantage of it. As from to-morrow morning I propose to do P.T. twice a day and to spend the rest of the time brushing up my Italian."

The other two looked at him.

"Are you serious," said Long, "or is that just a line?"

"Dead serious," said Byfold. "I got a good many chances to talk to those characters who were guarding me, and they all said the same thing, carabinieri and all. Once Italy gives up the war you can go anywhere you like in this blessed countryside and count on help. Now that the Fascists are going, that's doubly true. If you were outside these walls now, you could walk the length and breadth of Italy, and count on a meal and a bed every night."

"And when do they think the shambles is going to occur?"

"As soon as Allied Troops land in Italy. And I reckon that that's going to be the time when we all have to prove whether we're mice or men. It's going to be the sort of chance no prisoner of war is ever going to get again."

"If he can get started."

"Yes," said Byfold. "*If* he can get started."

"You don't sound too happy about that," said Goyles. "Any special reason? The tunnel's five-sixths done. It's well past the outer wall. We three are almost first on the roster to go out of it. It ought to be money for old rope."

"I suppose so," said Byfold.

"What's on your mind?" said Long.

"I—look here, you've got to keep quiet about this, because I may be quite wrong. I didn't say anything to the S.B.O. or Baird, although they both asked me—but something *did* happen whilst I was in the carabinieri hut. It was the first morning I was there. I wasn't in the end cell, where they put me later, but in a room next to Benucci's office. It hadn't got a spy-hole, so I couldn't see who went past, but there was a good deal of coming and going, and I couldn't help thinking that some of it was probably on my account, so I listened as carefully as I could to see if I could pick up anything that was being said next door. It wasn't at all easy, and you couldn't hear anything very distinctly, but I suddenly realized something rather odd was going on. At least one of the voices was English."

Goyles remembered Meynell's story.

"Could it have been the wireless?" he suggested.

"It didn't sound a bit like the wireless. You could hear that all right, when it was on. Dance music and announcements and so on. This sounded quite different."

"Educated or uneducated?" said Long.

"Educated, I thought. You could only pick up the general tone of it, but there were occasional words—I heard 'roll-call' more than once. No Italian says 'roll-call' in just that way."

"Could it have been the S.B.O.?"

"I don't think so," said Byfold. "According to Pat the only time he's ever gone over there to talk to them was when I saw him on the morning after the shooting. Before that, Benucci always used to come in here."

"Was it distinct enough?" said Goyles, "for you to pick up any sort of intonation?"

"Yes," said Byfold, "that's just it. There was. I'm prepared to swear it was either an American or a colonial speaking."

He paused, and added unhappily, "That's what makes me wonder about our tunnel."

VIII

That afternoon, as he had half been expecting, Colonel Lavery was summoned to a conference by the Camp Commandant.

"No doubt," said Colonel Aletti, after the preliminary courtesies had been exchanged, "you will have been thinking about the somewhat startling news which was received this morning."

Colonel Lavery agreed that he had been thinking about it. Conversation was not easy. Colonel Aletti spoke slow, grammatical English, but he had nothing like Benucci's smooth competence. Nevertheless he seemed to understand Colonel Lavery fairly enough.

"I am not a man who interests himself in politics," went on Colonel Aletti. "I am a simple soldier. I receive orders from my superiors. I carry them out to the best of my ability."

Colonel Lavery indicated that this was roughly the system in the British Army, too. As he spoke, he was weighing up the man in front of him. He thought that Byfold's diagnosis might prove to be reasonably accurate. Colonel Aletti did not look to him like a strong man. He had the long, sad, aloof, slightly petulant face which many Englishmen imagine to be typical of the Italian upper class because it is the face they most often see, in the good clubs in Rome, the villas above Firenze, and the *salles privées* in casinos up and down the Corniche. With his well-pomaded grey hair, his correct carriage, his bemedalled uniform and his thin, neatly booted legs, he looked, thought Colonel Lavery, quite strikingly like the late Sir Henry Lytton in his rôle of the Duke of Plaza Toro. He also reminded himself that this was the man whose decision, or lack of it, might mean the difference for all of them between a chance of liberty and an unthinkable prolongation of their imprisonment, and chose his next words carefully.

"I take it," he said, "that the case against Captain Byfold may be assumed to be at an end."

"Certainly," said Colonel Aletti. "The process was conducted, at the instigation of Captain Benucci, under the orders of the Fascist hierarchy; such orders are no longer effective."

"I am glad to hear it. Now with regard to the camp. Have you any idea what will happen to us?"

"My orders, at the moment, are to carry on as before. Marshal Badoglio has published a communiqué, proclaiming Italy's unalterable intention of fighting on until victory is won."

"Yes," said Colonel Lavery, "I read it in the *Corriere*. Might I suggest, however, as men of the world, that we are entitled to look beyond the words and consider the realities behind them."

"Certainly," said Colonel Aletti cautiously. "What particular realities had you in mind?"

"When the English land in Italy, what will the Italians do?"

"Since you ask the question frankly, I will answer it frankly. Much depends on where they land."

"Yes," said Colonel Lavery. There was plain sense in that. He shifted his ground slightly. "I take it that pending this happy outcome, it should now be possible for us to co-operate more than we have done in the past."

"Nothing will give me more pleasure. It has often pained me in the past that we could not conduct affairs with more amiability."

"I agree," said Colonel Lavery, rather grimly.

"Such trouble as there has been, you must realize, has been of my making. I was under the necessity, in many respects, of taking orders from Captain Benucci. Nominally, he was my subordinate. But being of the Party, he had authority exceeding mine in many matters. Many of his actions I did not approve of, but could not prevent."

"I quite appreciate that."

"I doubt it," said Colonel Aletti frankly, "for it is a system which would be inconceivable in any but a Fascist country. I was responsible for all matters of routine administration, but where there were questions of policy, I had to accept the Party decision—as announced by Captain Benucci. All security matters, too, were controlled by him, through his senior carabinieri officers. I was left almost entirely in the dark. They had their own methods. You may know, for instance, that they employed spies in the camp."

"I had heard it suggested," said Colonel Lavery, "that Coutoules—"

"Was Coutoules in the pay of Benucci, then?" Colonel Aletti sounded genuinely surprised. "I did not know that. I was told nothing. The identity of the other was also kept from me."

"Of the other?" Colonel Lavery hoped that his voice did not sound too eager.

"You did not know, then," said Colonel Aletti, "that there was a German Intelligence Officer in the camp?"

CHAPTER TWELVE

"THE BARRETTS OF WIMPOLE STREET"

I

"HE SAID *what*?" SAID COLONEL BAIRD.

Colonel Lavery repeated the information.

"He must have been pulling your leg," said Colonel Baird. "The idea's fantastic. Did he give you any idea who it was?"

"He couldn't. He didn't know himself."

"Then how did he come to know about it?"

"I asked him about that. Apparently Benucci was rather tight one evening and was boasting that nothing went on in this camp without him knowing about it. The Commandant, who hadn't got much use for Benucci, suggested he was laying it on a bit thick. Benucci said, far from it. The English were so stupid that they didn't even realize that they'd got a fully fledged member of the German Intelligence Service planted amongst them."

"He might have meant Coutoules."

Colonel Lavery considered this. "He might have done," he agreed. "Coutoules didn't look much like a German."

"Did he say whether he was posing as an officer or as one of the orderlies?"

"He didn't say."

"If it's one of the officers," said Colonel Baird, "I'll eat my desert boots, in public."

II

When he thought about it afterwards Colonel Lavery came to the conclusion that the most remarkable feature of this period was the slow, almost imperceptible, but very steady rise in the *morale* of the camp. There was no lack of grumblers when his orders were first made known, but the majority opinion was so solidly behind him that he felt strong enough to ignore them.

Through that boiling month of August—and it was hot even by Italian standards—organization and discipline improved and the camp ceased very gradually to be a collection of individuals and became a community, inspired by an object. What that object was—what precise hand fate and the Italian Government were going to deal—nobody knew. It was sufficient, at the moment, if they put themselves in the best position to play the cards as they fell.

Hut Commanders instructed their assistants and cursed their black sheep. Colonel Baird drove his digging teams to more and more furious endeavour and Colonel Lavery found every morning on arising one new grey hair on his head.

Some of the most surprising converts to military enthusiasm were the Old Hirburnians.

"I must confess, I never saw much sense in that escaping nonsense," said Tag Burchnall, "but give me a decent, limited, military objective and I'm for it. It might be an idea if we green blancoed our webbing, don't you think, before parade to-night. It'll wipe the eye of 'B' Section, if it does nothing else."

It was about this time also that Roger Byfold began his keep-fit campaign. Like everything else that he undertook he went into it with a rational and compelling enthusiasm.

"I've given the matter a good deal of thought," he said to
Goyles and Long. "As I told you, it's quite clear that the time is
coming when some special effort will be demanded of everyone.
I am not sure what form this effort will take. It may demand
a rapid gymnastic feat, such as the scaling of these walls, or
the jumping from a moving lorry or train—we must therefore
maintain bodily suppleness and agility by means of Muller's
exercises before breakfast and a regular physical training class at
least once a day. Further, since the initial break will undoubtedly
be followed by a long period of marching, we will harden our
feet by making first ten, then twenty and later thirty circuits
of the compound every evening, in our heaviest boots. Finally,
since we shall be traversing a friendly or neutral countryside,
we had better brush up our Italian. Tony is the best linguist—he
shall give us both an hour of colloquial Italian each day after
lunch. Thus, when the moment comes, we shall be armed at
all points."

"*Speriamo*," said Long in his best colloquial Italian.

It was during this period, too, that Goyles realized the truth
about the death of Coutoules. He did not reach his conclusions
by any blinding flash of intuition. Like all problems long and seri-
ously thought over, the answer arrived in instalments. New and
apparently irrelevant facts came to light, and old facts, long sifted
and half-forgotten, assumed a new significance, until finally, as to
one who stares into the red heart of the fire, the shapeless began
to assume a shape and the formless to take form.

One such odd fact came out of a conversation with the *padre*,
a tall Etonian, who had done good work all the previous winter in
one of the "other-ranks" camps; had nearly died of enteritis, and
had been moved to Campo 127 direct from hospital.

He and Goyles attended the same Greek class, and it was coming away from a morning session that the conversation turned to the remarkable difference between the ancient and the modern inhabitants of Greece, and so, by easy stages, to the late Cyriakos Coutoules.

The *padre* said, "I suppose I was the only person who met Coutoules before he came to this camp."

"How's that?" said Goyles, surprised. "I thought this was his first camp."

"Indeed not. He was in the Modena other-ranks camp with me last autumn. I believe there was some doubt at that time about his officer status. Then he got himself shifted to Cremona."

"Was that the camp at Modena where they nearly had a mutiny?"

"That was the one."

"What exactly happened?"

"The prisoners found out that the Italian staff were appropriating Red Cross parcels for their private use and lodged a complaint. The authorities then stopped *all* Red Cross issues and halved the ration—"

"And a lot of the prisoners nearly starved?"

"It wasn't a question of 'nearly'," said the *padre* shortly.

"I see," said Goyles. He turned this over for a moment in his mind. "Is it known who was responsible?"

"I think so," said the *padre*. "Yes, I think we know all right. Nominally it was the commandant who gave the orders, but I think the real villain of the piece was his second-in-command, Captain Bernadi."

"A carib?"

"Yes."

"Well, I hope someone's got a note of it," said Goyles.

At the time the information made no further impression on him.

It was some days later that he heard the word Cremona mentioned in conversation and linked it up by an effort of memory with what the *padre* had told him.

The speaker was a submariner, a naval lieutenant who contrived (it is a secret known only to the Navy) to combine a look of youthful innocence with a huge red beard.

"Were you at Cremona?" said Goyles.

"For my sins, yes," said the submariner.

"Was it a *strafe* camp?"

"Not really. We called it the sorting house. I think it was the sort of camp you got sent to if the Italians weren't certain about you. If they came to the conclusion that you were a hard case you probably went up to Campo 5 at Gavi. They evidently decided that I was innocuous and sent me on here."

"Do you remember Coutoules at Cremona?"

"Yes, more or less. His last week there was about my first. We weren't chums. Anyway, there wasn't much time for beautiful friendships at Cremona. Life was grim and life was earnest and the end, in a number of cases, was the grave."

"I heard it wasn't very pleasant," said Goyles. "Who was the cause of it all?"

"The real villain was the Italian Intelligence Officer, a deep blot called Marchese. He had one eye and no morals."

"He was a bit of a terror, was he?"

"He was a swine," said the submariner.

"He can't have been much worse than Benucci."

"Put them in the same cage in the Zoo," said the submariner, "and there wouldn't have been a cloven hoof's difference between them."

"Hmph," said Goyles.

He picked up the next thread in the Theatre Hut. He had strolled in one morning and was sitting quietly at the back watching one of the final rehearsals of *The Barretts of Wimpole Street*.

He could not help thinking that Rolf-Callender, for all his faults, was an extremely accomplished actor. On the stage, even without make-up or broad-cloth, he opened out, somehow, into the flamboyant personality of Robert Browning. Off-stage he was insignificant. Behind the footlights he was a person.

As the rehearsal was breaking up Captain Abercrowther caught sight of Goyles and came across to talk to him.

"Good show, Angus," said Goyles. "You looked as if you really enjoyed bullying all those children."

"It answers a deep-felt want in my nature," agreed Captain Abercrowther. "But that wasn't what I had to say to you. There's something I've been meaning to tell you for some time."

Whereupon he repeated to Goyles the observations which Captain the McInstalker had already made to him about the strange movements of the Italian laundry van.

"Look here," said Goyles, "are you absolutely certain that was the night that Coutoules—"

"July 1st?"

"Yes."

Captain Abercrowther took out a small diary and consulted it. "There's no doubt about it," he said, "we were both going to dinner that night with Lady Pat Keyne—Basingstoke's youngest, you know—and that was why we particularly wanted our shirts."

"Did you see where the van stopped on its way round the camp?"

"It only stopped in front of the Senior Officers' Hut. We were hoping it would come on here, but it didn't. When it went, it went straight out."

"What time would that have been?"

"Between half-past nine and ten. It was getting a bit dark."

Goyles mentioned this conversation to Tony Long that evening, and Tony was able to confirm it.

"I saw the van going out," he said. "I was at the cooler window. I should have said that it was nearer ten than half-past nine. What's it all about?"

"I'm not quite sure," said Goyles.

Nevertheless, the pieces were beginning to join together.

III

"I'm afraid," said Colonel Lavery to his Adjutant, "that the Commandant is no longer quite the old friend that he used to be."

"I thought it was too good to last," agreed the Adjutant. "I expect yesterday's fiasco upset him a bit."

He referred to an unfortunate moment on roll-call on the previous evening. Evening roll-call, under the new régime, was now a smart, reasonably well-turned-out parade. It was also becoming apparent to the Italians that it was a parade which was conducted almost wholly by and for the benefit of the prisoners themselves.

Companies fell in under their Company Commanders, were inspected, and stood at ease. When the Italian orderly officer was signalled, Colonel Lavery appeared, and the parade was called to attention and handed over to him. At the end of the roll-call—which took about a quarter of the time it had done in the old, disorderly days—the parade was again called-up and properly dismissed.

On the evening referred to Colonel Aletti had elected to come and watch proceedings for himself.

At the conclusion of them, when the last name had been called, he had given the order, "You may fall out." No one had moved an inch. Thinking that he might have been misunderstood, he had repeated the order. Upon which Colonel Lavery had given the order, "Parade dismiss."

It was not perhaps the most tactful way of demonstrating to Colonel Aletti that the control of his camp was changing hands.

"We shall have to butter him up a bit," said Colonel Lavery. "We can't afford to get at cross-purposes just now."

"The Italians will have to make their minds up soon which way to jump," said the Adjutant. "It's more than a month since Sicily was finished. We must land in Italy before long."

"I wish we weren't quite so far north," said Colonel Lavery. "With the best will in the world, it's going to be tricky, and if the Italians turn sour— Yes, who is it? Oh, come in, Baird."

"I thought you'd like to hear this," said Colonel Baird. It was difficult to say whether he was amused or annoyed. "We've just had our first security search since the fall of Mussolini."

"Was it a thorough one?" said Colonel Lavery. "Did you lose much?"

"I should have described it as concentrated rather than thorough," said Baird. "Paoli brought in a dozen soldiers and caribs and a few workmen. They went straight to the kitchen and took up the whole of the floor, including the stove which they removed bodily and the slab it stands on—they seemed mighty suspicious of that stove."

There was a moment of horrified silence.

"Then they've found the Hut C tunnel," said Colonel Lavery.

"Fortunately no," said Baird. "Indeed, they had very little chance of doing so, since the kitchen they elected to demolish so thoroughly was the one in Hut A."

"But—" said Colonel Lavery.

"What—?" said the Adjutant.

"By the time they had finished operations," went on Colonel Baird smoothly, "and had discovered absolutely nothing for their pains except the undisturbed sub-soil of the hut, I had caused to be gathered a large and sympathetic crowd of onlookers who gave them very generous applause as they came out empty-handed. They didn't look pleased."

"So I should imagine," said Colonel Lavery. "What's your idea of it?"

"Unless we're being made the victims of a gigantic and rather pointless double bluff, the answer seems to me to be plain. Benucci and his immediate circle knew about the Hut C tunnel. When they quitted the camp in such a hurry they either forgot to tell—or didn't bother to tell—anyone else."

"The latter, I should think," said Colonel Lavery. "It would suit their book much better if the opposition made fools of themselves."

"Well, I should imagine that Paoli—who was about twenty-five per cent in Benucci's confidence—may have had an idea that the tunnel started from one of the hut kitchens—or he may have been deliberately misinformed, and told that it started from Hut A. Hence this afternoon's demonstration."

"It's possible," said Colonel Lavery. "How is the tunnel going?"

"Much too well to want to lose it now. We've taken it straight on, without raising the level at all. That means that it is going to run out into the slope of the hill over the crest from the camp wall."

"How long will it be before you're out?"

"We could break any day. We're going slowly and tidying it all up as we go. It's a beautiful job."

"I hope you're right about Paoli," said Colonel Lavery thoughtfully.

IV

"Tony," said Goyles, "will you cast your mind back to that evening you were in the cooler."

"The night Coutoules was killed?"

"Yes. What I really want to establish is some definite timings."

Long cocked an eyebrow at him.

"The great detective?"

"Yes," said Goyles. "The great detective at work. And I'll tell you something about this detecting business which you may find it hard to believe. Once you pick it up you can't put it down even if you want to."

"Like a dog with a piece of stinking rabbit," suggested Long helpfully.

"Perfectly," said Goyles. "If you want the truth, I don't believe anyone ever will be able to say exactly what happened to Coutoules that night—not so as to prove it. A lot of people who know about it are scattered already, and when the British land in Italy the rest of the cast will be dispersed too. All the same, I can't stop. The fascination of guessing and filling in the gaps is too strong. It's like trying to finish a crossword puzzle in a train going headlong towards a crash."

"All right," said Long. "What do you want to know?"

"I want to establish the times," said Goyles—he sounded quite serious—"when the wireless set in the carabinieri quarters was playing jazz that evening."

"You mean when they had the set full on?"

"Yes."

"It was rather odd, now you come to mention it," said Long. "It wasn't just loud, it was *fortissimo*—almost as if someone had turned the control knob full on and forgotten about it. We heard it from time to time afterwards, but nothing like that evening."

"When did it start?"

"Now you're asking something," said Long. He reflected. "I was standing looking out of the window—I think it was about ten o'clock when the laundry van went out—I was noticing all the absurd precautions they took at the two gates. I stood there for quite a long time, waiting for it to get dark enough for me to start up on to the roof. I guess it was about eleven before I was able to get going. I should have said that the wireless came on at about half-time."

"That would be about half-past ten?"

"Yes. I remember hoping that it would keep going long enough for me to get up on to the roof under cover of the row it was making."

"And it did?"

"Yes—just. It was switched off or turned down about five minutes after I got up."

"Fine," said Goyles. He made a methodical note in his book.

"Glad to be of assistance," said Long. "Don't get carried away by it, though. Remember you're due on P.T. in ten minutes' time. After that, colloquial Italian till lunch."

That afternoon Goyles sought an interview with Colonel Lavery and put a question to him which seemed to puzzle the S.B.O. considerably.

"Yes," he said. "I'd forgotten about it. But as a matter of fact it's quite true. Coutoules came to see me that afternoon. In fact, it was the last time I spoke to him—and the last time but one that I saw him—"

"The last time but one, sir?"

"Yes. I saw him, of course, on roll-call that evening. Not being attached to any hut he was one of the last to have his name called. He walked off just ahead of me, towards our hut. As far as I know he was making for his room."

"That afternoon," said Goyles. "Can you remember anything— did anything strike you as out of the ordinary?"

"The whole thing was extraordinary. He was easily the most unpopular person in the camp. I'd arranged for him to have a room by himself, partly to stop stories that he was spying on people, but chiefly because I didn't want to see him lynched."

"And then he asked you to have him moved back?"

"Asked," said Colonel Lavery, "is an understatement. He begged me to put him back. He practically went down on his knees."

"Did he say why?"

"Nothing that I could really get hold of. You know he spoke English quite well, but he was liable to get a bit incomprehensible when he was excited. He repeated two or three times that he didn't want the room and he was sure there were many people who deserved it more than he did—which was true enough in a way. Right at the end, when he saw that I wasn't going to change my mind, he did say something which I thought rather odd—"

"Yes?" said Goyles.

"He shrugged his shoulders, in a sort of resigned way, and said, 'To think that I had only myself to blame for coming here.' I said, 'I suppose we might all of us say that.' He said, 'Ah, but I'm the only one of you who actually prayed for my move.' Then he went out."

"Are you sure he said 'prayed'?" said Goyles.

"It was either 'prayed' or 'paid'," said Colonel Lavery. "It didn't seem to make a lot of sense either way."

v

MONDAY, SEPTEMBER 6TH, AT 8.30 IN THE EVENING

Positively the first performance in
Campo 127 (And probably the last)

THE BARRETTS OF WIMPOLE STREET
(A Comedy in Five Acts, by Rudolf Besier)

With the following Distinguished Cast:

As Elizabeth Moulton-Barrett—your favourite Star
CAPTAIN THE HONOURABLE PETER PERSE

As Robert Browning
LIEUTENANT RUPERT ROLF-CALLENDER

As Edward Moulton-Barrett, that accomplished character actor (remember *The Man Who Came to Dinner!*)
CAPTAIN ANGUS ABERCROWTHER

And full supporting cast

"Roll up in your thousands"

There was no need for the last exhortation. The theatre hut had a maximum seating capacity of two hundred and tickets were strictly rationed. A seat in the front row was reserved for the Camp Commandant. (He liked to attend all such functions; though in view of the nature of some of the jokes in the previous Christmas pantomime it was perhaps fortunate that his knowledge of colloquial English was limited.)

The Old Hirburnian Rugby Football Club occupied a block at the back of the hall, and, in the interval before the curtain went up, seemed to be continuing an argument from some earlier occasion.

"Anyone with an elementary knowledge of tactics," said Tag Burchnall, "would see at once that no general would land his forces at the toe of Italy when he could just as easily land them half-way up."

"It isn't only a question of landing them," said Gerry Parsons. "You must remember that you've got to supply them, too. From a logistical point of view the further south the better."

"All you've got to do is land a force half-way up the peninsula, on both sides, and you'll cut off half the German Army."

"Then why not land at the top of the peninsula and cut it all off?" said Rollo Betts-Hanger.

"Logistics—"

"The obvious place to land a large force is Ancona. There's practically no tide in the Adriatic—"

"Lines of supply."

"On the other hand, if they establish their forward base in Northern Corsica and land between Livorno and La Spezia that gives them a straight run to the Po Valley at Modena—"

"Certainly no further north than Naples."

"Here comes old Aletti," said Burchnall. "I suppose it would be a civil gesture if we all stood up."

VI

"Why the devil didn't someone think of it before?" said Rolf-Callender.

"What's wrong?"

"It's the window at the back— You know Mr. Barrett has to throw it open just before the final curtain. Now it seems it can't be opened."

"What's wrong with it?"

"When we put the set in we put it too far back. It jams on that side beam."

"Has anyone got a saw?"

"What are you going to do? For God's sake don't bring the whole thing down."

"It's all right," said Captain Abercrowther, who had removed his morning coat and rolled up his sleeves. "I'll just take a bit out of the end of that cross beam, knock it along a trifle, and then the window will open fine."

He was far too old a hand at amateur theatricals to let contre-temps of that sort worry him. In his experience it would only have been surprising if nothing *had* stuck at the last moment.

"Astounding," said Colonel Aletti, as the curtain fell for the first interval, "such acting, such *décor*. And that young lady on the otto-man, is she in reality one of your officers?"

"Indeed, yes," said Colonel Lavery. "I'm glad you are enjoying it."

"It seems unbelievable," said the Commandant. "The voice— the gestures—so anatomically correct. Will there be rapine?"

Colonel Lavery cast his mind over the plot. "So far as I can remember," he said, "the ardours in this play are more poetical than physical."

"Incredible," said Colonel Aletti. "Incredible. And the enthusi-asm when the name of Italy is mentioned!"

"Incredible," agreed Colonel Lavery.

★

"Damned good," said Goyles, as the curtain came down for the second interval.

"It really is extraordinary," said Byfold, "what a complete twerp a chap can be off the stage and how damned entertaining when he's on it."

"I can't take my eyes off that dog," said Long. "Every time he wags his tail I'm sure it's going to fall off. And it beats me how they keep him from licking off his make-up. Are we going out for a quick breather?"

Though all the windows were open the packed hut was as hot as an oven.

"We'd better stick it out," said Goyles. "We'll never get in again if we move."

The play had come to its tremendous last minute. The lovers had stolen away. The empty room at Wimpole Street had filled with members of the Barrett family. Last of all had come Edward Moulton-Barrett—papa in person.

Captain Abercrowther, who really was an actor of considerable parts, had his hand by now on the pulse of the audience. For those few minutes belief was suspended, and the hatred, fear and pity of two hundred souls was following him as he walked to the window at the back.

In a moment the curtain would fall, illusion would depart and the present would rush back.

As he laid his hand on the casement window he sensed that it was going to prove difficult to open. He thought for a moment of abandoning the gesture. It would be almost as effective if he simply stood with his back to the audience, staring out of the closed window. Then he took a grip of himself, seized the bottom of the window, and threw it up. It resisted; then, when he applied his strength to it, it came with a rush.

At this moment, unperceived by anyone in the theatre but himself, the amazing thing happened.

As the window came up, a small square of boards at the very back of the stage, behind the backcloth, hinged downwards. A beam from the overhead spotlight shone straight through this cavity and lit up the shaft beneath it. It lit up also what lay at the foot of the shaft, and with incredulous eyes Captain Abercrowther picked out the word IMPAIR in red on a green background.

He realized that he was looking directly down at a roulette board.

Behind him the curtain fell to a solid roar of applause.

CHAPTER THIRTEEN

THE WHEELS OF CIRCUMSTANCE

I

"If I hadn't seen it with my own eyes," said Colonel Baird, "I should never have believed it."

It was nine o'clock on the following morning and the Escape Committee, with Goyles and Abercrowther in attendance, were examining, behind carefully locked and guarded doors, the stage in the Theatre Hut.

"It was some finale," agreed Colonel Shore. "I thought you seemed a little anxious to head-off the Commandant—otherwise I didn't spot anything particularly wrong."

He referred to a difficult moment on the previous evening when Colonel Aletti, who had evidently planned to congratulate Elizabeth Browning personally, had been kept with some difficulty from the stage.

"How does it work?" said Colonel Baird.

"What actually happened, I think," said Captain Abercrowther, "was that, when we were originally fixing in part of the set, we put it too close to the framework at the back of the stage and the window wouldn't open. At the last moment I had to shorten and lower one of the side stays. I was cutting the end off with a saw about five minutes before the curtain went up. You may have heard me. Even then we couldn't lower the window until I'd knocked this bit of bottom studding along about six inches"—he demonstrated. "You see what happens. It looks like studding, but it's really the bolt which keeps this little trap-door shut."

"Then from the moment you did that there was nothing keeping it up at all?"

"No, except that it was a tight fit. The jerk I gave to the window was the thing which finally loosened it. It just fell open."

"Yes," said Colonel Baird. He was standing on the stage, straddling the trap-door, staring down into the shaft. What had looked, in the dark and from below, like a partial collapse of the tunnel roof, was now only too obviously man-made. The trap-door was skilful enough, but apart from that there had been no attempt at concealment. The excavated sand lay in heaps under the back of the stage.

"Who do you imagine—?" began Captain Abercrowther, and caught Goyles' eye and stopped.

"Look here," said Baird. "You're a bit of a carpenter, Abercrowther. If I get a small party in here to shovel back the sand into the shaft, could you fix this trap-door so that it can neither be opened nor spotted?"

Captain Abercrowther nodded.

"And if you gentlemen would come with me for a moment, I think I'd like a word with you about this."

Goyles waited to see if he was being included in the invitation. When he saw that he was not he had to make a very quick decision.

What he did was to move across, catch Colonel Baird as he was about to leave the hut, and say something to him.

Colonel Baird looked startled.

"I take it you know what you're talking about," he said.

"I'll explain as soon as I can, sir," said Goyles.

Colonel Baird hurried after the other members of the Committee and Goyles walked slowly back to his own hut. Although his body moved with deliberation his mind was at stretch.

The first person he looked for was Doctor Simmonds, whom he found in his room turning over the pages of a six months' old copy of the *Lancet*.

He came straight to the point.

"You examined Coutoules' body, didn't you?" he said. "Did you have the opportunity to do it thoroughly?"

"Reasonably so," said Doctor Simmonds cautiously. "I had one quick look at him when you first discovered the body. Then the Italians gave me a further opportunity of examining him when he was brought up for the second time—largely, I surmise, to make certain that I should agree with their own diagnosis."

"What was the exact cause of death?"

Like most doctors when asked this particular question, Doctor Simmonds took a few moments off for thought. Then he said: "Asphyxiation caused by sand. There was sand in the stomach and in the trachea—a little in the lungs—not very much. You wouldn't expect much. The reflex would have kept it out until the moment he lost consciousness."

"It wouldn't have been possible to fake that effect after he had died from some other cause—shock or heart failure?"

"You mean by pouring sand into his mouth?"

"Yes."

Doctor Simmonds considered the suggestion carefully and shook his head. "Quite impossible. You wouldn't get any sand into the stomach at all, if he was already dead. Or it would be very difficult. You'd need a force-pump to get it down, and that would leave obvious signs."

"Was there *anything*," said Goyles, "anything out of the ordinary at all? Anything that shouldn't have been there if he simply died under a fall of sand? Was there anything to suggest—I don't want to put ideas into your head you know—but was there anything at all to suggest that he might have been killed by being *held* face downwards in sand."

"How exactly do you visualize it being done?"

"If I am right the operation would have been carried out by two or three men—men who wouldn't make any very obvious mistakes—I mean they would know about post-mortem bruising and that sort of thing. I thought that one of them might perhaps have got hold of each of his arms *by the sleeve of his coat* and twisted his arms behind his back to force his head down and prevent him moving, whilst the other would press his head down into the sand—"

"Hold it a moment," said the doctor. "That rings a bell. I'll just have a look at the notes I made at the time." He took a notebook out of the drawer of his desk and turned the pages—"Yes, I thought so. There was a slight but distinct marking on the nape of his neck. I discussed it with that professor and we rather assumed at the time that it was done by a stone in the sand which fell on him—"

"But it might equally have been a hand holding him."

"More probably, I should say."

His next visit was to the Quartermaster.

"You remember," he said, "some weeks ago, getting hold of one of the Italians for me—a chap called Biancelli—?"

"The one that shot himself?"

"The one that was said to have shot himself," amended Goyles. "But that's not the point at the moment. It's the other man."

"The other man?"

"When you found out about Biancelli for me, you told me that the name of the carib who was with him—I think it was Marzotto. Could you fix it for me to have a word with him?"

Captain Porter looked doubtful.

"I wouldn't ask you," said Goyles, "only it's hideously important."

"Of course I'll do it for you if I can," said Captain Porter. "It isn't that—but I've got a sort of feeling—wait here a moment, would you?"

He was back inside five minutes.

"You're out of luck," he said. "Marzotto left with the other bunch of thugs when Mussolini fell. I fancied I remembered the name. He was the only carib who went with them."

"Thank you," said Goyles.

Although he was well aware that time was running against him, he hesitated before taking the next step. He stood for quite ten minutes watching a basket-ball match which was being contested with more venom than science, on the dust pitch between A and B Huts. Outwardly the microcosm was unchanged. It was underneath the surface that the sands were shifting and the currents running.

Not so far under the surface, either, thought Goyles. He walked across to the Infirmary Hut. Its only occupant was Hugo Baierlein. The health as well as the *morale* of the camp was evidently on the up grade. The beds, which were usually all occupied, were now empty. Even Baierlein was out of bed. He was hobbling very slowly across the floor, both legs swaddled in plaster.

"I've been across the room four times," he announced. "I feel like a very old, very depraved man with the gout which his forefathers have visited upon him."

"Good show," said Goyles. He sat on the bed for a moment swinging his legs, and Baierlein, having finished his fifth crossing, came to rest opposite him.

"What's on your mind?" he asked.

"I'd like to put a question to you," said Goyles. "I just want an honest, unbiased opinion. I wouldn't bring this up if it wasn't so desperately important, and you're the only person left who can give me an answer."

"Go on."

"When you were going up the ladder that night—you and the others and the searchlights came on again and the machine guns opened up—did you think it was a ghastly fluke—or did the thought come into your mind that you might have been given away?"

It was some time before Baierlein spoke, and when he did so he did not appear to have heard the question. He said, "Alec was to go first up the ladder, then Grim. Desmond was next and I was last. We were all lying out in the deep shadow between the Theatre Hut and the Chapel. It's one of the places no searchlight can reach. We had fifteen yards of open to cover before we reached the wall. We lay in reverse order—that is to say, I was nearest the wall, Alec furthest away. That was so that when we came to the wall the first man could throw the ladder up and steady it, whilst the back men went up it first. Immediately the arc lights started to dim we got going. I've never moved faster in my life. I swear we had the ladder in position before the searchlights started to fade."

"I estimated there was about two seconds interval between the arc lights and the searchlight," said Goyles.

"Then it proves you can go fifteen yards in two seconds if you really try," said Baierlein. "I felt at that moment we were going to pull it off. I was half-crouching under the ladder, holding it, and

Desmond was standing on the foot of it. Grim was half-way up and Alec—he could have got away altogether, you know, if he'd just considered himself—was lying on the wall, holding the top of the ladder. Then the fresh searchlights came on."

He paused again.

"I don't think any of us moved whilst you could count five. The searchlights were flicking about all over the place, but not systematically, and too fast to be much use. I couldn't see what happened next, but I fancy Alec got up to jump—anyway he must have moved. All the lights swung round at us and the shooting started. Alec rolled off the wall, right on top of me. I think he was dead before he fell. Grim tried to go on up the wall—he got up about three rungs before they finished him. Desmond was on the ground. I didn't even know I'd been hit till I tried to move."

"I see," said Goyles. "So you think—?"

"I've thought about it, on and off, ever since. I can't honestly come to any other conclusion. They weren't expecting us. They were alert, and quick on the trigger—and when they did spot us they did a lot more shooting than was necessary. But I don't think they were waiting for us. If they had been—if they'd known what was happening and where it was going to happen—they'd have had plenty of time to get the searchlights on to us *after* the arc lamps went out and before the searchlights themselves were cut."

"Yes," said Goyles. "I thought of that."

"Then again, even when the spare searchlights came on it stuck out a mile that they hadn't a clue what to look for. But it was more than that. I was listening to the sentries on the nearest platforms when the lights first went out. They were surprised out of their wits. No. I'm sorry. If you want me to say that we were framed, I shall be a bad witness."

"I don't want you to say anything of the sort," said Goyles. "In fact, if it's any consolation to you, you've taken a load off my mind."

He left the hut and went back to his own room, where he found Tim Meynell and a fellow Sapper Officer. "I heard you wanted to see me," said Meynell. "I brought Punch along with me. He knows more about these gadgets than I do."

"Punch" Garland grinned down his enormous nose. "I'm a bit out of date now," he said, "but I'll do what I can. Where do you think the instrument is?"

"In Colonel Baird's room," said Goyles. "Come on."

They found Colonel Baird waiting for them.

He said, "When you asked me not to hold another committee meeting in my own room I guessed what was in your mind. In fact we were fools not to have thought about it before. I've had a rough search but I can't find anything obvious."

"The microphone they make nowadays," said Garland, "is a tiny little thing. I saw one the Americans were using in their interrogation centre at Tozeur. I knew the man in charge. He showed me the corner of the room it was in and bet me five dollars I couldn't find it in half an hour. I lost."

"What about following the wire?" said Meynell.

"That's almost the only way to do it. It shouldn't be too difficult here. The hut's raised on brick piles. Let's dig round outside."

The two experts disappeared and Colonel Baird said to Goyles, "What put you on to this?"

"It was the very first real clue I was given," said Goyles. "And I threw it away. Tim Meynell told me how he'd been under the carabinieri office in one of his sewer crawls, and heard what he thought was an American or a colonial voice. Roger heard the same thing later, when he was shut up in one of the rooms in the block."

"And they were listening to a relayed session of the Escape Committee?"

"That's about it," said Goyles.

"Got her," said Garland, his great beak appearing at the window. "She comes in under the lintel—run the top of your knife in, Tim."

"I fancy the whole thing comes out," said Meynell. "It's only held by a couple of screws!" He was busy unscrewing them as he spoke. Then he drove in the end of his jack-knife and, levering outwards, brought away the whole of the piece of wood which framed the sill of the window.

Colonel Baird looked into the cavity. "I can see the end of the wire," he said. "Nothing else."

"It's inside the wood," said Garland. He pointed to a knot-hole in the underside of the sill. He put the point of his knife into the hole and moved it, and they could hear that there was something metallic inside. He turned the piece of wood over.

"No join at all," he said. "They make the whole thing out of plastic wood, and paint it to match the surrounding woodwork. Neat, isn't it? Practically a standard fitting in all the best prison cells."

"Do you think that the other rooms in this hut—?"

"I shouldn't imagine so," said Garland. "However cleverly they hide the mike, the wire's always the weak point. They wouldn't want wires trailing all over the place. So far as I can see this is the only lead-in, and it stops here." He was screwing the window-sill back into position. "It's quite harmless now."

"But look here," said Baird. "Why pick on this room? They didn't know I was going to use it. The chap who ran the Escape Committee before I got here had a room on the other side of the passage."

"That's what I meant when I said it was a standard fitting," said Garland. "An experienced workman could instal the whole thing in about an hour—provided the approach line had been laid."

"And I think I know when it was done," said Goyles. "Do you remember that *strafe* search we had—after the first wall break—just after you arrived, sir. They kept us all out on the courtyard from morning roll-call till after lunch. That would have given them time to instal half a dozen microphones."

"If there's nothing else we can do—?" said Meynell.

"No, that's all right," said Colonel Baird. "I don't think I should say anything about this, just yet. Thank you very much."

When they had gone he stood looking at Goyles, who could see that he had worked out all the first implications of the discovery and was beginning to feel his way towards a second instalment.

"Goyles," he said, "I think it's time you came out into the open."

"I was thinking the same myself, sir," said Goyles. "I've got one or two ends still to tie up. I'd like to say my piece this evening. Could you ask Colonel Lavery if that will suit him?"

"Colonel Lavery?" said Baird. It was difficult to say whether he was surprised or annoyed. "Yes—I suppose so. After tea, then—in his room."

II

"Colonel Baird says you have something to tell us, Goyles," said Colonel Lavery.

The three members of the Committee were seated on the bed; Colonel Lavery and Goyles had chairs. The Adjutant was perched on the table. Although it was after six o'clock the heat was still intense and all of them were in their shirtsleeves.

"What I'm going to say," said Goyles, mastering the feeling that he was facing a board of viva-voce examiners, "is every bit as much surmise as anything else you've heard. But I think, if you'll hear me out, you'll come round to my way of thinking in the end. I'd like to start by reminding you of a remark made by Colonel Shore—to the effect that when you have a situation which is starkly impossible, then *any* logical explanation stands a good chance of being the right one. So I'm going to start with what I might call my basic supposition. At all events it's the key which seems to unlock the door. And that is that we have all of us greatly misjudged a very courageous and very loyal little man—Cyriakos Coutoules."

Goyles paused, but the only person who broke the silence was Colonel Shore. He said something under his breath that sounded like "Check".

"I've done what I can to confirm this," went on Goyles, "but we shan't know the truth until we can get in touch with one of the high-ups in our own M.I. But it seems the likeliest explanation. It's common knowledge, I think, that there are a few 'phoney' prisoners on both sides. The Germans use them, and so do we. I think Coutoules was a British agent. I don't think his job was strictly military intelligence. I think that he was put in to keep trace of potential war criminals so that they could be dealt with promptly and effectively after the war. At each of the camps he was in before coming here there was at least one Italian whose conduct would be likely to bring him before an Allied tribunal. Here, of course, he was angling for the biggest fish of the lot."

"Captain Benucci," said Colonel Baird softly.

"It's an attractive theory," said Colonel Shore, "but can you explain one thing? How does any prisoner get moved round as he wants to?"

"I'm no expert on these things, but if you sent me into Italy with a million lire carefully concealed about me and a few contacts I reckon I'd manage it," said Goyles.

"So that's what he meant when he said he'd paid to get here," said Colonel Lavery.

"Yes. That remark was one of the things which confirmed my suspicion."

"And you're saying that Benucci spotted him and had him put away?"

"Benucci had him put away," said Goyles. "Whether it was he who spotted him I don't know. I should say not. I should think it was more probably Benucci's assistant who spotted him."

"Assistant?"

"I'm afraid there's little doubt about it. Colonel Aletti, though indiscreet, was being perfectly truthful. There is, in this camp, a German Intelligence Officer. He worked under Benucci—or it may even have been that Benucci was subordinate to him. He was—and still is—close to the heart of our counsels. He is an excellent actor and, I need hardly say, a brave and ruthless man. He escaped suspicion because it never occurred to anyone to suspect him."

"Do you know who he is?" said Colonel Baird.

"I think so," said Goyles. "In fact, it's so perfectly plain that anyone who reasoned the thing out must come to the same conclusion as I have. For the purpose of what follows, once his existence is accepted, his identity is not of any great importance. If you don't mind, I'll take the traditional line for the moment and refer to him as X. X had at least one accomplice, among the orderlies. I have no idea who that orderly is, and unless X himself tells us I doubt if we shall ever know. They are a mixed bag. When I put this point, in a roundabout way, to Corporal Pearce, he said it was probably one of the South Africans. The South Africans no doubt equally suspect the Poles. And the Poles the English. The point is that they are not a homogeneous body, and it would be very simple for a traitor to exist among them. Also, in the peculiar way in which things are run in a prisoner-of-war camp, whilst the officers are segregated, the orderlies have every chance of talking to the guards. Amongst the orderlies was X's assistant. He sent information direct to Benucci, or possibly through Benucci's familiar, Maresciallo Butsi. Apart from the orderly, I fancy that Benucci was the only person who knew who X was. Once, in a fit of bravado, he revealed the fact of X's existence to Colonel Aletti. He must have been kicking himself ever since."

"What was X's job?" said Colonel Lavery.

"Military Intelligence, sir. Or so I think. He and Benucci weren't really interested in camp security. Benucci had to pretend to be— that was his job. But in my view he was a genuine, Nazi-trained, case-hardened Intelligence man. One of Himmler's own. Anything which X could tell him—it might be of Intelligence value, or it might more often be of propaganda value—would go straight to the top. We may not have any high-ranking officers here, but remember we've got a Cabinet Minister's nephew, two pre-war M.P.s and one of the Staff Officers who helped to plan the battle of Alamein—to say nothing of representatives of almost every arm in the service. A prisoner of war is taught to keep his mouth shut when he is first captured, but once he gets into a permanent camp, amongst his own friends—what subjects under the sun are not discussed in the long nights? It must have been rather like having an enemy microphone in the lobby of the House of Commons—"

"More like the smoking-room of the Guards' Club," said Colonel Lavery. "But please go on."

"Well, the next thing is that Coutoules realized he had been spotted. He was nervous about it—but he may have reckoned that he could hardly be kidnapped from the heart of the camp. Here he underestimated his enemies. That is exactly what they did do. But before they did it, they had certain preparations to make. Benucci could have had Coutoules arrested and shot any time he liked. He wanted something more out of it. As has already been suggested, he wanted revenge. And he thought out an idea which appealed profoundly to his peculiar sense of humour. He and his own band of cronies started a little counter-sapping. At night they would climb the east wall of the camp—seen by the sentries, but, of course, not challenged—and would disappear into the Theatre Hut. That, by the way, is no doubt why they were so keen to stop 'visiting' between the huts after dark. If they had been seen by one of the prisoners it would have blown the gaff. They cut a trap-door in the stage of the Theatre Hut and sunk a vertical shaft to meet the head of the Hut C tunnel. With plenty of time, all the tools they wanted, a good space under the stage for sand disposal, and no fear of interruption, they probably completed the job very quickly. It doesn't take long to sink a shaft under those conditions."

"But, good God," said Commander Oxey, "if they knew enough to be as accurate as that—?"

"Yes—" said Goyles. "I see that you take the point. I did warn you that once you examined the evidence the identity of X would not be in any great doubt."

"Go on," said Colonel Lavery sharply.

"When they were ready—that is to say, when their shaft was just about to break into the Hut C tunnel—they carried off Coutoules. Two carabinieri came in with the laundry van. I fancy Benucci was actually talking to you, sir, whilst it was being done. Two caribs knocked Coutoules on the head, tied him up, gagged him and rolled him in a bundle of washing, and drove him out of the camp. There was one typical little incident at the gate. The sentry—who wasn't in the know—spiked two of the bundles with his bayonet. I don't know whether one of them was Coutoules or not. Possibly so. The caribs thought it was a tremendous joke. Their sense of humour was pretty well in evidence all that evening. Later that night they took Coutoules into the carabinieri office and questioned him. That was when his finger-nails came off."

"Not under the sand?"

"No," said Goyles. "Not under the sand. There was a lot of loose thinking about that and it needed a ton or so of sand on my own head before I saw the truth of it. If ever you have been in a tunnelling collapse you will realize the fallacy of the suggestion. You are knocked flat and pinned. All your energies are spent in trying to breathe—and that doesn't last long. Even if you did have your hands free you couldn't pull your nails off—not in sand. It's a pretty toughly rooted growth, a nail. You might bruise the tips of your fingers or even scrape them raw. But you wouldn't pull a nail off. It was Benucci and his fellow humorists who did that. Incidentally that was why they had to have the wireless on so loud."

"Poor devil," said Colonel Lavery. "When they'd got what they wanted out of him, I suppose they finished him off by holding him face downwards in a box of sand."

"That's about it, sir," said Goyles. "The medical evidence suggests that. Then they carried him over the wall, by ladder—Biancelli and Marzotto were the only sentries close enough to see what they were doing. Marzotto was safe, but Biancelli wanted to talk later. That's why he was removed. Then they dropped Coutoules down the shaft, and tumbled enough sand in on top of him to partly fill the hole and make it look like a fall."

"Benucci must have had a good laugh when we served up Coutoules in the Hut A tunnel," said Colonel Shore.

"He had us on toast," said Commander Oxey. "And was he loving it!"

"To say nothing of the fact," said Colonel Baird, "that with his microphone in our committee-room he could forestall any move almost before we made it."

"There's one thing I can't understand," said Colonel Lavery. "Why are we still being allowed to use the Hut C tunnel?"

"I think that's quite easy, sir," said Goyles. "The whole Coutoules business was a Benucci ploy. It was him and his particular stable companions who plotted and carried out the whole thing. *They* knew about the tunnel—everything there was to know about it—to the nearest inch and the nearest degree. But neither they nor X cared much about escaping. If Benucci had stayed in power I have no doubt he would have stepped in at the last moment and staged a pretty little massacre at the tunnel mouth. The moment he went into opposition his feelings naturally altered. I don't suppose he minds now if the whole camp escapes—I don't mean that he's become Anglophil, but anything that upset the existing régime would naturally be in his favour—as for X, now that all his contacts at the top have gone, I don't quite know *what* his plans are. I expect he aims to escape with everybody else when the armistice comes, and carry on the good work from somewhere else—possibly from a German prison camp."

"I see," said Colonel Lavery.

"Yes—" said Colonel Baird.

"Yes, but—" said Commander Oxey.

"Look here, Goyles," said Colonel Shore, "who is this chap X?"

"See who that is, Pat," said Colonel Lavery. "I said we weren't to be disturbed."

The Adjutant went to the door and opened it. He said something to someone outside. Inside the room everyone was silent with his own thoughts. The door closed and the murmur of voices went on.

Then the Adjutant reappeared.

"It's Captain Meynell, sir—I think you ought—"

"All right," said Colonel Lavery. "What is it?"

Tim Meynell looked with some surprise at the crowded room, then he said to Colonel Lavery, "I'm sorry to butt in, sir, but I thought you ought to know at once. I was under the Commandant's office about half an hour ago. If everything's just right it's possible to pick up scraps of conversation. The Commandant was talking to someone. I guessed it was some sort of foreigner, because he spoke so slowly that even I could understand what he said, and I'm no wizard at Italian. Then the other chap said something and I caught that too—it was German—"

"German," said six people simultaneously.

"Yes. German's one of the things I know. I got the gist of it quite easily. The German is C.O. of an armoured car unit in this area. Apparently they've got wind of the fact that the Allies are going to announce the Italian Armistice at eight o'clock to-morrow evening. At one minute past eight the Germans are going to take charge here. The Commandant has sold us up the river."

CHAPTER FOURTEEN

THE GREAT CRAWL

I

THOSE WHO POSSESSED WATCHES LOOKED AT THEM.
It was exactly eight o'clock.

Colonel Lavery said to the Adjutant, "I shall want the Hut Commanders over here. Tell them not to come over in a bunch. I think the Quartermaster is in his room. You might pass the word to him. Oh, and tell R.S.M. Burton I shall want him—but he's not to come before nine o'clock."

As Colonel Lavery spoke, Goyles realized one thing very clearly. Any chance that they had lay in the fact that the S.B.O. was a man who had mastered the technique of command. This did not imply that he was a captain of men or the leader of forlorn hopes—but simply that he was a professional soldier who, by long practice and usage, had acquired the ability—that deceptively easy, much under-rated ability—to formulate a plan and put it into operation.

"I don't think we need you any more, Meynell—thank you very much. You won't say a word about this to anyone, of course. That's right. You can stay, Goyles. We shall want someone who knows the ins and outs of that tunnel. Now then, Baird. How long's it going to take you to break out?"

Colonel Baird pondered. "It's easy to be too optimistic about a thing like that," he said. "I should say, at least four hours—not more than eight."

"Shoring it as you go and making a decent exit hole at the end?"

"Certainly. I'll guarantee we'll have the whole of Hut C out of it before roll-call to-morrow morning."

"That you won't," said Colonel Lavery. "I'm not going to throw away eighty per cent of this camp unless I have to."

There was a moment's silence.

"I don't quite see, sir—" said Colonel Shore.

"You might get half a dozen people from the other huts across in the dark to-night," said Colonel Baird. "Particularly if the sentries aren't particularly alert. I don't think you'd get more—"

"No one's going to stir out of their hut to-night if I can prevent it," said Colonel Lavery. "I shall evacuate the camp—to-morrow."

"But—?" said Colonel Baird.

"How—?" began Commander Oxey.

"By Christopher Columbus," said Colonel Shore. "That'll be something, won't it?"

"See here," said Colonel Lavery. "You told me that, with any luck, you could get that tunnel out over the brow of the hill—out of sight of the sentries—right?"

"I think so, yes."

"Then Hut C shall do that, to-night. They've got the whole night to do it in. It doesn't matter where they put the sand—that's not important now. They can store it in sandbags under their beds. They can use any woodwork they like. We must have a perfect job. If you can bring it out somewhere that'll give a hidden crawl right down to the river, so much the better. As soon as you cross the river you're in the wood, so you'll be all right."

"By Abraham Lincoln," said Colonel Shore again. "Four hundred men—in broad daylight."

"Why not?" said Colonel Lavery.

"Why not, indeed?" said Colonel Baird. He brought his big hand down with a gentle smack on to his knee.

"There's a lot to be thought about," said Colonel Lavery. "Oh, come in, Hugo. This is an orders party. Find somewhere to sit down. As soon as the others are here, I'll start."

With a queer pang, Goyles was suddenly reminded of hundreds of orders parties he had attended during the war. The Colonel standing, talking. The quiet men sitting round him busily writing it all down in little notebooks. How much tragedy and comedy, how much destiny, how much death and destruction, how many famous last words had been scribbled down by quiet men into little notebooks?

"Now we're all here," said Colonel Lavery, "I ought to say one thing. And that is that I lately received—in the usual way—an order from the War Office that in the event of an armistice everyone in prison camps was to stay put. I think—I hope and believe—that that order is now out of date. I think it was given under a misconception about the tactical situation. I intend to disregard it anyway—but I think perhaps you ought to know of its existence. Now then, there's a lot to do before lock-up to-night. And a lot to do after lock-up for that matter. This isn't a formal party, so I'm going to welcome suggestions—though I'll make the final decision. The first thing is that if the plan's going to work everyone will have to go out through Hut C. That means that everyone in the camp has got to go into Hut C in broad daylight to-morrow. There's no reason they shouldn't, but it's going to take some organizing. First of all, quite clearly, they won't be able to take much kit with them. Even the dumbest sentry's going to begin to get ideas if he sees squads of men filing into Hut C in full marching order—"

"If I might say so," said Colonel Baird. "I don't think anyone needs to take anything except a small reserve of food, a good pair of boots, and compass and map if he's got them. After to-morrow night it's going to be a reasonably friendly countryside. You can pick everything else up as you go."

"That's what I feel," said Colonel Lavery. "I'd like Hut Commanders to inspect every man in their hut to-night in the kit *he actually proposes to go out in*. There are bound to be some fools who'll give the game away by trying to take too much. The next point, I think, is this. We're not going to send out a complete hut at a time. We'll have ten serials—call them A to J—each composed of a mixed bag of people from all huts, and a few orderlies."

Out of the corner of his eye Colonel Lavery saw Goyles move and said, "Yes. I know what you're going to say. I'll tell you what I've got in mind about orderlies in a moment."

"Timing for serials," suggested the Adjutant.

"I don't think we can be too rigid, Pat. We've none of us any idea how long it's going to take forty men to crawl through a tunnel and disperse—"

"Longer than you think—always," said Colonel Baird, out of his experience of tunnels.

"I agree. I think that the answer is that we stick up a letter on the main notice board immediately we're ready for the next serial. The Italians are used to seeing a crowd round that notice board—and with things as they are a bit of an extra crowd won't look out of place. I'll leave it to each hut to decide what men go in what serial because quite obviously the men in A and B are going to be a lot happier than the ones in I and J."

"Draw for it."

"Something like that. The only party whose composition I'm going to lay down is the rear party. I'm afraid it won't be a very popular party. I shall be on it. I'd like you to stop, Pat. Also the

Escape Committee—and a tunnel party; I think that must be you, Goyles, and Byfold and Long."

"Yes, sir," said Goyles. He tried to sound cheerful about it.

"Also the provost section. I don't anticipate trouble at the tunnel mouth, but it's as well to be sure. We shall want about six tough and willing types. They'll be armed with sticks. They can operate from the room next to the tunnel mouth in Hut C. They'll have two jobs. One will be to turn back anyone who tries to beat the pistol—"

"And I suggest, sir, anyone who's late. Let people know that they'll go to the back of the queue if they're not punctual—"

"All right. Their other job, of course, will be to deal with any Italian who wanders into Hut C. I don't want that to happen—but if any Italian does stick his nose in he'll have to be dealt with. Any weapons he has on him can go to the provost."

"If we get at all far with this," said Colonel Baird, "one of the things is going to be to prevent the camp looking empty."

"The last serials out will have to keep busy," said Commander Oxey. "They'll have to show themselves all over the shop."

"Like a stage army," suggested Colonel Shore.

"I'll put something in orders about it," said Colonel Lavery, making a note. "The last serial out must organize two open-air classes and half a dozen pairs to walk round the circuit. If we get that far it'll be late afternoon and the camp's pretty dead by then. The serials before will put on two games of basket-ball and a cricket practice. The serial before that can play rugger—they'll need time to change back and cool off before they go out. Now—the orderlies. There's a snag here." Colonel Lavery turned to the Hut Commanders. "We were discussing it just before you came in. We've got reason to suppose that one of the orderlies is in touch with the Italians. At least"—he looked at Goyles—"that's part of the danger we anticipate."

"I think that's about the strength of it, sir," said Goyles. "X couldn't do anything direct. He'd have to do it through the orderly—"

All the Hut Commanders looked up, but since nobody seemed to want to explain about X they simply refrained from writing anything in their notebooks.

"Keep all the orderlies until last," suggested Baird.

"I think that'd be a bit unfair," said Colonel Lavery, "and it might start trouble—which it would be very difficult to put down without drawing attention to ourselves."

"Send them out first, in one party," said Colonel Shore, "and get them as far away from the camp as possible."

"They'd be very difficult to control once they were out," said Colonel Baird. "I think we'll have to compromise. Here's R.S.M. Burton. He's just the man we want. Look here, Burton, I'd better put you in the picture—"

"Do I understand, sir," said the R.S.M. finally, "that from now on I'm to take my orders from you and not from the Italians?"

"That's it."

The R.S.M.'s chest expanded about four inches and his shoulders became miraculously even squarer. "Sir," was all he said.

"Now, then. I think the orderlies had better be told after lunch to-morrow. There's no need for them to know before that. If they spot anything out of the ordinary they'll just think it's a normal escape. Parade them after lunch in their own hut, R.S.M. I'll give them their orders myself. They'll go out together as one complete serial—we'll call it serial 'O' so as not to confuse it with the others, and we'll give them timing—let's think—if we allow one minute per man—that's forty minutes a serial—say fifty to allow for accidents. If we start at nine o'clock we should do five complete serials before lunch. We'll have one more after lunch, then the orderlies."

"Serial 'O' after Serial 'F' and before Serial 'G'," wrote R.S.M. Burton in his little notebook.

"My orders will be that when they are out, they must travel in parties of not less than six for the rest of the day. If anyone tries to leave his party of six before nightfall the other five will have to stop him—by force if necessary. After to-morrow night they can please themselves."

"Very well, sir," said the R.S.M. He had no idea of the reasoning which lay behind this order, but it seemed quite straightforward—indeed, a good deal more reasonable than many orders to which his service in the Brigade of Guards had accustomed him.

"Do you think they'll do what they're told?"

"They'll do what they're told, sir," said R.S.M. Burton.

"Now the other parties—once they're out. They must keep their heads well down until they are across the river and in the wood—they won't need telling that."

"After that it's going to be a bit more tricky, isn't it?" said Colonel Shore. "We don't want an aged Italian peasant tottering up to the front gate of the camp at about midday saying he met a file of escaping *Inglesi* in the wood and what is the Commandant going to do about it?"

"I think that's one of the real snags," said Commander Oxey. "And I don't honestly see how you're going to get over it."

"I do," said Colonel Baird. "Make everyone travel in parties of five or six for the first day. Any Italian they meet, they kidnap him."

"We don't want to start by—"

"I don't think there's any choice," said Baird. "The Italians won't know about this Armistice until to-morrow evening. Technically, until then, we're enemies. We ought to keep out of sight as much as possible, but if any party *does* run into an Italian—they should, I suggest, persuade him to accompany them for the rest of the day."

"I don't like it," said Colonel Lavery. "But I agree it's the best we can do. What next?"

"Food."

"That's the Quartermaster's department. I don't think anyone should bother to take perishable food. Things like tea and coffee and tinned porridge might be useful—I suggest that Serials 'A' to 'E' draw what they can at breakfast. The rest at lunch."

"I'll have it taken over to huts first thing to-morrow," said Captain Porter. "Luckily it's a distribution day anyway, so the orderlies won't get wondering—"

"All right," said Colonel Lavery. "Has anyone else got any points. I don't want to hurry you, but I've got to get out written orders, and that's going to take time. I don't think it's avoidable though. Once things start to-morrow we shan't be able to hold conferences to sort it all out if it goes wrong. It's got to work automatically or not at all. If I haven't got the orders ready by lock-up I'll need a volunteer from each hut to carry them across after dark. It's a risk but it's one I'm prepared to take."

"Invalids," said someone.

"Hell, yes," said Colonel Lavery. "I'd forgotten them."

"There's only one," said Goyles. "That's Baierlein."

"Can he be moved?"

"He can move himself, slowly," said Goyles. "If you put him in an early serial he should be all right. Anderson and Duncan will look after him."

"Anything else?"

"Synchronize watches, sir," suggested the Hut C Commander happily.

II

"Just stay behind a moment, would you, Goyles," said Colonel Lavery, as the crowd dispersed.

"I think," he went on, "in view of what's happened—and still more, in view of what may happen—I ought to know—"

"Can I just say this, sir," said Goyles. "If the arrangements you have just made come off, in the sort of way you've arranged them X can do us no harm. He's snookered."

"I see," said Colonel Lavery.

"If they don't come off, then we shall all have plenty of time to talk about it."

"All right," said Colonel Lavery. "We'll leave it like that."

III

It was two o'clock on the following afternoon, and Goyles, with Long and Byfold, was sitting on his bunk. He had never before realized that time could stand still. He had appreciated that there might be some difference in its apparent duration—a minute in the hands of the Spanish Inquisition might be longer than an hour in the arms of a lover—but he had never before realized that time could actually stop—that the sun and the moon could stand still and the chronology of the human race be suspended.

There had been minutes in the previous twelve hours which no one was ever going to forget.

Night in Hut C. Hot, sticky darkness. The lights were turned out at eleven and the Hut Commander had banned all torches. Into one room, carefully screened on the blind side of the hut, they had come, in batches of twenty, to hear their orders. Later they had come back to the same room, one at a time, to have their escaping kit inspected. Some of them had been sent back more than once before the Hut Commander would be satisfied. "Since you have the good luck to live in Hut C," he had told them, "you will be able to take more with you than the other chaps—they have to walk here across the compound under the eyes of the sentries. But that doesn't mean you can dress yourselves like Christmas trees. You've got to crawl, remember, at fair speed, through a tunnel nearly two hundred feet long. If you stick, or bring part of the tunnel down, you will wreck the chances of every single man behind you in the queue. Go back and think again."

Goyles had seen very little of this. He had been down in the tunnel itself with a select band of experts. They knew roughly where they were in relation to the slope of the hill, for metal rods, thrust upwards, had shown daylight at decreasing distances for the last few days, but precise calculation was still impossible.

"It isn't an even slope," he said. "We may be running under a level patch or even into a small piece of up-hill. We must reckon on eight feet of digging, and allow for more." After that they had worked in nightmare, non-stop shifts. As the sand came out it was packed in bags and laid first in a wall up the side of the entrance shaft; after that it was carried out and stacked under beds.

It had been just after three o'clock in the morning that they made a perfect out-fall. Goyles was at the face when it happened. His trowel ran first into a layer of packed flints, then into pebbles and thin dirt; then a spout of gloriously fresh air, and a star appeared. He had given the order to dowse lights and as they had worked on in the grey dimness of the tunnel mouth the extent of their luck had become apparent. If the choice had been in their hands, they could not have chosen better. They had come out underneath a considerable boulder, actually in a dry stream bed, at a point where a small vertical drop must have made a little waterfall during the winter rains.

In the end Goyles had decided to stop all shoring about three feet short of the boulder. He realized that it was a choice of evils. If no props were put in, the boulder might collapse under use. If the entrance was shored, there was a chance it would be spotted from the opposite hill-side when day came.

"Better leave it as it is," he thought.

When everything was ready, and in the last moments of dimness before the true dawn, he had crawled out, down the stream bed, to the river at the bottom. The lips of the runnel, he was pleased to see, were masked almost all the way down with tufts of low scrub and grass. He sat for a moment, trailing his hand in the water, and wondering what would happen if he disappeared into the silent woods opposite—woods behind which lay freedom.

He had no illusions about his own chances. If he was to be one of the last out of the tunnel he had, he considered, no chance at all. The question in his mind was not whether the scheme would work—it was how many would get away before it was stopped. Places in the early serials, he knew, were already being bought for large sums.

He had come to the conclusion that if he had any sense he would cut straight off into the darkness. Nevertheless, as he crawled back along the tunnel, made some last adjustments, closed the trap, and got into bed, he felt obscurely pleased with himself and he slept soundly until eight o'clock—and was one of the few people who slept at all that night.

On roll-call that morning, each Hut Commander had made to Colonel Lavery the agreed sign that meant "All well—so far". The Italian Orderly Officer left the camp at ten minutes past nine. At a quarter past nine Major Gibb posted a news bulletin on the Intelligence Board. It was evidently intended to be the first of many, for it had a large letter "A" in the top left-hand corner.

After that, time stood still.

As Goyles realized, one thing alone had saved them that morning, and this was that the sentries themselves had something else to think about. Some whisper of the coming Armistice was already in the air. It was known, too, that there were German forces in the neighbourhood. The soldiers on the walls must have been wondering what the immediate future would bring forth. Otherwise, being trained guards, they could not have failed to notice the signs that were displayed before them—the purposeful coming and going of prisoners—the steady dribble of men towards one hut—men who went in, but never came out again—the crowds round the notice board—the self-conscious groups, who suddenly realized that they might be attracting attention and scattered for no apparent reason.

Serials "A" and "B" had run to time. Serial "C" had congregated in the hut when the first hitch occurred. The mouth of the tunnel was showing signs of collapse. Against such a contingency Goyles had had two complete sections of boxing cut and fitted and painted black. The tunnel had been cleared and whilst Serial "C" sat on the floor of the hut and sweated through a hideous hour the new sections had been installed. After that the pace had been increased and sometime had been made up until an irresponsible pair in Serial

"D" had tried to take out a home-made cooking stove. They were now under open arrest in the kitchen.

Lunch had been a nightmare meal. Half the places had been empty. The occupants of the other half had eaten with little appetite.

"It's the first time in a prison camp that I've ever seen food sent away from a meal," said Long.

"Did you see Rolf-Callender?" said Byfold.

"No—I missed him—he was dressed as a girl, wasn't he? What was he like?"

"Gorgeous," said Byfold. "I hope he got through the tunnel without wrecking his corsage. He said he was making for the Vatican City."

"Should give the Pope something to think about," said Long. "How are we doing?"

Goyles looked at his list. "Half-way through 'E'," he said.

"That's half the camp. They ought to give Lavery a gong for this."

"If the whole camp gets out," said Byfold, "you can make it a knighthood. It wouldn't be excessive."

IV

At eleven o'clock that morning Joseph Rocca, farmer, received a fright. He went straight home and reported it to his wife. Together they considered the matter, and came to the reluctant conclusion that they should do something about it. Joseph got on to his bicycle and rode downhill towards the village. There he stopped to consult with his brother. His brother proved sceptical. A second brother and a cousin were summoned. They thought there might be something in it. "You must ride to the camp and tell the Commandant," they said, "it is your duty."

"It is up-hill to the camp," pointed out the first brother, "and it is now half-past twelve. Let us eat."

At two o'clock Joseph arrived outside the gate of the camp and attracted the attention of the guard. He had, he said, information for the Commandant. He was allowed inside the wire and given a seat. A messenger went away, and came back to say that the Commandant was having his siesta. Could Signor Rocca wait? Joseph hesitated, but, having come so far, he decided he would wait.

At half-past three he was taken in to see Colonel Aletti, whom he knew slightly. Signor Rocca was a well-known local farmer, and the camp purchased provisions from him. "This morning at ten o'clock—" he began.

The Commandant listened patiently. At the end, he smiled and said, "See for yourself."

The two men stood at the window of the Commandant's office and looked down on the camp. All was peace. Groups of prisoners lay out, listening to lectures. A game was in progress on the sports field. The sentries paced the walls.

"They looked like prisoners," insisted Joseph. "Five of them—large men—definitely of Anglo-Saxon type—a sort of criminal look, you understand."

"All were present at roll-call," said Colonel Aletti. "None have been through the gates or over the walls. They could hardly dig their way out in broad daylight."

Signor Rocca felt that honour had been satisfied. He shook hands with the Commandant and departed. Lieutenant Paoli, who had been present at the interview, was not so sure.

As soon as he could he excused himself, and wandered into the camp. Once he was inside, every police instinct that he possessed told him that he was right. There was a current of feeling which hit him as soon as he got inside the gates.

Every group that he passed shouted a silent warning at him. He wandered slowly towards Hut C. Here the feeling was stronger still. He considered for a moment whether he should fetch some assistance and start an immediate search. Something was going on. That was plain. But what? Better to make sure first. He opened the door of Hut C and walked slowly down the corridor. He made his way to the kitchen and opened the door. The time was exactly four o'clock.

v

At twenty minutes to five Colonel Lavery, accompanied by the Adjutant, came out of the Senior Officers' Hut. He made his way slowly across to Hut E and went in. He walked down the corridor, noticing that every door was propped open with a chair or a bench. It had been the duty of the last man out in every room to wedge the door open. The two of them left the hut and walked to the next one. They visited each hut in turn.

It had been their custom, for some weeks, to make an unofficial inspection of this sort during the evening meal.

As they passed the notice board they stopped for a moment to look at the bulletin. It was Bulletin No. 12 and had the words "Rear Party" in small letters across the top. At the bottom an unknown hand had scrawled *"A Rividierci"*. Colonel Lavery smiled.

He and the Adjutant turned together and made for Hut C.

"Is it just my guilty conscience," said the Adjutant, "or do things feel not quite as they ought to be? The compound's often empty at this hour—"

"It's the silence," said Colonel Lavery. "No talking, no shouting, no jazz bands; I believe even the sentries are beginning to cotton on to it."

They disappeared into Hut C and shut the door behind them.

In the first room they found Colonel Baird. He had gone early into the hut to avoid attention and had stayed there all day.

"Operation crawl completed," he said, as he stood up. He added, "Would it be in order for me to congratulate you?"

"Thank you," said Colonel Lavery.

They went down the passage. All doors were open except for the kitchen. Inside they found Long, Byfold and Goyles; also a bundle on the floor wrapped in an army blanket, that jerked from time to time like a fresh-landed salmon.

"Paoli, sir," said Goyles. "I think he's quite all right, really."

"Better be sure about it," said Colonel Lavery. "Some of us are going to be recaptured." He smiled for the first time that day. "We don't want another murder trial. After you, Baird." He turned to the other three—"There's no means of shutting this trap behind us, is there? I'd like to give them the maximum trouble."

"I'm afraid not, sir," said Goyles.

Five minutes later he was at the edge of the wood. He turned to look back. From where they stood even the top of the camp wall was invisible, but he could see, half a mile away across the valley, the road which came down the hill in a series of loops to the village which lay at the camp foot.

He felt Byfold's hand on his elbow.

"It's them, all right," said Long.

Like six grey mice, each with his flickering tail of white dust, the German armoured cars crept down the hill.

CHAPTER FIFTEEN

"OVER THE HILLS—"

AN OBSERVER WITH A GOD'S-EYE VIEW OF ITALY THAT LATE summer and autumn would have witnessed strange things. In the south the dust of a moving battle; in the centre and the north, on every road, the coming and going of a German army that had belatedly made up its mind to stop and fight; and on the hills, down the thorny backbone of the Apennines, through the scrubland that borders the Po valley on its south side, in the tall forests of the Abruzzi and the chestnut groves that ring Florence, over every piece of country which height or depth or hard going put out of the reach of the mechanized Germans, a moving chain. Refugees walking south, in an effort to get back to the homes from which war or dictatorship had uprooted them; deserters of both armies creeping back to their homes; and above all, distinguishable by their size, their vigour, their Nordic colouring and their indescribable garments, a steady stream of British prisoners of war, moving from the great officer prison camps in Northern Italy, some north to Switzerland, some more ambitious of fame or danger towards their own lines four hundred miles to the south.

All moved with steady purpose, for all were aware that there was a deadline set against such travel. It might be the end of October or it might be the first weeks of November, but sooner or later the snow would cover the hills; movement, except on the roads, would be difficult, and both armies would settle down along a fixed winter line which it would be perilous indeed to try to cross.

Meanwhile, they kept going. As they went, treading in each other's tracks, passing through defiles, crossing rivers, skirting valleys, avoiding main roads, they formed a highway of their own—something which might, in time, be looked on as a folkway like the Pedlars' road or the Pilgrims' Way about which people would say, in years to come—"That was where the prisoners went that summer".

Goyles, Byfold and Long took this hard road. Their bodies were as fit as conscientious training could make them, but their feet still a bit soft. None of them looked much like an Italian. They had discussed the advisability of wearing British uniform and had decided against it. "If the Germans catch us, I don't think what clothes we happen to be wearing will make much difference to our treatment," said Goyles, and the others agreed. They dressed for comfort. They had corduroy or battle-dress trousers and coloured shirts. They carried their belongings in sacks. Long had a panama hat, which was voted by the others to be too conspicuous, and which he soaked for a whole night in the mud of a stream bed, after which its shape and colour passed beyond description.

They rose early and went to sleep early, setting their movements by the sun. It would be between four and five in the morning when they slipped out of the barn where they had spent the night. That was the easiest and the safest part of the day, when everything was quiet and the most active enemy was snoring in his blankets two thousand feet below. One morning they were paid an additional dividend for their early rising: when they stood on the flanks of Monte La Croce and saw across the tops of the featherbed mist which still filled the Lombardy plain below them purest white touched with pink under the level rays of the early morning sun, the peaks of the High Alps more than a hundred miles to the north.

They took their meals where they were offered, and though they were sometimes hungry, they never had to touch the small reserves that they carried. These were the iron rations, saved up for the day, still far ahead, which they sometimes discussed. It was for "when they got nearer the lines", of course "things wouldn't be so easy then".

By four o'clock in the afternoon their eyes were skinned for a night's lodging—though they might have to walk for another three hours before they found exactly what they wanted. Best were lonely farm houses up in the hills, separated by ten kilometres of tracks from any made road. Here, whatever the real feelings of their hosts, they felt tolerably secure for one night at least. Once a farm had been decided on, they would perch patiently above it, waiting for the dusk. Then the descent and the entry. *"Siamo tre ufficialle inglesi. Si, vero. Sono tedesci qui?"* The patter soon got mechanical. Even the jokes, with much repetition, *"Sporsati? Non, vero. Questo* (indicating Long) *troppo giovanne. Questo* (Goyles) *troppo vecchio: e questo* (Byfold) *troppo bruto"*. Then a hot meal—at its best an enormous bowl of *pasta* with perhaps chicken giblets and an end of ham. Once, bread boiled in water with a little salt. Then into the barn, with the loan of a blanket and Goyles would settle himself into the straw with a sigh of thankfulness for one more day achieved. His preparations for bed had the merit of simplicity. If the farm felt secure he removed his boots. If not, he kept them on. He hung his sack of belongings by his head, put his glasses in a safe place—one of his chief worries was what might happen if he lost or broke them—and in a few minutes he was asleep.

After fourteen days the power of routine had asserted itself. All that was past was history. All that was to come was surmise. They might have been living so all their lives.

There were, of course, panics. Small panics, as when Goyles found, one morning, that his glasses were no longer in his sack, and an hour was spent raking through the length and breadth of the haystack on which they had slept, before the glasses came to light in Byfold's sack where Goyles must have put them in a sleepy moment the night before. More serious panics—like the sudden, inexplicable meeting with a German officer on a motor bicycle on a mountain ridge near Scai. Without a second's hesitation or a word said, they had taken to their heels and scampered down the hillside into a wood. The German had sat, sourly unmoving, on his machine. No doubt he was used to Italians running away at the sight of him.

If everything else failed, there were always the four hundred Roumanians. These Roumanians, deserters and killers to a man, were normally reported to be bivouacked in the nearest village down the valley. Sometimes they were Albanians, and on one occasion, Cossacks—but always four hundred. After a time they grew to expect them, and if their presence was not reported by their hosts they would enquire after them. It gave them a feeling of stability that they should be escorted down Italy by this phantom bodyguard.

Goyles had, in his sack, wedged down among the tins of porridge, the khaki pullover, the skeletons of two pairs of socks, the motoring map and the tiny but precious piece of soap, a cheap, black-covered Italian notebook into which he would enter, as he sat over his evening meal, a few words to recall the stages they had made that day. It was both route-card and diary. Often a single word was enough to sum up the events of the last twenty-four hours. "Rain" marked the thirteenth and fourteenth day. It was an exception in that autumn of fine weather. *"Castagnacce"* was their first taste of the peculiar sweet polenta made from chestnuts instead of flour, which was their staple diet for three cloying days to the north of Monte Verdi.

"Crypto-Fascist" recalled an uncomfortable night neat Norcia when, after trying and rejecting several harbours, they had chosen, against their better judgment, a lonely but pretentious building, more a villa than a farm. The master of the house, a big man, had served them the finest evening meal of their journey, and had sat down to it with them himself, dressed in a neat linen evening coat, and accompanied by two subdued daughters. Over the wine their host's true political feelings had begun to peep through. Most of what he said went past the elementary Italian of Goyles and Byfold, but Long picked up enough to be cautious, and, that night, after being shown by their host to a fine barn where mattresses and *coperte* were laid out for them, they had rolled quietly off the straw, padded for a mile up the valley, and spent an uncomfortable night in a bean stack.

It was their rule that they moved on every day, and there was only one entry which bracketed two days—the thirty-seventh and thirty-eighth of their journey. It was a time when Byfold's right heel was causing him a lot of trouble, and he was in some pain that evening when they hobbled down into the courtyard of the monastery of Monte Catria. The monks had dressed the hurt and had prescribed at least a day's rest. There was, they explained, only one road which led to the outside world, and this was continually watched. They had slept that night, all three of them, with a fourteen-year-old Yugoslav boy, also a fugitive, in a huge bed. They had been further surprised to be woken, in the morning, by a black woman, who told them that she came from Georgia and would be a mother to all of them. She had darned Tony's socks, and they had spent the day sitting about the monastery and listening to an organ recital by an accomplished young monk from Eritrea. On the second morning they had moved on, refreshed but bewildered.

In the traffic of this unofficial highway they met old and new friends. Stopping for a midday meal at a shepherd's hut they found before them at the table a black-bearded giant. They knew that he was English, but it was ten minutes before Goyles realized that he was talking to an old school friend, a man he had met perhaps half a dozen times since leaving school, who had made a big name in civil engineering. Goyles knew that he had been constructing airfields in the desert, but had not previously realized that he had been captured. They shared ten years' experiences over the lunch table and then parted. The engineer was making for the Adriatic, where he had heard that the S.A.S. were arranging pick-ups from the beaches.

More than a week later, and a hundred miles further south, they came to their night's lodging at the top of a straggling village to be told by the priest that there were *"due inglesi"* about a mile further down the valley. Normally, this information would have left them unmoved, but they gathered also that there was trouble, so after eating they walked down and found Captain the McInstalker and Captain Abercrowther. Abercrowther had his hand wrapped in a mountain of stained bandages. He had been carrying water in a glass wine flask and going down a steep hillside to fill it had slipped, broken the flask, and cut his hand deeply at the root of the thumb. The cut had never healed and was now in a very bad way indeed. The Italians had been helpful but had few disinfectants and no drugs. If the hand was no better in a few days' time it would mean a German field hospital. Meanwhile, the two of them were lying up.

It had been a stupid accident and it was a reminder to them how much they lay at the mercy of the smallest mishap.

That night, not for the first time, they discussed the question of whether they ought to come down from the mountains and risk a quick journey by rail or road. Once more they decided against it. Liberty was too precious a coin to risk on the hazard. Their progress in the hills was mortally slow, but it was certain—or as certain as anything could be in an enemy country. If they walked twenty miles every day, crawling from upland to upland along the spine of the mountains, it might, at a hard day's end, measure only twelve miles on the map of their progress. But if you advance twelve miles a day, for seven days a week, for week after week, you get somewhere in the end.

For the first two weeks they made very little real headway, for they were working their way into the mountains, travelling at right angles to their eventual course. They followed the Ronco upwards until it diminished from a broad river to a tiny mountain stream which split up and disappeared on the flanks of Monte Falterona. Then they turned south-east and for the next month only the smudged entries in Goyles' notebook marked their progress. Indeed, they were sometimes hard put to it to say themselves how far they had come. The shepherds and the woodcutters and the charcoal-burners whom they met had little idea of distance. They cared nothing for kilometres. It was *"una Mez' ora"*—a half-hour:

or something less definite even than that—*"una mez'oretta"*, which Tony Long translated for them as "a dear little sort of half-hour".

And so, as September passed, and as October lengthened towards November, slowly—slowly as the sun crossing a window on a drowsy afternoon—slowly as the sap creeping down the branch of a tree—they swung east and south-east, and then, as the Gran Sasso rose along their horizon, majestic and menacing under its cap of unmelting snow, they found themselves looking south and even to the west of south.

Under this constant, slow, unremitting effort their bodies grew hard and serviceable again. Mentally, they drew apart. Talking afterwards to others who had had similar experiences, Goyles found that this was a normal result. At the time it worried him. He had imagined that their common experiences, the drive of a common purpose, would have cemented the friendship they had already formed. Instead, it was shaking it to pieces. At the time it was a thing he accepted without speculating about it. Tony Long was more and more silent. Roger Byfold's humour turned first to cynicism, then to open sarcasm. It was only later that he tried to rationalize it, and came to the conclusion—helped by a hint from the diary of Scott, the explorer—that a party engaged on an uncommon enterprise needed the bond of a leader. The harder the circumstances, the less could you dispense with the discipline which flowed naturally from an established order. Every day decisions had to be taken—whether to turn left or right—whether to stop or go on. Nor were they light decisions. If the answer was wrong the most unimaginable consequence could flow from it. Being equals, none of them could lead. So the decision had to be made by the worst of all possible means—by debate and argument. It was like trying to fight a total war with a democratic government, Goyles decided.

The first outward sign of strain was when Goyles found himself addressing Tony formally as "Long". This was so stupid that they almost managed to laugh themselves out of it. The habit nevertheless persisted. Shortly after that Byfold, temporarily defeated in some argument, sulked for a whole day. These spells of childishness were not continuous. There were long periods when they behaved like friends and adults. The symptoms of strain were usually underneath the surface.

On the fortieth day Long walked out on the other two.

There had been an argument the night before—not a very serious one—as to where and when they should halt for the night. Goyles and Byfold had wanted to stop early and in the end they had had their way. Long had been silent that morning. They were crossing some very difficult country north of Scai; every valley ran perversely across their line of advance, and the undergrowth was thick enough to make walking difficult without affording either cover or shade. All three of them were hot and ill-tempered. They were walking, as they usually did in open country, about a hundred yards apart, and when they came to a small coppice, a tangle of dwarf oak and juniper crowning the divide of the two valleys, Tony went to the right of it; the other two thought the left-hand side looked easier and took it. That was really all there was to it.

On the further side of the wood the valley forked, and the two of them were some way down the left-hand arm before they realized that Long was not with them. They kept on their way, moving up, gradually, on to the intervening ridge from where they were confident they would be able to see him. Sure enough, there he was, well on down the right-hand valley, four hundred yards ahead and going fast.

Goyles and Byfold shouted. First singly and moderately. Then loudly and in unison.

Long kept on. He didn't even turn his head. Byfold looked worried. Both of them knew that the hills and valleys played strange tricks with sound.

"Perhaps he can't hear us and thinks we're still ahead of him," he said. "If we run we might catch him."

"You can run if you like," said Goyles. "The pig-headed basket. He can hear us perfectly."

He sat down on the bank.

"Then what's wrong with him?" said Byfold.

"He's been working up to it for days. He thinks we're slacking. I expect he also figures we're holding him back."

"He travels the fastest who travels alone, that sort of thing, you mean?"

"That's the idea," said Goyles.

"Let him go, then," agreed Byfold.

After a few minutes they got up and went on. It felt strange at first being only two.

When this happened they were twenty miles north of Vallemare. The next obvious move was to go down into the Sangro road and river loop. The southern and eastern boundaries were the River Sangro and there was talk of a German winter line here, and airfields on the Ventimiglia. The Eighth Army was known to be well north of Campo Basso. They had picked that up on the wireless two nights before, listening to the B.B.C. Italian broadcast. They had felt a tightening of the stomach muscles as they heard this.

All that day they walked across the uplands. It was high plateau, sheep country, and absolutely open; it was said to be free of Germans. They made good progress and were across the Cocullo road by lunch-time. They crossed carefully, between German Army convoys, and were cheered by the sight of five Spitfires, red and blue and silver, playing in the sky ahead of them.

That afternoon they climbed again and came to a sheep settlement. It was a ramshackle place at nearly six thousand feet, used only in summer and autumn. They were glad of a blanket each in the straw that night, but slept peacefully in spite of the cold. It was to be almost their last undisturbed night.

Next day they kept to their mountain crest, leaving Cocullo on their left. The going still looked good, but they were uncomfortably conscious that they were walking into a cul-de-sac.

The first sign of this was when they met a party coming back. They had passed stationary parties before—people whose nerve or initiative had given out and who had talked themselves into lying up "until the English advance caught them up". Cold or starvation would drive them down sooner or later into the villages and most of them would be picked up by the Germans before spring set the armies on the move once more.

This party was not sitting still—it was coming back. Possibly this showed more spirit. Nevertheless it was startling. There were three sergeants from the H.L.I. They had come all the way from a working camp near Modena.

"It's pretty dead hopeless down there, sir," said the leader of the party. "First you've got to get across the Sangro—that's a road, river and railway. We did that all right, but then you run into an open bit, about ten miles across, where there's a battle going on. Not much movement—observation and fire and that sort of thing."

"Don't forget the mine-fields," said the small, dark sergeant.

"All the *casas* are full of parties who've tried it and got turned back. They're the lucky ones. Most of them started out and got picked up—"

Goyles and Byfold thanked them and moved on. They knew that a thing always sounded worse when talked about by someone who had tried it and failed. All the same, they weren't underestimating what was ahead. They spent that night under a heap of sacks in an empty charcoal-burner's hut.

Next morning they made their way quietly down to within distance of the Sangro, and lay up all day watching the road.

The sergeants had not exaggerated. The traffic was continuous. But there was more to it than that. When they looked closely they noticed that the same sort of truck would come backwards and forwards, once or twice in the hour. They were small German troop carriers, and they were not part of the through traffic. They were patrolling.

In the early afternoon an even more alarming thing happened. One of the trucks which they had been watching stopped and spilled out a dozen men; small men in the dark green uniform of the Alpini. The party disappeared into the wood below the point where Goyles and Byfold were lying. An hour later they reappeared, got into the truck and moved slowly off.

"Lucky we weren't too close to the road," said Byfold.

"Very lucky," said Goyles. "The thing may look a bit more practicable by night."

As soon as it got dark they moved down towards the road. They had never tried moving by night before—certainly not across broken country—their progress was slow, painful and noisy.

They were still a hundred yards short of the road when they noticed the lights. These were coming on and off, irregularly; when one suddenly turned on immediately below them they realized what they were.

"They're headlights," said Byfold. "The bastards have got lorries parked up and down the road. When they hear anything they turn the lights on—"

Goyles was looking ahead, at the country on the other side of the river.

"They've got patrols out there, too," he said. "You can see the lights from time to time. Defence in depth."

"What's it all about?" said Byfold. "They can't have laid it all on, just for us."

"I expect this is one of the check points," said Goyles. "It's one of the obvious places. Whenever we've looked at the map we've agreed we'd cross about here. They can't be as thick as this on the ground all the way round the Sangro. We'll go back and try again further to the east."

It was very late indeed, and they were very tired by the time they got back to their charcoal-burner's hut. They turned in without a word. They had hardly realized until then what a bad effect on their *morale* the act of turning back would have. Also they were running short of food.

Things looked more cheerful in the light of morning. It was late when they got up and set their faces northward up the valley. After a short walk they stumbled into a camp of Italians—refugees from a village which the Germans had taken over. They were unaccountably cheerful, and, since they had killed a sheep the night before, Goyles and Byfold were able to eat a satisfying breakfast of mutton broth and limp *polenta*.

They went on up the valley.

"We'll go well to the east, this time," said Goyles. "Towards Agnone."

"We mustn't funk it again," said Byfold. "It's like jumping in the deep end of the swimming bath. Anyone can be excused for fluffing it once, but if you fluff it twice you're finished."

A little later they caught sight of a figure, some way ahead of them on the path and coming fast.

They removed themselves circumspectly into the undergrowth.

A few seconds later Byfold raised his head, took another look at the advancing figure, scrambled to his feet and ran forward.

Goyles put out a hand to stop him, but Byfold said, "It's all right, Cuckoo. I'd know those trousers anywhere. It's Tony."

He ran on to the path. Goyles sat watching him.

CHAPTER SIXTEEN

"—AND FAR AWAY"

I

IT WAS LONG ALL RIGHT.

In a few minutes they had heard each other's stories. In an hour it was as if they had never parted.

Long didn't say much about his defection and the others refrained from pressing him. "I heard you shouting, all right," he said, "but I didn't take any notice, because I was fed up with you. I very soon got un-fed up. In fact, I was pretty lonely. I'm glad to see your faces again."

He asked them about their adventures and they told him.

"Yes. I gather that crossing isn't healthy," said Long "I fell in yesterday with an S.A.S. type—chap called Morgan—regular cloak-and-dagger merchant. As a matter of fact I'd met him once before when I was training in England. Apparently he and two or three others have been sent to tell us to get a move on—"

"Hell," said Byfold. "What do they expect us to do—double smartly across the lines?"

"It's not us," said Long. "In fact, he admitted we'd done very well getting as far as we had in the time—but apparently there are a lot of parties just sitting on their bottoms waiting to be rescued—people who, anyway, started from the southern camps, and have come about fifty miles in two months and got tired. His job is to whip them on as quickly as possible—"

"The implication being," said Goyles thoughtfully, "that the British Army has done all the advancing it's going to do this year."

"I think so, yes. He couldn't say so, of course. However, I got some tips off him. One was on no account to try to cross that bit of road you two types seem to have taken a running jump at—"

"Thank you for nothing," said Byfold.

"The other was more constructive. He gave me a route towards the Adriatic. The fighting's pretty fluid there, and it's not armoured country, so you've got nothing but patrols. I wrote down the key points, but a lot of it's in my head. You start from San Lorenzo—that's two cottages and a sheep-run about ten miles east of here. Cross the Ventimiglia upland—you've got to be careful about that. Pietransieri—Agnone—Trivento—"

They spent some time working it out on Goyles' map.

They got to San Lorenzo that evening. The farmer welcomed them without embarrassment. He seemed quite used to British prisoners.

When they were sitting over their evening meal Goyles, remembering his breakfast, said, "Do you think he'd sell us a sheep. We've still got quite a lot of money—"

"Drive it in front of us, do you mean?" said Byfold. "Sort of camouflage?"

"Ass. No. Have it killed and boiled. Food's not going to be so easy now, especially if we have to move at night."

"Quite an idea—what do you think, Tony?"

Long came out of a deep reverie and agreed that it was a good idea.

Fortune favoured them. The farmer was not even interested in their money. He would give them a sheep. "Normally," he explained, "in the autumn, we drive them down to the plains at Campo Basso. Now both armies are across the road. The sheep must stay in the hills. When the snow comes, most of them must die."

The butchery took place promptly and the meat was boiled there and then with salt—they had to pay for the salt—in a huge cauldron. They had a second supper of mutton broth and they breakfasted off mutton chops. When they started out the next morning each of them had a cold joint of mutton in his sack. There was no paper of any sort in the house. Goyles wrapped his in his spare pullover.

The sky that morning was grey, with a promise of rain before the evening. They made their way slowly up a long neck of the valley, Long with his eye constantly on the compass and the map. At eleven o'clock he called a halt.

"Here's where we have to make a detour," he said. They turned off the track and went up the left-hand side of the valley. It had looked innocent enough when they were walking along a made track at the bottom, but it was a rough and exhausting sixty minutes before they had pulled themselves up and could look over the crest into the valley which paralleled them to the east. This was a much shallower valley—almost an upland. It was full of sheep. There were thick woods crowning the bluff on the other side, and beyond the woods the ground fell away, presumably to the river, which was out of sight.

"What are we waiting for?" said Goyles. "The sooner we're in those woods the better."

"That's what you're meant to think," said Long. "Do you see those huts?"

"Shepherds' shelters."

"They're guard huts," said Long. "Just you watch them."

An hour later they saw a German make his way carefully up behind one of the huts and disappear into it.

At four o'clock it started to rain, a maddening, persistent drizzle which always promised to stop and never did. If they had been on the move they would have thought nothing of it. They lay in the shelter of a large rock and cursed.

"Shelter, my foot," said Roger. "All it does is to collect the rain and empty it down my neck."

Goyles said nothing. He was carving his leg of mutton with a safety razor blade. Darkness seemed a very long time coming.

With the darkness the rain stopped. They got up, shook themselves together and went on slowly. The sky was still overcast and it was pitch dark. Long led; of the three his night sight seemed best. All they knew was that they had to keep straight on across the shallow dip ahead of them, find a way down the side valley masked by wood, get down to the river, road and railway, cross all three and take the first valley to the right as far as the village of Pietransieri. It was a journey which would have taken less than two hours in daylight.

After midnight the sky cleared, there was the rind of a moon, and they were able to go a little quicker. By three in the morning they were safe in a hay-loft at Pietransieri. Goyles was the most exhausted. He found it difficult to see at night and so he had fallen most often.

That day they lay very close. Two or three times people came into the barn below them, but no one came up the ladder into the loft. They made themselves an inner shelter, deep down in the hay in one corner, to which they could retreat if they had to with some hope of avoiding detection if the loft was entered. There was no question of going out or seeking help. The village was thick with German troops. It looked like an anti-aircraft unit. Their chief trial was an entire lack of water. During that day Goyles' dislike of cold mutton became an obsession.

When it was dark they let themselves out of the back of the barn and dropped down to the cobbles. They paused for a quick drink in the communal wash-house at the foot of the village street and then moved out on to the hillside. There was more light, but the going was worse. Goyles remembered that night as the incidents of a nightmare. As a result of the wet and cold his feet and legs soon lost their power of feeling—which may have been as well, for he seemed to bump his shins or stub his toes every few paces.

The only serious accident occurred in the early hours of the following morning. They were making slow but steady progress round the upper slopes of Monte Agnone. The ground was a series of scrub-covered slopes cut by small ravines—the beginning of numerous mountain streams, now dry. Byfold unexpectedly slipped the last ten feet into one of these, and turned his right ankle. He could still move slowly, with help, and they hobbled and crawled for another mile, into the outskirts of a fairly large wood. Here they tried to get some sleep. At first light they heard men and animals moving quite near them.

They lay still because there was nothing much else to do.

A moment later they saw—and had been seen by—a party of woodcutters. This turned out to be the finest stroke of luck imaginable, for the woodcutters proved not only friendly but refreshingly tough. They had little use for the Germans, and were of the opinion that liberation by the Allies was round the corner. They put Byfold on one of their mules and led the three of them back to their encampment—it was a sort of summer house of logs and brushwood—where they were given a meal and a blanket each, and where they slept the sleep of the dead, waking when the sun was going down and the woodcutters were coming back from their day's work.

In front of a huge fire, in the mouth of the shelter, they talked it over. The woodcutters were unanimous in their advice that the Englishmen should stay. They would not be breaking their encampment for another ten days, they said, and during that time the English Army might be with them. They were well hidden in the woods far from all made roads.

In a way, the answer lay with Byfold. He said that his ankle, though stiff, was serviceable. He could go on if necessary. Long said that he was in favour of going on.

Goyles for a time said nothing. He had been in a very odd mood for some time. Neither of the others had seen anything quite like it before. Since they had met up again with Long, three days previously (it was difficult for any of them to realize that it was only three days), he had been unusually quiet, alternating fits of silence with an equally unusual jumpiness. This was more surprising because until that moment he had been the steadiest of the three.

Now, as he sat in front of the blazing fire, he would neither look at his friends, nor address them directly. Instead, he aimed a rapid-fire of questions at the leader of the woodcutters.

"How far was the nearest point in Allied hands? (Ten miles, perhaps fifteen.) What was the route? What German posts were there? Had anyone been that way before? English prisoners or Italians?"

When he had listened to the answers Goyles said, "We should be able to make it to-night. I'm going to try, anyway."

He stated it as a fact. It was hardly an invitation.

There was an awkward pause; then Byfold said, "All right, that makes it unanimous. We'd better start as soon as it's properly dark."

"We'd better eat first," said Long.

The woodcutters seemed unoffended by the abruptness of these proceedings. They served a meal of vegetable stew and pancakes. Ten minutes after finishing it the three were off. Long led, suiting the pace to Byfold, who came next, using a sort of crutch the woodman had made for him. Goyles brought up the rear.

"You might have been a bit more polite to those types," said Byfold, as they moved on.

"Was I being rude?" said Goyles. "I'm sorry, I didn't notice."

Nothing more was said for some time.

About an hour later Long said, "We ought to press on a bit if we can. We want to be well out of the patrol zone before light."

"I could go faster," said Byfold. "It's Goyles who keeps hanging back."

"I'm sorry," said Goyles. He was certainly walking well behind the other two. "I must be getting jumpy."

After that he closed up a bit, but not much.

Their route lay, as the woodmen had explained, diagonally across three broad valleys. The first two were in German hands, patrolled, but not held. There were German posts on the road which crowned the second ridge and this was the danger spot.

The third valley was No-man's Land. Beyond it was Trivento, held by neither side, but visited, so it was said, by British patrols.

Short of the second ridge they called a halt. A thin drizzle of rain had started, but at that stage this did not worry them so much as the fact that they were walking, blind, into what they knew was a patrolled line.

They were crossing a vineyard and they found a small shelter. It was the sort that is used before the grape harvest by a watchman, and was now empty. Except for the low doorway it was completely covered and once they were inside Byfold risked the use of his torch whilst he and Long took a quick look at the map.

Goyles sat on the couch in the corner and said nothing. It was difficult, in the dim light, to be certain whether the moisture on his face was rain or sweat.

"I should say it's a toss-up," said Long at last. "We must be just below that wood—it runs right up to the ridge."

"We can't go through the middle of it," said Byfold. "It would take too long and would make too much noise. On the other hand, the edges of it are just the place for a post."

They sat in the darkness listening to the steady patter of rain on the vine-leaves. It felt warm in the hut—warm and deceptively secure. Long broke the silence.

"I think," he said, "that it's the moment for a reconnaissance. It had better be me."

There was no denying that. Byfold was still lame and Goyles was almost blind in the dark.

"I'll be about half an hour," he said.

"Don't get caught," said Byfold.

Goyles said nothing. Long looked towards him curiously for a moment. They were dim shapes to each other in the darkness. Then he turned, ducked to the entrance, and was gone.

Goyles got off the bed, moved across the hut, and stooped to look after him. They heard Long's steps as he moved away, then silence. A single white Verey light went up from the ridge ahead of them, curved over in a lazy arc, burning as it fell. Byfold saw

Goyles' face for a moment, and was shocked. "What is it?" he whispered. "What's up?"

"Roger," said Goyles. "I've got something to say, and I reckon perhaps I've got twenty minutes to say it in. Will you save the questions for afterwards?"

"You can say almost anything in twenty minutes if you give your mind to it," said Byfold quietly.

"All right. Here goes—"

As he spoke his whole personality was changing. The lassitude of the last few days was slipping from him. It was like a boxer stepping out of his corner at the sound of the bell.

He spoke for some time. His voice ran on and on in the darkness. He was unravelling a long and tangled skein, but he had done it so often before, in his own mind, that he had no need to fumble.

When he had finished, Byfold said, "If that's right, Cuckoo, what are we waiting for?"

"We're waiting for Long to come back."

"Waiting for—?"

"Look here," said Goyles. "Why do you think I haven't run away twenty times before? Every time I've thought about it I've sweated—but since we've played the hand so far, we'll play it out. We've got to hear what he's going to say. It's our only way of being quite sure about this last bit."

There was another silence, and in the silence they both heard the "clink" of a stone moving under a metal-shod boot. Then Long was coming down the path and into the hut.

He was breathing fast.

"I've got the dope," he said. "The left side's no good—there's a proper reception committee up there. It's an ack-ack post, I think, but there's an infantry section there, too. The right-hand side looks O.K. I didn't go across, but I poked my nose out and it looked clear."

Byfold got up so that he was standing in front of Long. Goyles was directly behind him. "This ought to be the last act, oughtn't it?" said Byfold.

"It's practically the curtain," said Long.

On the word "curtain" Goyles hit him on the back of the head with the bottle he had been holding in his hand. There was a dry splintering as bone and bottle broke together. Long fell on to his knees and folded slowly forward. Before his face touched the floor Goyles and Byfold were out of the hut and moving fast up the hill.

II

Half an hour later Goyles and Byfold were sitting under an over-hang of rock in a moderately dry river bed. They had crossed the road, with every confidence, on the left of the wood. They were now six hundred yards down the hill, on the further side of it. Verey lights were going up—but from behind them.

"Better sit tight till the fuss dies down," said Goyles. "They won't find us now unless they fall over us."

"Do you think the reception committee's still waiting for us on the other side of the wood?"

"Could be," said Goyles. "Long may have got up to them again by now."

"You don't think you killed him?"

"I don't think so. I hope not—I certainly didn't mean to."

"Why not?" said Byfold. "The bloody swine—" He was still confused by it. To him there were still two different people. There was "Tony" whom he had liked and trusted, and there was "Long" who, for his own ends, had cold-bloodedly tried to walk them into a trap.

"You'll get used to the idea in time," said Goyles. "Remember he was a German. Remember he was doing a job."

"He was doing a job all right," said Byfold. Another thought struck him. "What about Grim and Alec—?"

"That stuck in my throat," said Goyles, "until I'd had a word with Hugo. Hugo was quite certain that no one gave them away. I must say I believed him. When you come to think of it, why should Long have betrayed them? He wasn't an anti-escape expert. His job was intelligence. As a matter of fact he tried like hell to stop it—he even came to see me about it in prison."

"And I suppose that pulling out Coutoules' finger-nails was part of the job?"

"Curiously enough," said Goyles, "not only did he not join in torturing Coutoules but, so far as the evidence goes, it was his arrival that stopped the party. As I was saying just now he got out of the window of the cooler and on to the roof at about eleven o'clock that night. The wireless was full on—I've had several versions of this, and they all more or less tally. About five minutes later—that's to say, about the earliest moment that Long could have got off the roof and down into the carabinieri block—the wireless stopped. So either his arrival restrained Benucci and his fellow jokers—or Coutoules was dead. Either way it lets him out."

"You may be right, Cuckoo," said Byfold. "I just find it difficult to be as dispassionate about it all as you are. I suppose it's this business of leading us up the garden path. I take it that that S.A.S. man he told us he'd met was all hooey?"

"Complete invention, I should say. He had to leave us to prepare the reception committee this end. Then, if it was to work, he had to lead us by the right route—"

"He led us all right," said Byfold. "Like little children he led us."

"I'm not making Long out to be any better than he was," said Goyles. "But we were part of his job—and whilst he was on the job, nothing else mattered. What he had to do was to get us all captured—at the last possible moment. If I hadn't known what I did about him, it would have come off very nicely—half an hour ago."

"Then what?"

"Then we should all have gone off to a prison camp in Germany—with a perfect background, and a wonderful bad-luck story. 'Long? Good chap, Long. You heard what he did in Italy. Walked for fifty days and got picked up as he was actually crossing the lines.'"

"I see," said Byfold. "And were we going to be with him—or were we going to be 'shot resisting capture'?"

"Oh—I think we were going to survive all right. After all, we were part of his cover story. Besides, everything being equal, I think he quite liked us. And you've got to remember—" Goyles broke off and eventually Byfold said, "Remember what?"

"He did save my life in that tunnel. I thought of that too before I hit him."

There was another silence. The fuss behind them seemed to be dying down. The rain had stopped and a freshening wind was rolling up the clouds.

"How long have you known all this?" said Byfold at last.

"It's hard to say. I think I was quite certain about a week before we left camp. I was pretty sure before. In fact, when you thought about it at all, it was so damned obvious that I imagined everybody would jump to it. It was the finding of that microphone that saved him, really."

"Saved him?"

"Well, it put off the evil day. It was pretty plain by then that things were getting back to the authorities—really secret things— things that only half a dozen people knew about. As soon as we found the microphone everyone said, 'Of course. That's the explanation.' Only it wasn't. Just think of some of the actual things that did get back. I don't mean general information about the progress of the Hut C tunnel—of course Long kept Benucci posted about that—but actual and concrete facts. Do you remember when you went down to bury Coutoules for a second time in the Hut A tunnel? Do you remember coming out and telling Long all about it—he was just back from the cooler? Do you remember what the Italians started to do when we gave them the tunnel—the usual drill—they roped it off and started breaking down the roof. Almost immediately you told Tony the story, that stopped. Instead, they got *inside* the tunnel and started taking photographs, showing how you'd brought the roof down with that pole—all that scientific stuff. That was a small thing, and I can't say it stuck out a mile, but I remembered it afterwards. The next thing was my effort to see that sentry, Biancelli. Apart from the Escape Committee, Long was the only person who knew about it. It had to be stopped, of course. Give me five minutes free conversation with Biancelli and I'd have known everything. He and Marzotto had the only post that was near enough to where Benucci and Co. took the body of Coutoules over the wall that night to be certain what was happening. No doubt one or two of the other posts could see that something was up, but they'd each had a 'carib' put alongside them, remember, to keep their eyes exclusively on the job. Even that time—when the answer was practically handed to me on a plate—I didn't see it. Then, you remember the plot to rescue you? That was obviously given away. I suppose everybody assumed that Benucci had picked the details up on his hidden microphone. That was nonsense. The plot wasn't hatched in Baird's room. It was originated and discussed in Colonel Lavery's room."

"And that was when you realized—?"

"No. What finally showed me the truth was Potter. Poor little Potter. His crime was that he had been to the school that Long was meant to have gone to, and at about the same time. I suppose he chose Shelton because it was a small school, and the chances were in favour of there being no contemporary of his in the camp. Potter *was* interrogated in Colonel Baird's room remember, and everything that he said went straight over the wire to Benucci. As soon as he said he'd been to Shelton he had to be got rid of—which he was, fairly smartly—and that was what ultimately and finally gave me the truth."

Everything was very quiet now.

Byfold and Goyles got stiffly to their feet. They made their way down the stream bed, and over the river at the valley bottom. It felt like crossing the finishing line at the end of a long race. They set their faces up the last hill and walked forward slowly but without undue precaution.

The wind had blown the clouds off, and ahead of them a single bright star was showing.

BRITISH LIBRARY CRIME CLASSICS

ALSO AVAILABLE

Many of our titles are also available in eBook and audio editions